"Ms. Malek's marvelous storytelling gifts keep us deliciously entertained!" —*Romantic Times*

DOREEN OWENS MALEK

Winner of the RWA Golden Medallion and the *Romantic Times* Reviewers' Choice Award!

TURKISH DELIGHT

"Are you going to rape me?" Sarah asked in English, trying hard to keep from revealing the fear in her voice.

Kalid Shah devoured her with the intense dark eyes she remembered from their previous meeting. The eunuchs on either side of her, their oiled black skins gleaming, held her in place with grips of iron.

"If I chose to do so, there would be no one here to stop me," Kalid replied flatly in the same language, with a British accent. He made a slight dismissive gesture and the eunuchs released her, stepping back. He said another short word abruptly and they left the room, bowing their way out.

Sarah looked around the ornate apartment in the Orchid Palace, then out at the flowering courtyard beyond, with its splashing fountain, marble bathing pool, and cages of colorful birds; it was a smaller, less elaborate version of Topkapi.

The pasha's dismissal of his servants was understandable. There was absolutely nowhere for her to run.

"Why am I here?" Sarah demanded, with as much spirit as she could muster under the circumstances.

"You belong to me now," Kalid said simply. "I may do with you as I please."

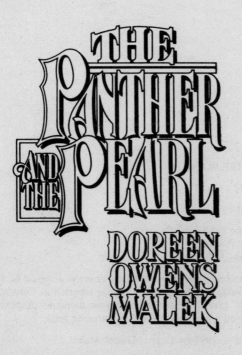

THE PANTHER AND THE PEARL

DOREEN OWENS MALEK

LEISURE BOOKS ▐ **NEW YORK CITY**

A LEISURE BOOK®

May 1994

Published by

Dorchester Publishing Co., Inc.
276 Fifth Avenue
New York, NY 10001

Printed in the United States of America.

For my lost daughter,
Megan,
Who dwells with the angels.
And for my found daughter,
Monica,
An angel on earth.

Prologue

Bursa, Ottoman Empire
August, 1885

"Are you going to rape me?" Sarah asked in English, trying hard to keep from revealing the fear in her voice.

Kalid Shah devoured her with the intense dark eyes she remembered from their previous meeting. The eunuchs on either side of her, their oiled black skins gleaming, held her in place with grips of iron.

"If I chose to do so, there would be no one here to stop me," Kalid replied flatly in the same language, with a British accent. He made a slight dismissive gesture and the eunuchs released her, stepping back. He said another short word abruptly and they left the room, bowing their way out.

Sarah looked around the ornate apartment in the Orchid Palace, then out at the flowering courtyard beyond, with its splashing fountain, marble bathing pool, and cages of colorful birds; it was a smaller, less elaborate version of Topkapi.

The pasha's dismissal of his servants was understandable. There was absolutely nowhere for her to run.

"Why am I here?" Sarah demanded, with as much spirit as she could muster under the circumstances.

"You belong to me now," Kalid said simply. "I may do with you as I please."

"In my country we do not purchase people!" Sarah burst out, indignation overriding caution.

"In your country, people were purchased regularly until quite recently—about twenty years ago, I think," he said, smiling slightly.

"Our late President Lincoln outlawed such slavery," Sarah replied, irritated at being corrected. "And anyway, I'm from Boston. We were not involved in that awful trafficking in human lives."

"Boston is not part of the United States?" he said dryly.

"When my cousin hears what has happened to me, you will be in serious trouble!" Sarah said angrily.

His smile widened. "I am the law here. Your kinsman . . ." He snapped his fingers " . . . is powerless in Bursa."

"The American embassy—" Sarah began.

Kalid threw back his head and laughed, displaying the striking white teeth of a predator. "Talkers," he said contemptuously. "It will take them six months to decide what to do and when to do it. In the meanwhile, you are mine."

Sarah stared at him mutinously, unable to reply. He had shaved off his short dark beard since she last saw him, revealing the smooth golden-olive skin of a face stamped with the aristocratic arrogance natural to a prince of Bursa. There were twin curves in his cheeks where dimples would appear when he smiled, and he had a shallow cleft in his chin. His nose, slightly beaked, rose above a sculpted mouth with a full, sensual lower lip. His hair—the dense, shadeless black of the east—curled over his high forehead and around his ears, glossy and thick. He stood a head taller than she did, slim and straight, his embroidered white caftan slit open at the throat to reveal the mat of sable hair on his chest. He was, in fact, quite startlingly handsome, which added immeasurably to the uncertainty and confusion Sarah was feeling.

Kalid reached out suddenly and lifted a lock of golden hair from her shoulder, wrapping it around his dusky finger. Sarah stiffened and pulled back; he drew her closer with a slight but insistent pressure until she succumbed and stumbled forward.

He let the hair fall and traced the line of her bare throat with his forefinger, down to the cleft of her breasts revealed by the deep neck of her gauzy blouse. Sarah sucked in her breath as he moved his finger and rested the tip of it lightly on her nipple. Rouged with henna by the harem women who had prepared her for him, it was easily visible through the sheer silk she wore. He circled it lightly, then more firmly, until it rose and hardened at his touch.

Sarah dropped her eyes as she felt the color climbing into her face, then forced herself to lift her head and meet his burning stare defiantly. Then she slapped him as hard as she could.

He didn't flinch, merely held her gaze for a long moment, then withdrew his finger. In a flash, he seized her hair again and wound the length of it around his hand, pulling her so close to him that she was trapped against his shoulder, his nose inches from hers. It was extraordinary; he wasn't hurting her, but neither was she able to move. She stared up at him, frozen, as his black eyes with their lush lashes seemed to fill the entire world.

"I could have you killed for that," he said softly. There was no mistaking the menace in his tone.

It was a long moment before Sarah managed a reply. She drew a breath and licked her lips. "But then you would lose your investment, donme pasha," she said levelly.

He released her so suddenly that she reeled; by the time she regained her footing, he was regarding her impassively.

"Perhaps I would consider it money well spent," he said.

"Are you disappointed, then?" Sarah said sarcastically. "Am I not as pliant as you anticipated? Perhaps for such a high price you expected a docile mount. You should have examined your prize a little more closely before buying. This filly bites."

"Any horse can be broken to the bit," he said quietly. "In time, even the wildest, fiercest filly comes to anticipate with pleasure the hands of its master."

"You will be disappointed," Sarah said tonelessly.

"I will not be disappointed," he replied confidently. "This is only the beginning."

"Sultan Hammid got the best of your deal, pasha," Sarah said. "He has your heirloom and your money, and you have a ringer for a courtesan."

"What is this, ringer?" he asked.

"Useless. No good."

"Ah, but you will be very good."

"So you do plan to force me."

"Force will not be necessary." He cupped her chin in his hand and turned her face to the light. "You will beg me to take you, *kourista*," he said silkily," and then beg me not to stop."

"Never," Sarah said through gritted teeth, jerking away from him. "I won't be worth the work, trust me. Just let me go."

"What, return you to the Sultan?" He seemed amused.

"He'll see that I'm released to my cousin. Maybe he'll even give you back what you paid for me," she said hopefully.

Kalid shook his head. "It is not a matter of price. Sultan Hammid is unaware that my bargaining was a game, a sham. I would have surrendered anything he asked for you."

Sarah was stunned into silence. Almost despairing, she realized that this man was long accustomed to getting what he wanted, and what he wanted now was Sarah Woolcott.

He clapped his hands suddenly and the eunuchs reappeared, as if from the air.

"What is happening?" Sarah asked, looking around in a panic. What was he doing now?

"They will take you back to your quarters in the harem," Kalid said, turning away. Before Sarah could say anything further, she was ushered into the tiled hallway and escorted back to her room.

Kalid listened as their footsteps faded in the distance, then walked over to the samovar and poured himself a cup of thick Turkish coffee. His father would have called a servant to perform even this simple task, but he was not his father, and therein lay his problem. His life formed an uneasy bridge between East and West, like the ancient city of Constantinople, and he was at home in neither hemisphere.

Kalid changed his mind and shoved the cup aside disgustedly, reaching for the decanter of *raki* on the table. He poured half a glass of the colorless liquid, added water to turn it white, then dashed it off in one gulp, inhaling as the fire spread through his belly.

It had not gone well. The American woman hated him. Kalid sighed; it was to be expected. The whole world knew how independent they were, Americans and their women. He had accepted the situation when he saw her in the Sultan's harem and heard who she was.

Kalid poured a few more drops of liquor into his glass and swirled it thoughtfully. She would set him a task, but it would be worth it in the end. She was fiery; together they would make a beautiful blaze. He wanted her to reciprocate in the Western way, to come to him willingly and meet his fierce desire with her own. There was no triumph in coercing an unwilling woman; that was for cowards. The real victory lay in transforming an initially reluctant opponent into an eager, trembling partner in love.

But that would take time. He'd made a bad beginning, acquiring her as brutally and bloodlessly as he had, but there was no choice. If he had not acted swiftly, she would have ended her stay in the Sultan's harem and gone back home. He would never have seen her again.

The idea was insupportable. He had to have her. His grandmother said he had been bewitched by the blue eye, just like his father, and perhaps it was true. He had a house full of women, and he wanted none of them—none but her. When he'd first seen her in the Grand Hall at Topkapi, she had met his gaze challengingly above her face veil, not averted her gaze in the coy manner of the harem women. He had been riveted. And when he noticed her pale gaze following him with undisguised interest, he had been lost.

She was not indifferent to him, no matter how haughtily she behaved. She felt something, and it was powerful, even if she wouldn't admit it to herself. He knew his effect on women, and he knew he was not wrong. But he must fan that spark hard enough, and long enough, to overcome her outrage at the way she had been taken.

She was proud and willful; very well, so was he. She would be a challenge. He was tired of the tractable harem women; this one would provide some sport. And what pleasure he would take in her when she finally submitted.

Kalid swallowed the rest of his drink and put the back of his hand to his mouth. He wanted her. He wanted her hot, searching mouth on his, her soft, long-fingered hands clutching him convulsively in a frenzy of passion, her pale, yielding body opening to receive his like a sheath accepting a sword.

He closed his eyes, the sweat beading on his forehead, his fists now clenched at his sides.

He would make it happen. He must.

Memtaz waited anxiously in Sarah's chamber; set aside for the *ikbal*, the favorite, it was the most luxurious in the harem, second only to the apartments of the Pasha's female relatives.

"What happened?" the little maid demanded.

"Nothing," Sarah replied.

"Nothing?" Memtaz echoed in puzzlement. A Circassian slave long in Ottoman service, she had been instrumental in Sarah's robing for the presentation to Kalid and was most anxious for her foreign charge to do well.

"He looked me over as if I were a prize heifer he had purchased at the county fair and then sent me back here," Sarah said.

"County fair?"

"Never mind."

"He didn't touch you?"

"He touched me."

"Nothing more?"

"No."

"He was not pleased with you?" Memtaz said, distressed. "How is that possible? You look so lovely, I don't understand. How could my master think he had made a bad choice?"

"He didn't think that, Memtaz," Sarah said wearily. "He said he would have paid anything to get me. He was satisfied. With my appearance, anyway."

Memtaz stared at her, dumfounded.

"Don't look at me like that. This is your cursed country," Sarah muttered, collapsing on a plush divan covered with satin cushions. She surveyed the opulent wall hangings indifferently and then looked once more at the servant woman.

"How is it that Kalid Shah speaks English so well?" Sarah asked Memtaz curiously.

"His mother taught him, and me," Memtaz explained. "She was a blue eye-*gavur* . . ."

"Foreigner?" Sarah said. "A captive?"

Memtaz nodded vigorously. "Yes, captured by the corsairs and sold to the valide pasha, Kalid's father. She was English, like you."

"I'm American."

Memtaz shrugged, as if the difference were of no importance. "The old master loved her very much and had no other kadin while she lived. He indulged her, and when she wished her son to be sent to school in England to learn the ways of her people, the old master complied. There is a university—oh, what is it called, Oxfar . . ."

"Oxford?" Sarah asked, startled.

"Yes, yes. The young master went to shool there before his father died and he returned here to claim his inheritance."

Good lord, Sarah thought. This barbarian who had bought her as if she were a length of yard goods had an Oxford education? His mixed parentage did explain some things, though—his height and the honeyed tinge of his skin, as well as his excellent command of her language.

"Memtaz, what is going to happen to me?" she asked the servant unhappily.

Memtaz shook her head. "Who can say? If you had been a gift from the Sultan, my master would have been forced to marry you, as is our custom. But since he gained you in this way . . ."

"Yes?"

"Most likely you will take your place in the pasha's harem as an odalisque."

"What's that?" Sarah asked quickly, but she knew. She had heard the term in the Sultan's seraglio.

"Female slave."

"Like you?" Sarah asked; she was sure not.

"No, I am *gedikli*, reserved for household tasks. You would be *haseki* . . ." Memtaz hesitated.

"Tell me."

"Reserved for my master's pleasure."

"You mean a concubine," Sarah said dully. She had known it, but saying it aloud somehow made it worse.

Memtaz did not disagree.

Sarah closed her eyes.

"Don't look so sad, mistress," Memtaz said soothingly. "You are really very fortunate. You will have a luxurious life, with nothing to do but bathe in the *hamman,* anoint yourself with fragrant oils and array yourself in splendid garments, smoke the *nargileh,* and eat the choicest sherbets and sweetmeats."

"I don't want to bathe in the hamman, Memtaz, or smoke hashish. I want to be free."

"And Pasha Kalid is young," Memtaz went on, as if Sarah had not spoken. "He is the most handsome man in Bursa, perhaps in the whole Empire. All the harem women sigh heavily for his touch and pray to be chosen for a night of love. You could be bound to an old, ugly, fat man who stinks of garlic. My master is very rich too. He inherited this palace and all its holdings from his father, the harem and the surrounding pashadom from the Golden Horn down into the Bosporus and up to the bedouin hills . . ."

Sarah held up her hand to stop the speech. "Thank you, Memtaz. I know you are trying to comfort me, but I need to be alone now, to think. You may go."

Memtaz bowed.

"And Memtaz?"

The maid turned.

"What does 'kourista' mean?"

Memtaz smiled. "Oh, it is a love term, a great flattering . . . you understand?"

"A compliment?"

"Yes. When a man calls a woman this, it means that she is the object of his aching longing, his strongest . . . desire."

Sarah looked away.

Memtaz withdrew quietly to the anteroom where she slept. Sarah turned and stared out the barred window of her chamber at the stone walls of the carriage house, which connected the pasha's harem to the outside world.

There had to be a way to escape from this place. But how to determine it?

Sarah sighed wretchedly. What was she going to do? She was thousands of miles from home with no way to get in touch with anyone. Even if Roxalena knew what had happened to Sarah, the princess could do nothing against her father the Sultan. James was the only Western person Sarah knew in the whole Ottoman Empire, possibly the only one who could help her, but her cousin was as lost to her as if she had been swallowed by an earthquake.

Sarah's throat closed in horror at her situation. She had been sold, *sold*, for God's sake, to a man who aroused such conflicting feelings in her that the very thought of seeing him again brought her to the verge of hysterical tears.

Chapter One

Constantinople
Capital, Ottoman Empire
July, 1885

"So you are curious about harem life?" James Woolcott said, smiling, taking a sip of his iced drink.

"Of course," Sarah replied. "Who wouldn't be?" His first cousin, she shared James's last name and his passion for travel abroad; they had been raised together in Massachusetts by James's father, Sarah's uncle, like brother and sister.

"Really, James, you should not spend Sarah's vacation with us discussing the immoral practices of these lewd foreigners," Beatrice said stiffly, rising to set her glass next to the silver pitcher on the table. She removed her lace handkerchief from the sleeve of her blue silk afternoon dress and dabbed at her temples with it. Her skirt, which was draped up to show a pleated, striped underpanel, rustled as she sat again and fingered the trailing wisps of her chignon.

"I'm afraid you are the foreigner here, my dear, and immorality is merely a matter of perspective," her husband replied, winking broadly at Sarah.

They were sitting on the second-floor terrace of the Woolcott home in the European section of the city, within view of the Galata Bridge, trying to catch an afternoon breeze from the water. Below them, the bustle of the market, the creaking of carriage wheels and clopping of horses' hooves, and the cries of the vendors near the docks were muted but still audible.

Beatrice picked up a folding fan, its handle inlaid with ivory, from the arm of her rattan chair and began to waft it vigorously.

"Is there any more ice?" she asked her husband.

"Not until the next delivery at the end of the week," he replied. James looked at Sarah. "The ice is brought from snow pits on Mount Olympus, but the trip is very long and arduous and so the ice is scarce and extremely expensive."

"But it helps to make these roasting summer

days bearable. I confess I have never gotten used to the heat, my dear," Beatrice said to Sarah, her freckled face scarlet. "I'm sure that it must be quite a bother for you, too."

"Actually, after twenty years of New England winters, I find the balmy climate a nice change," Sarah said. "The train trip from Paris on the Orient Express gave me plenty of time to adjust to the weather."

"I think Sarah is already in love with the East, Bea, and don't change the subject," James observed. "We were discussing Sultan Hammid's harem."

"I wasn't," Beatrice replied darkly, fanning herself even more vigorously.

"Is there more than one?" Sarah asked.

"Oh, yes. Each of the regional princes, or pashas, has a harem, but Sultan Abdul Hammid's is the largest. It is called the Grand Seraglio, sometimes known as the Sublime Porte, and is said to contain the most beautiful women in the entire world. Hammid's agents scour the Egyptian slave markets and deal with the Barbary pirates in order to acquire the most succulent ladies for their master."

Beatrice made a disgusted sound, annoyed at Sarah's obvious fascination.

"Where is the seraglio?" Sarah asked.

"Deep within Hammid's palace, Topkapi, built on the isthmus between the Sea of Marmara and the Golden Horn."

"What lovely names," Sarah murmured.

"Turkish is a remarkably expressive language, very moving in its images," James remarked.

"I prefer English," Beatrice said.

"Yes, my dear, I know you do, but unfortunately I cannot operate a rug exporting business from Boston Common," James said briskly, setting his sweating glass on the table. "You might adopt Sarah's attitude and look upon our time here as a learning experience rather than as a sentence to purgatory."

"It's hot enough to be purgatory," Beatrice murmured. She adjusted the waist of her fitted bodice, wincing as the whalebone corset pinched her flesh.

"So the Sultan is the chief ruler of the whole Ottoman Empire?" Sarah asked.

James nodded. "He is the padishah, or king pasha, and all the lesser pashas, though in command of their own districts, are his subjects. And the Sultan rules with an iron hand; he is an absolute monarch. To thwart his will means death."

"These people here have no rights, not as we know them in the West," Beatrice interjected, shuddering. "It's very frightening."

"But how can the Sultan sleep with all those women in the harem?" Sarah asked. Her blue eyes were wide.

James burst out laughing. "I see which subject interests you the most! The answer is that he doesn't—only one at a time—and he has his favorite mistresses, as well as kadins, or wives, up to four by law. But the women are all available to him at any time. Their lives consist mostly of waiting, keeping themselves ready to please and entertain should they be called."

"Despicable practice," Beatrice muttered.

"And do they stay there always?" Sarah asked.

"Unless they are given away to one of the other pashas, married off, or sold," James replied, smoothing his neat blond hair, which was the same pale gold as Sarah's.

"And the people here just accept this system?" Sarah said incredulously.

"Oh, there are always insurrections, but so far no one has been able to unify the tribes scattered throughout the empire against the Sultan. And of course the bedouins are constantly fighting with everybody."

"Bedouins?"

"Desert gypsies, Arabs, mortal foes of the Turks. They dwell in tents and live by selling whatever comes their way. They are always staging raids on the outlying districts, as well as attacking traveling caravans, that sort of thing. They resent any attempt to rule them and consider themselves subject to no one."

"It's all so . . ." Sarah groped for a word.

"Uncivilized?" Beatrice supplied, bobbing her head so that her earrings, marcasite-studded beads dangling from silver wires, danced with the motion.

"Very different from teaching fourth grade at

the Southport School," Sarah finished lamely.

"Would you like to get inside the palace to see the seraglio?" James asked Sarah suddenly.

Beatrice stared at him. "You told me visitors are never allowed inside the harem," she said.

"That is traditionally true, but Sultan Hammid is a despot, and he can change his mind at a whim. It so happens that I have heard he's looking for a Western tutor for his daughter, Princess Roxalena. Roxalena is the Princess Sultana, Hammid's oldest daughter—very spoiled, I'm told, but supposedly very bright. She's immensely curious about life outside the Empire. Your cultural twin, Sarah, an Eastern sister."

"So?" Sarah said, interested.

"Well. Roxalena was betrothed at birth to some friend of her father's, a caliph in Damascus, but that fellow was killed in a skirmish a few years ago. Then there was some talk of her marrying the Pasha of Bursa, a chap called Kalid Shah, whom I've never seen but who is said to be quite the young fellow in these parts, the local equivalent of a dashing cavalier. But that didn't happen for some reason, and Roxalena is now sixteen, almost past marrying age. I suspect the Sultan is indulging her in order to get her assent to marrying his choice, sort of a parting gift, if you will. He seems unwilling to force her, which is amazing when you consider how women are usually treated here. But then, people indulge their children, and I assume the Sultan is no exception."

"You are quite well versed in the local lore," Sarah observed with admiration.

"I have to be. My business depends upon my ability to shift with the wind, and to do that I have to know what's going on."

"James, you are not seriously suggesting that Sarah go into the Sultan's harem and tutor that girl," Beatrice said, horrified at the prospect.

"Why not? Her teaching credentials make her the perfect choice, and she would be doing me an immense favor. I operate my business here at Hammid's sufferance and it wouldn't hurt to ingratiate myself by supplying him with the tutor he's seeking. He would be indebted to me, and Sarah would be able to satisfy her own curiosity at the same time. You don't have to be back for the school term until mid-September, right, Sarah?"

"But how could I communicate with my pupil?" Sarah asked. "I don't speak Turkish, not more than a few words and phrases."

"The Princess Sultana speaks some English. There were missionaries in the palace when she was a small child, before her father banished them for stirring up unacceptable ideas. Either age has made him more lenient or he's desperate to marry the girl off soon. Anyway, one of your tasks would be to make her more proficient in the language."

"James, I forbid it!" Bea said sharply. "Sarah came all this way to visit us, not to languish with a bunch of heathens in some glorified brothel."

"Sarah?" James inquired.

"I'm thinking."

"You could find out the secret of the harem and write a book about it when you go home," James said.

"The secret of the harem?"

"Why the women are content to stay and wait to be chosen." James leaned closer to Sarah conspiratorially. "The reason, according to the stories I've heard, is that Turkish men have studied the art of pleasing a woman sexually, and once loved by one of them, a lady will never voluntarily leave his bed."

"James, for heaven's sake!" Beatrice said in an outraged tone, blushing furiously.

James chuckled. "You would have to observe their customs while in the palace, adopt the Ottoman style of dress, and wear the veil in the presence of men other than eunuchs—all of that, Sarah."

"About the eunuchs . . ." Sarah began.

"I've had enough of this," Bea said briskly, rising. "I'm going in to see about dinner."

James and Sarah looked after her.

"I don't think she's very happy here, Cousin James," Sarah observed quietly.

James sighed. "I know. I plan to make as much money as I can for the next four or five years, then go back home and invest in a business there. I hope she can take it for that long."

He looked at Sarah. "Her chief complaint has been that there are no women like herself to talk to—that's why your letters always cheer her. And your visiting was even better. But you've already been here for weeks and seen the local sights. You've been to the covered bazaar and the Byzantine churches and the Roman ruins. Going into the harem would be a chance for you to expand your horizons beyond what most tourists ever see. What do you say, Sarah? I can talk to the *khislar* whenever you want."

"Who is the khislar?

"The chief black eunuch. He serves as the liaison between the harem and the outside world. He is the Sultan's messenger and advisor, very powerful in the palace."

"Why would a man like that consent to become a eunuch?" Sarah asked slowly.

"There's usually no consent involved," James said. "The eunuchs are generally captives of war or caravan raids, even sometimes boys abducted off merchant ships. They are always foreign, the whites usually from the Caucasus, Armenia, and Georgia, the blacks from Abyssinia, Nubia, and the Sudan. Their lot is forced upon them."

Sarah fell silent, shocked.

"A less than charming custom, to the Western mind," James said softly. "But widespread in the East all the way to China, and completely accepted."

"Why do they do it?" Sarah asked.

"The harem women are certainly safe from male servants who are unable to perform with them," James said.

"So everything in their lives is done for the convenience of the Sultan."

"Everything."

Sarah shivered. "I don't know. It's a very brutal world you describe. I'm not sure I should investigate it."

"So we shall have to see whether your curiosity is stronger than your fear." James sat back and folded his hands over his waistcoat, surveying her with a slight smile on his lips. "I do not hesitate to predict that curiosity will win."

Beatrice appeared in the doorway. "Come inside, you two. The insects worsen at dusk, and you will be eaten alive."

Sarah and James rose together, obeying Beatrice's call.

A week later, Sarah and James peered out the side windows of their carriage, coughing as the wheels kicked up dust during the climb toward the Sultan's palace. The building was huge and glitteringly white, with many wings and minarets spiraling toward the sky, the mica in the stone sparkling in the sunlight reflecting from the water below it. The road leading up to it was thronged with traffic, many of the travelers workers at Topkapi, some of them eunuchs in the palace uniform of loose shirt with baggy cotton trousers fitted at the ankle, red waist sash, and black waistcoat embroidered with gold. Sarah patted her chip-straw bonnet and fingered the collar of her brown lightweight summer suit nervously, then bent to dust the draped skirt where it was drawn up to reveal a cream silk ruffle.

"Stop fussing, you look fine," James said reassuringly.

Sarah glanced up to see the gates of the carriage house looming before her, forty feet tall and manned on either side by a halberdier carrying a fearsome axe with a gleaming, slanted blade. And in the exact center of the closed wooden gates stood a huge black man wearing a gorgeously striped silk caftan, belted at the waist with a cloth-of-gold sash, with a headband of the same material worn low on his brow. He was posed with his massive arms folded across his chest and his feet, encased in knee-high black boots, planted far apart.

"There's the khislar," James said. "I believe that he is waiting for you."

Sarah looked at the gates and at her reception committee and felt as if she were entering a forbidden city. She glanced at James anxiously.

"You don't have to go through with it," James said, reading her expression. "I'll just tell the khislar you've changed your mind and we can go home."

Sarah squared her shoulders and sat up; she had initiated this, and it would not look well for James if she backed out at the last minute and disappointed the Sultan.

"No, James, I'll be all right. I would appreciate it if you would accompany me to the gates."

They descended from the carriage, and Sarah felt the khislar's eyes on her as they approached. They examined her closely with an alert, measuring gaze that made her distinctly uncomfortable.

"You've told him that I'm not destined for the usual fate in the harem?" Sarah said sharply.

"Of course," James said. "If you were meant for the Sultan's pleasure, he would undress you and examine you like a physician to see if you passed muster. Just let me emphasize that you are to be returned to my house in the city whenever you request it."

Sarah nodded.

James had a conversation in halting Turkish with the khislar and then turned to Sarah, kissing her on the cheek.

"Good-bye, my dear," he said. "Enjoy yourself. I will expect to see you in a few weeks."

"Good-bye, James," Sarah said, clutching the carpetbag containing her things.

The khislar extended his hand, and after a moment's hesitation, Sarah gave him her satchel. The gates swung open behind them at the same instant, and James's carriage turned around in a circle to begin the downhill journey. Sarah looked after it briefly, then followed the khislar through the carriage house entrance.

Inside the gates, it was another world. People bustled everywhere, each of them seemingly with a purpose, as Sarah trailed the khislar past several guard posts and the quarters for the halberdiers and the eunuchs into an open, cobbled courtyard. All around her workers swept the stones and toted water and carried out their tasks in slavish dedication to their assigned duties. Soldiers marched past in formation, wearing navy uniforms shining with gold buttons and topped off with red flower-pot hats.

Sarah's eyes roamed freely, trying to take it all in. A myriad of corridors led off from the courtyard in all directions; she would later learn that one went to the main gate, another to the school for the young princes, a third to the infirmary, a fourth to the kitchens, and so on. It was all so immense and complicated that she could hardly grasp it, and since she was the subject of much staring and covert commentary, she kept her eyes on the khislar's broad back and concentrated on getting where she was supposed to go. Directly ahead of them was an elaborate arch decorated with lapis lazuli tile; it rose above intricately carved double doors of brass inlaid with stones and sealed with golden handles. Parrot cages with squawking, multicolored birds flanked it, and the birds flapped about as another pair of halberdiers stepped aside when the khislar gestured for them to open the doors.

This was the harem. Sarah tried not to stare rudely, but the spectacle was overwhelming. She had never seen so many women gathered together in one place—so many lovely young women in rich, flowing, albeit scanty garments. They were everywhere, reclining on cushions, sitting on the edge of the marble pool in the center of yet another courtyard, leaning against the columns which surrounded it, bending over the second story balcony which led to the private apartments. Some of them were naked to the waist, draped in heavy gold necklaces hanging between their breasts, their ears decked with similar adornments. Some wore the traditional Turkish garments—a long gown with hanging sleeves which fitted at the back and buttoned up the front, or trousers, very full from waist to knee, with a trim waistcoat. Some wore headdresses; others had their uncovered hair plaited into complicated styles. Most were laden with sumptuous jewelry. All racial types were represented, their skins of every color, their eyes and hair of every hue—though none that Sarah could see was as fair as herself. A quartet of blindfolded musicians played stringed instruments in one corner next to a softly splashing fountain, and small animals—cats and dogs and even a monkey—ran underfoot. Low tables set upon Oriental carpets were heaped with fruit and other delicacies, and Sarah watched the monkey steal an apple and then swing out of sight to eat it.

The khislar halted before a side staircase and looked back at Sarah, who hastened to catch up with him. She could feel the stares, hear the escalating chatter behind her as she climbed the steps and followed him into a private chamber at the end of the upper hall.

A young girl was reclining on a divan in a room as ornately furnished as the lower floor, reading a book. She jumped to her feet, and the slim volume slid to the rug when she saw Sarah.

She was exquisite, her shining black hair falling loosely to her waist, her huge doe's eyes as dark as onyx and fringed with heavy lashes. She was wearing pink silk harem trousers with a full-sleeved, amethyst blouse and a wide silver sash encircling her tiny waist. Heavy pearls dangled from her ears and hung from a silver choker about her slender throat. A matching cap of silver mesh thickly embroidered with seed pearls was perched rakishly on her small, neat head.

She startled Sarah by seizing her hand, kissing it, and then holding it to her brow.

"My English teacher!" she said, beaming. "I am Roxalena. I am so happy to have you here. *Tessekur ederim.*"

"You are welcome, Princess," Sarah replied. "I am very happy to be here."

Roxalena made a gesture dismissing the khislar, who set down Sarah's bag, bowed, and left the room.

"My English is most very bad, please to excuse it," Roxalena said, leading Sarah to the divan she had vacated and indicating that she should sit. Roxalena then curled up like a cat next to her. "How are you calling yourself?"

"My name is Sarah."

"And you are from the U.S. of America. My father's mapmaker has been showing me this place on his charts. It is very far?"

"Yes, very far."

"And are all the women there dressed like you?"

"Most of them, yes."

"But these are ugly clothes!" Roxalena said, with a sweeping motion of her hand. "Why do you wish to look like an old brown hen?"

Sarah smiled, thinking that the princess's English was much better than she professed.

"I assure you, your highness, that this is the latest fashion in my country."

"And your yellow hair, that is common too?"

"Common enough."

"And is it always bound up so?" she said, twirling her finger to indicate Sarah's bun.

"Usually, your highness."

"Bah!" Roxalena said. "I will give you some of my fine things, and you will be looking most beautiful very soon, hair let down, most very pretty. And my father is the highness, not me. You have no highnesses in the U.S. of America, true?"

"True."

"And the women walk about the streets unveiled and run the government?" Roxalena said eagerly.

Sarah laughed. "Well, we don't wear veils, and we *are* campaigning for the vote. . . ."

"Vote?"

"I'll explain it all in due time, your . . . Roxalena."

Roxalena nodded eagerly. "How long have you been in the Empire?" she asked.

"For several weeks."

"And you had a sea journey to get here?"

"Yes, from New York to Paris. Then I took the train from Paris to Constantinople."

"I am longing most sincerely to see Paris, France," Roxalena said, sighing. "I have many books, but old ones mostly, in Turkish. They have pictures, but it is not the same, is it?"

"No, it's not the same."

Roxalena looked around the gorgeous room, as if surveying the walls of a prison.

"I will never see Paris," she said mournfully.

"Maybe you will."

Roxalena shook her head. "It is written on my forehead that I will live out my life here." She seized Sarah's hand again. "That is why you are so important. You must be my eyes and ears, my window on the world. First, I must learn better English to read your books."

"Princess, your English is excellent."

"But I cannot read, I can only speak! It is

most important that I learn your letters and the writing."

"I can teach you that."

"But will there be enough time before you go?" Roxalena said anxiously.

"We will work hard," Sarah replied, smiling.

Roxalena clapped her hands delightedly. They were interrupted by a loud burst of girlish laughter from the first floor.

"What is that?" Sarah asked.

Roxalena put her finger to her lips and grabbed Sarah's wrist with her free hand. She led Sarah out to the balcony, and they both looked down into the open courtyard. The young women splashing gaily in the marble pool spied them and suddenly erupted into more giggles, covering their mouths.

"Silly asses," Roxalena muttered wryly.

Sarah stared at her, trying not to grin. She wasn't sure what she had expected of an imperial princess, but Roxalena was not it.

"Why are you annoyed with them?" Sarah asked, nodding toward the girls.

"Annoyed?"

"You just said they were silly."

Roxalena shrugged. "They have heard today that Kalid Shah will be paying my father a visit on the Feast of the Flowers. They are plotting what to wear and how to act to catch his eye."

"Is that the Pasha of Bursa?"

"You know of him? I was almost pledged to him, but I told my father I would not marry him, that if he sent the betrothal ring I would take the almond poison and kill myself."

"Why?" Sarah asked, aghast.

"I have met Kalid, and there was no fire in his eyes at the prospect of our marriage. I will not go to a man who does not want me."

Good for you, Sarah thought. Unfortunately, the rest of Roxalena's countrywomen did not have her latitude to refuse.

"These silly girls," Roxalena said, waving toward the bathing pool, "all hope that he will single one of them out and ask the Sultan to take her back to Bursa with him. Kalid has no kadin and, it is often said, no favorite."

"Is that unusual?"

Roxalena rolled her eyes. "He thinks he is unusual, *guzdar* . . ."

Sarah raised her brows inquiringly.

"Special," Roxalena said.

Several black eunuchs, their ebony hair covered with turbans, walked below them and began clearing away the food from the tables.

"Are there no white eunuchs in the harem?" Sarah asked.

"No, they attend upon my father in the *selamlik*, where he meets with his male visitors," Roxalena replied.

As they watched the women in the pool, one of the girls put her arm around her companion's shoulder and bent to kiss her neck. The recipient of the kiss tilted her head back and then slipped her hand inside her friend's blouse, caressing her breast. They whispered together for a moment and then climbed out of the pool. They ran, hand in hand, into an adjoining room.

Sarah looked away, embarrassed, but Roxalena merely shrugged philosophically.

"Often they are not chosen by the Sultan for a long time," she said simply. "They make do with each other. And still others become addicted to the poppy and spend their days in opium dreams."

Sarah listened in silence. She was not surprised to learn that harem life, seemingly so indolent, had its dark side.

Both women turned as the khislar appeared behind them and said something to Roxalena.

The Princess smiled at Sarah.

"My father wishes to meet you," she said, obviously pleased. "To be summoned by the Sultan so soon, it is a very great honor. Come, we must make ready to see him. And after that we will have my very first English writing lesson!"

Chapter Two

"Tell her to take off her clothes," Kosem said.

The slave trader translated the order into Greek, and the girl obediently shrugged off the robe she wore. The folds of cotton fell to the floor as the girl stood with downcast eyes, her naked beauty revealed to the world.

"Well, Kalid," Kosem said, "isn't she lovely?"

Kalid Shah glanced at his grandmother, then at the unfortunate young woman standing before them. Her hair, coated with butter to make it shine, was plaited elaborately, glowing like onyx in the lamplight. Small, perfect breasts jutted forward from her slender form, and a concave belly led down to a thick pubic bush curling densely between her long, graceful legs.

"From Thessaly," Kosem said with satisfaction, nodding at the slaver. "What do you think?"

"Very pretty, grandmother," Kalid said.

"Very pretty? I pay thirteen hundred *kurush* for this girl and all you can say is 'very pretty'?"

"I didn't ask you to buy her," Kalid said.

"Take her away," Kosem said to the trader, who spat a harsh syllable, and the girl scurried from the room. The trader bowed his way out. Kosem waited until they were both gone before she said to her grandson, "Kalid, I am old and likely to die soon."

"You'll outlive me," Kalid replied, smiling.

"I want to see your son before I go. I want to know that your father's name will live on."

"Grandmother, we've had this conversation before."

"And I'm not getting any younger."

Kalid sighed.

"Yes, I know," the old lady said sarcastically, "none of these girls is good enough for you."

"I never said that."

"You wouldn't have the Princess Sultana!"

"Roxalena refused me."

"She refused you because you obviously had no interest in her! You weren't even polite enough to pretend."

"She doesn't want me and I don't want her."

"Want, what is this 'want'? An idea for children! Do you think I 'wanted' your grandfather

43

when I came to him? This grows with time. It is enough that you are man and woman, young enough to produce children, and your families wish the alliance."

Kalid's mouth tightened. "Talk to Roxalena, old woman. She was no happier about the match than I was."

"She's the Sultan's daughter—do you think she would have a reluctant man forced upon her? She's the toast of the empire! A chance to marry into the Sultan's family and you throw it away. *Masshallah*, son of my son, you are a fool."

Kalid took a sip of his *boza*, not bothering to reply.

The old lady leaned forward eagerly. "Kalid, get married. Marry anybody—this girl you have seen tonight or another one like her—so you can produce a legitimate heir. Then you can have other wives or as many courtesans as you want. Is it so much, to ask you to do this one thing for me before I pass from this world?"

"Grandmother, you are not passing anywhere."

"There are rumors that you do not marry because you are useless with women and cannot father a son," Kosem said craftily.

Kalid shot her a disgusted glance. This was beyond ridiculous, even for her.

"If your father were still alive, he would order you to marry!" Kosem burst out, changing tactics again.

"My father is dead, and you are boring me," Kalid said. "Watch your tongue, old woman, or you will wind up restricted to the harem with nothing to say."

Kosem eyed him narrowly; his tolerance for his grandmother was legendary, and she could get away with telling him things no one else would dare mention.

"You think I don't know where you have gotten these ideas," Kosem said flatly.

Kalid met her eyes, then looked away.

"Your English mother filled your head with English fairy tales, then died and left me to deal with the consequences!" Kosem added in a strong voice, shaking her finger at him.

"Enough!" Kalid said, rising. "Go to bed."

Kosem didn't move.

"Didn't you hear me?" Kalid said softly.

The old lady gathered herself up with great dignity and stalked from the room, her head held high.

Kalid smiled to himself at her theatrics. Then his smile faded as he considered what she had said.

She was right about one thing.

He didn't want any woman in his kingdom, and he was beginning to wonder if he ever would.

"Bah! I cannot say it!" Roxalena threw the book on the floor.

"It's a soft *g*, Roxalena—it's pronounced like

a *j*," Sarah said patiently, retrieving the book from the carpet and opening it again to the page they had been reading.

"Then why not use the *j?*" Roxalena demanded. "Hard *g* and soft *g*, hard *c* which is really a *k*, and soft *c*, which is really an *s*—this is all so confusing!"

"I don't know why there are two pronunciations for the same letter. I didn't invent the language. English evolved over a long period of time and borrowed from many other languages in the process. . . ." Sarah stopped when she saw that Roxalena was staring at her.

"Never mind," Sarah said, closing the book. "I think you have had enough for today." Both women looked toward the door as a eunuch entered the room and bowed low before Roxalena.

"Your clothes are here!" Roxalena said delightedly, taking the package from the servant and waving him away. She ripped open the package and held up a gauzy blouse of sapphire blue with a matching wisp of silken veil.

"What do you think?" she asked eagerly.

"I am supposed to wear that for Kalid Shah's visit tonight?" Sarah asked incredulously.

"Certainly."

"It's transparent!"

"It's just the right color. I chose it especially to flatter your eyes. And this with it"—she held up a pair of linen trousers, embroidered with silver thread—"and these shoes." She held out a pair of kid slippers with upturned toes, also decorated with silver.

"Where did you get these things?" Sarah asked in amazement, watching her.

"I ordered them from my tirewoman. And you will wear my sapphire-and-pearl earrings, with my diamond necklace and the girdle of opals and pearls."

"Roxalena, I couldn't possibly—" Sarah began.

Roxalena held up her hand. "You would embarrass me in front of my father's pasha?" she inquired archly.

"Of course not, but all of this is unnecessary."

"You must be suitably dressed or Kalid Shah will think the house of Sultan Hammid has fallen on hard times, and he might perhaps be inspired to rebel."

"I see," Sarah said, smiling. "I could cause a revolution if I don't wear those clothes."

"Who knows?" Roxalena replied, grinning impishly. Her smile vanished abruptly as she placed the shoes at her side on the divan and a folded piece of paper fell out of one of them. She snatched it up and held it to her bosom protectively.

"What's that?" Sarah asked.

"It's for me," Roxalena said hastily, looking out into the hall to make sure she was not observed.

"You didn't answer the question."

"It's best you know nothing of this," Roxalena said soberly. "Such information could be dangerous."

"It's from Osman Bey, isn't it?" Sarah asked, and the expression on Roxalena's face told her she was right.

"How could you know?" Roxalena whispered, frightened and growing pale.

"I've seen the way you look at one another," Sarah replied. "You're meeting him in secret, aren't you?"

Roxalena hesitated, then nodded.

"I thought he seemed particularly attentive to you at the bathing outing the other day. But why conceal your relationship? He's the captain of your father's halberdiers. That's an important position. Aren't you allowed to talk to him?"

"He's a commoner," Roxalena said sadly. "I must marry one of the nobility. A liaison with such a one as Osman is forbidden. If it were discovered, Osman would be put to death."

"And he's willing to take such a risk?" Sarah gasped.

"We both are," Roxalena replied, meeting her gaze. "You must say nothing of this to anyone."

"I won't, but—"

Roxalena motioned for silence as they heard running footsteps coming closer and the women calling to one another excitedly.

"What is it?" asked Sarah, who could not understand their garbled cries.

"Kalid Shah is arriving. His caravan is on the road leading up to the main gate. We can see it from over there."

They both hurried to the window she indicated and knelt on the silk cushioned seat before it. The view from the second story harem quarters looked out over the red tiled roofs of the other wings. In the distance, raising a cloud of dust, they could see a procession of horses and wagons making stately progress toward the palace.

"Which one is he?" Sarah asked, craning her neck.

"Kalid?"

"Yes."

Roxalena peered over her shoulder. "At the head of the column, on the white horse draped with gold hangings. The two men riding just behind him are supposed to be his guards."

"Supposed to be?"

"He won't let them do their job. He thinks he can take care of himself. He only consents to have them with him to humor the valide pashana, his grandmother. The old lady is superstitious, and since she's the only family he has left . . ." Roxalena shrugged.

"He's arrogant, then."

Roxalena snorted.

Sarah chuckled.

"Why do you laugh?"

"Arrogance is a trait that seems in abundant supply around here," Sarah commented.

Roxalena took a second to register what had been said, then grinned delightedly.

"I suppose you have no arrogant men in the U.S. of America?" she teased.

"Quite a few," Sarah admitted. She stared down at the robed figure riding at the head of the moving column.

"He seems quite a bit taller than everybody else," she said thoughtfully.

"He is. When he visits my father, the Sultan always invites Kalid to sit very quickly so that the pasha does not tower over him." Roxalena covered her mouth with her hand and giggled.

Shirza, Roxalena's personal servant and hairdresser, appeared in the doorway and bowed gracefully.

"Will your Majesty be needing my services soon?" she asked respectfully.

"Yes, yes. It is time for us to dress. My father will require the women to attend upon him after he has dined and conversed with Kalid in private. Go and fetch what you need, and send Alev for my jewel box."

Roxalena turned to Sarah and smiled.

"We must all be very beautiful for my father's guest," she said charmingly.

Sarah surveyed herself in Roxalena's standing pier glass and did not recognize the woman she saw. The material of the silk blouse she wore was so thin that her arms were visible through the sleeves, and its scoop neck revealed the tops of her breasts and the diamond pendant which hung about her neck. The full linen trousers, known as *shalwar*, nipped in at the waist and ankle and were fastened at the hips with Roxalena's jeweled girdle. The misty blue veil covered but did not conceal her hair, and its accompanying drape hid her face except for her eyes, which glowed in complement to the fine materials and luxurious ornaments.

"*Seker*, yes?" Roxalena said from behind her, pleased.

The word meant sugar, and by reference sweet, or desirable.

"Roxalena, this ensemble is scandalous beyond description," Sarah said softly.

"What means this, scandalous?" Roxalena asked.

Sarah sighed. How could she communicate the mores of Victorian society to this woman whose whole life had been a preparation for seduction, a training ground in the art of pleasing men? Roxalena would find her objections ridiculous, and Sarah had promised to abide by Ottoman customs if she came to Topkapi.

"Nothing," she said, smiling slightly, shaking her head. "Thank you. I am grateful for your efforts and happy that you're pleased with the result."

Roxalena beamed. "Now you must remember to keep your veil in place unless you are asked to remove it by my father. And you must not speak unless you are spoken to by one of the men, and keep your eyes downcast during the performance."

"What performance?"

"The *chengis*, a group of women skilled in dance, have prepared a traditional entertainment for Kalid's pleasure."

"I don't know, Roxalena, I'm sure I'm going to do something wrong," Sarah said nervously.

"If you make a mistake I will shake my head, so, and you will stop, yes? Most likely you will not be required to do anything except watch the performance and then leave with the other women."

"All right."

Two eunuchs came to the door and folded their arms in a waiting stance.

"It is time," Roxalena said.

Sarah took her place beside the princess, and they walked out into the hall.

The marble-floored *Hunkar Sofasi*, the Hall of the Sultan, was almost empty as the harem women entered it. At one end was a raised platform under an ornamental canopy, or *baldachin*, with an elaborate throne for the Sultan and smaller gilt chairs for his kadins and guests. Before the throne was a silk carpet embroidered by tirewomen, with comfortable tasseled cushions arranged for the favorite concubines, and above it was a balcony where the *sazende* were tuning their stringed instruments. Tapestries suspended from the ceiling wafted back and forth, acting like fans to stir the warm air.

Sarah had barely entered the huge, columned room before cymbals clashed and the musicians began to play a slow, stately march. From the double doors at the rear, guarded by Osman Bey and his halberdiers, the Sultan advanced into the room, followed by his honored guest, his retainers, and his women at the rear. Sarah watched as Roxalena moved to take her place in the procession next to the first and second kadins, and then Sarah's gaze fell on Kalid Shah. Thereafter she saw only him; it was as if everyone else in the vast chamber had disappeared.

He was dressed in a scarlet robe edged with gold, the hanging sleeves slashed to display tight-fitting white silk armlets beneath them. The dagger at his waist was studded with diamonds, and a white aigrette in his turban held a cluster of rubies, diamonds, and pearls. He turned slightly, as if he sensed Sarah's eyes on him, and she felt a shock as his imperious gaze met hers.

He had the darkest eyes she had ever seen, heavily marked by black brows and thick lashes, and tendrils of glossy black hair escaped his headdress at the sides to curl about his ears. His short sable beard framed red lips that parted as he looked at her, and for the long moments that they gazed at one another time seemed to stand still. Then the Sultan clapped his hands, Kalid looked back toward the dais, and the spell was broken.

Sarah looked around almost wildly, as if afraid that her thoughts were visible, disconcerted to find that her heart was pounding and her mouth was dry. She deliberately unclenched her fists as the Sultan took his seat and the others settled around him, the novice concubines leaning against the wall, as they were not permitted to sit in the presence of the Sultan. The kadins and Roxalena sat on his left, Kalid Shah on his right. Just before the Sultan clapped his hands again and the dancers scampered into the room, Sarah was sure that Kalid's dark gaze swept the crowd and settled on her once more.

What transpired next was a blur. The musicians began to play a lively tune that soon had the dancers whirling. They wore low-necked muslin blouses, embroidered vests, and capacious skirts that opened like fans as they spun. There were twelve of them—the leader, ten dancers, and an apprentice. As one tune concluded, it led into another, and a fine sheen of sweat soon appeared on their bodies as they leaped and capered to the music. When the Sultan became bored, he signaled to the musicians, and the music changed to a slow, seductive melody. The dancers filed to the side of the floor as the leader doffed her skirt and blouse and moved into a belly dance.

Sarah was hardly aware of the spectacle taking place; her eyes were fixed on Kalid Shah, who was watching the performance expressionlessly. When the dancers left, they were succeeded by a band of gymnasts, and then by a magician, and it seemed an eternity before the women were dismissed and the men were left to their pipes. Sarah got a last glimpse of Kalid Shah as she filed out of the hall behind the eunuchs on her way back to the harem. He was leaning forward, saying something to the first kadin, who nodded and smiled.

Sarah had hardly returned to her apartment when Shirza bustled in after her, quite out of breath. She bowed hastily and then said, "My lady requests that you attend upon her immediately, Miss Sarah," she said slowly in elementary Turkish, with explicatory gestures, so that Sarah could understand.

"Where is the princess?" Sarah asked, surprised.

"In the Sultan's private audience chamber," Shirza replied quietly, obviously impressed.

"But why does she want me to come there?" Sarah asked.

"I know not, miss. Your escort is waiting."

Sarah stepped into the hall, and two eunuchs fell into step beside her. They led her to a small, expensively furnished room off the great hall, and she stopped short on the threshold when she saw who was waiting for her there—the Sultan, Roxalena, and Kalid Shah.

"Come in, Sarah," Roxalena said carefully, indicating with her eyes that Sarah was to proceed cautiously. Roxalena approached the Sultan, who was reclining on a divan, smoking, and made a low obeisance before him. When she looked up, he nodded and smiled, saying something she could not follow.

"My father, Sultan Abdul Hammid IV, Lord of the Golden Crescent, Lion of the Desert, sends you greetings, Sarah Woolcott," Roxalena translated into English, "and would present you to his Pasha of the District of Bursa, Kalid Shah."

Her pulse racing, Sarah turned her gaze on the pasha. He regarded her intently, reclining on one elbow, his deep red robe open now to reveal a supple brown throat and an undershift of white silk. At close range, he was even more impressive, his coloring more vivid, his presence impossible to ignore. Sarah bowed gracefully in his direction. He inclined his head.

The Sultan spoke again.

"My father instructs you to drop your veil," Roxalena said.

Sarah looked at her sharply.

"It is the Sultan's wish," Roxalena added meaningfully, nodding vigorously.

Sarah swallowed hard, then loosened the clips which held the the face piece to her veil. It came away in her hand, revealing her features.

"And the rest," Roxalena said, interpreting

her father's impatient gesture. Kalid Shah said nothing, merely watched as Sarah swept the veil from her head, uncovering her bound hair.

The Sultan murmured approvingly, puffing on his pipe.

"Why am I doing this?" Sarah asked Roxalena, who shook her head warningly.

Sarah subsided, remembering her instructions. She was not supposed to initiate conversation.

The Sultan regarded Sarah imperiously, annoyed by her question. Then he barked a further order, his benign mood dispelled.

"My father would have you unbind your hair," Roxalena said, her eyes directing Sarah to obey without objection.

Sarah removed the pins from her chignon, wondering if she would be required to disrobe next. Then she bent and shook out her hair, throwing her head back to loosen the tresses. When her gaze settled on Kalid, he was leaning forward, regarding her fixedly.

"Will they want to count my teeth?" she asked Roxalena sarcastically in English, unable to stop herself.

Roxalena shook her head violently, her eyes round as saucers, her expression apprehensive.

Sarah settled for running her fingers through her hair luxuriously, eyeing Kalid Shah defiantly.

When he spoke, she jumped; it was as if a

beautiful statue in the room had come to life and talked.

"Pasha Kalid asks why you have come to the Topkapi harem," Roxalena said cautiously.

"Doesn't he know?" Sarah countered, watching his face.

"Answer the question," Roxalena hissed.

"I have come to teach the Princess Roxalena English and to learn something of Ottoman culture," Sarah replied obediently.

Roxalena murmured a Turkish translation.

Kalid spoke again, his voice low and modulated.

"Pasha Kalid marvels that your husband would allow you to come so far alone and undertake such a mission," Roxalena said.

"Tell him that I have no husband and that I do what I like," Sarah said firmly. She watched Kalid's reaction as Roxalena translated her statement. His lips never moved, but she could have sworn she saw a smile in his eyes.

The Sultan said something abruptly, waving his hand in a gesture of dismissal.

"We are free to go," Roxalena said, rising and bowing to the two men. Sarah did the same. The princess and her tutor left the room, and the door was closed behind them by a servant.

"What is her name again, the American woman?" Kalid said to the Sultan, as soon as the women were gone.

The Sultan turned to look at him.

"Sarah Woolcott," he replied.

"I want her," Kalid said flatly.

The Sultan smiled.

"Did you see him?" Roxalena exulted, laughing delightedly. "His tongue was hanging out like that of a parched dog! Oh, that I should live to witness it. The great Pasha Kalid pining for a woman! I can die happy now."

"What are you talking about?" Sarah asked in irritation, still smarting from the humiliating interview. She lay down on the plush divan in Roxalena's apartment and rested her head on a satin pillow, settling herself wearily.

"He is besotted with you!" Roxalena said, grinning. "If my father hadn't gotten bored when he did, Kalid would have stripped you to the skin and filled his eyes to brimming with your beauty."

"Not without a fight, he wouldn't," Sarah replied grimly, adjusting the pillow under her head more comfortably and sighing.

Roxalena chuckled, enjoying herself immensely. "I always knew that someone would come along . . ." She looked at Sarah, a measuring expression in her eyes.

"What do you mean?"

"I mean someone who would strip him of that indifference and make him . . ."

Sarah waited.

"Hot," Roxalena concluded. "Who knew it would be you?" She lifted the diadem from her hair and handed it to a waiting servant, dissolving into chuckles again.

"Roxalena, I'm glad you find all of this so amusing, but being paraded in front of your father and his guest like a fatted calf . . ."

"What's that?" Roxalena inquired, removing her earbobs and sitting next to Sarah on the divan.

"Never mind," Sarah said.

"My father was only accommodating his visitor," Roxalena went on, as if Sarah hadn't spoken. "Kalid saw you in the crowd and wanted to get a better look at you. He requested that you be brought into the antechamber so that he might examine you."

"That he did," Sarah said dryly.

Shirza appeared in the doorway, carrying an elaborately carved wooden tray.

"What is it?" Roxalena asked her.

"A gift for Miss Sarah from my lord the Pasha of Bursa," Shirza recited ceremoniously, kneeling and proffering the tray.

Roxalena giggled and elbowed Sarah in the ribs.

"Please," Sarah said, closing her eyes.

"Bring it in here," Roxalena said eagerly, eyeing the tray's contents avariciously.

Shirza entered and placed the tray on a table inlaid with ivory, setting it in front of the divan.

"Bursa perfume, made for the house of Shah's women alone, blended of the essence of jasmine and rosemary, sandalwood and ambergris," Shirza said, indicating a carved crystal bottle.

It was decorated with cobalt flowers and capped with a silver stopper.

Roxalena nodded approvingly. "Very costly," she said.

"A jeweled hairpin, for a lady with such wealth of tresses will surely have need of it," Shirza went on, indicating a golden bodkin, such as Oriental women used to skewer a bun, displayed on a white linen napkin. It was studded with diamond chips and featured a pigeon's-blood ruby at its rounded crest.

"Tasteful," Roxalena said.

"And coffee from Yemen, specially prepared," Shirza concluded. "Kalid Shah instructs that it is for the palate of Miss Sarah alone, as it is his special gift to her." Shirza poured the dark, steaming liquid from the *jezve* into an enameled cup which already contained a quarter inch of froth. She handed the cup to Sarah.

"Well, drink it," Roxalena said, smiling. "It would be an insult not to do so."

Sarah drained the small cup, grimacing at the bitter taste. She would never get used to Turkish coffee.

Shirza waited expectantly.

"Have you nothing to say to the sender of these offerings?" Roxalena asked Sarah, wide-eyed with innocence. "It would be very bad manners not to respond to such lavish presents."

"Tell Kalid Shah I thank him very much for his courtesy," Sarah said tightly.

"That is all?" Roxalena asked.

"That is all."

Shirza bowed and left the room.

"Kalid will be disappointed," Roxalena said gravely.

"What would he expect me to say?" Sarah asked, yawning.

"That you will join him in his chamber for a night of passion?" Roxalena suggested.

"Very funny. To tell you the truth, my first instinct was to send it all back, but I realize that such an act would not be in accordance with your customs."

"Certainly not," Roxalena said, shocked. She watched as Sarah rose and then staggered slightly.

"I must be more tired than I thought," Sarah said, passing a hand over her eyes. "I'd better go to bed."

"What about all this?" Roxalena asked, indicating the tray.

"You keep it. In the morning, we'll try the c's and g's again."

Roxalena made a face.

"Good night," Sarah said in Turkish.

"Good night," Roxalena said in English.

In the hall, the eunuchs who accompanied the harem women everywhere fell into step beside Sarah and followed her to her room. By the time she approached her sleeping couch, she was so dizzy that she sat down harder than she had intended. Then she found she could not get up again to undress.

What on earth was wrong with her? She lay back on the cushions, the light from the long tapers burning in the sconces blurring when she looked at it.

She closed her eyes. Time for a little rest. Then she would get up and find out what was going on.

When Sarah woke, it was several seconds before she realized that she was not in her room at the Topkapi harem. The divan was covered in different fabric, a rose brocade, and the walls were pink sandstone, hung with lighter tapestries than the white walls of the Sultan's palace. She sat up abruptly, alarmed, and a bolt of agony shot through her head at the movement, making her groan. She held her head for several seconds, waiting for the wave of pain to recede.

Then Sarah realized that she was not alone, and she blinked rapidly, trying to bring the figure sitting at her side into focus. When her vision cleared, she saw a diminutive woman, who could have been anywhere from thirty to fifty, attired in a simple muslin gown. She brought her hands together and bowed deeply from the waist.

"I am Memtaz," this person said. "I have been assigned to you because I speak English, as does my master."

"Where am I?" Sarah gasped.

"At the Orchid Palace, the home of Pasha

Kalid Shah. He has bought you from the Sultan at an enormous price, and you are now his property. Come, you must prepare yourself to see him."

Chapter Three

The khislar stepped aside to admit Roxalena to her father's presence. She bowed low and performed the customary obeisance, waiting for the Sultan to command her to rise.

"Well?" the Sultan said abruptly, helping himself to a piece of *halvah* from a silver salver held by a slave at his side. Behind him two Nubians stood waving elaborate feathered fans rhythmically, stirring the draperies of the throne room.

Roxalena looked up, judged that it was permissible to stand, and did so. She waited.

The Sultan gestured impatiently with the sweetmeat.

"My English teacher has disappeared," Roxalena said bluntly. She always knew when coquetry would work with her father, and

65

this was not one of those times.

The Sultan said nothing, merely looked bored, as if this inconsequential matter had nothing to do with him.

"I am worried about her," Roxalena added.

"Western women should not come to this country," the Sultan said airily. "Strange things happen to them here."

Roxalena knew that her father had his finger on the pulse of everything that took place at the palace, but to inquire further when he clearly had no wish to discuss the matter was dangerous, for herself as well as for Sarah.

"I miss my English lessons," Roxalena said, trying another tactic with him.

"Teachers are easily bought. I will instruct the khislar to find you another," the Sultan said with finality. He made a dismissive sweep of his hand, indicating that the interview was concluded.

Roxalena bowed and withdrew, then scurried out of the throne room and down a side corridor. She drew her veil over her face and bent her head, taking care to stay close to the walls and avoid being noticed. As she neared the kitchen, servants bustled past her carrying covered baskets and bales of fruit and bundles of linens, intent on their tasks. Behind the main kitchen was an alley where refuse was dumped, and Roxalena opened a small metal door and stepped into it, holding a scented gauze handkerchief to her nose delicately.

Osman Bey emerged from an alcove across the way and embraced her immediately, almost lifting her off her feet.

"You got my message," Roxalena said against his shoulder, closing her eyes and inhaling his clean masculine scent, her cheek crushed against the tunic of his uniform.

"It isn't safe for you to come here," Osman said. "Are you sure you weren't seen?"

"I was very careful. This is an emergency."

"What happened?"

"My friend Sarah, the teacher who has been giving me English lessons, has vanished from the palace."

"Kidnapped?" Osman said, holding her off and looking down into her face.

Roxalena shrugged worriedly. "I have no idea. Of course my father knows what happened, but he won't tell me anything. He probably had a hand in it."

"You want me to ask some questions, see what I can learn?"

Roxalena nodded. "Please. Sarah hasn't been in the East very long and I don't know what will become of her. She volunteered to teach me and I feel responsible for bringing her to Topkapi."

"Consider it done," Osman said, and kissed her forehead tenderly. "Tomorrow night, in the boathouse?" he asked.

"Tomorrow night," Roxalena said, squeezing his hand.

"Don't worry. I will have some word of your friend by then," he said reassuringly, and Roxalena slipped out of his arms, running back through the door.

It was two days before Sarah was summoned before Kalid Shah once more, and during that time Memtaz undertook to instruct her in some aspects of harem life, but Sarah proved an unwilling pupil. She stared sullenly as she looked on during the rituals of the hamman, the bathing pool—dying the hands and feet with henna, scrubbing the skin with pumice stones, washing the hair with egg yolks, and perfuming the whole body with sandalwood, ambergris, and myrrh. Sarah wasn't interested in making herself beautiful for Kalid Shah, but just as when she was first presented to him as his captive, it was clear that she would have little choice in the matter. She sat like a statue while a coterie of slaves, under the direction of Memtaz, removed the almost invisible hair on her body with *ada*, a lemon-and-sugar paste. This was a stinging ritual which left her gasping with rage and indignation as well as pain, but when she struggled, Memtaz summoned two eunuchs to hold her down, and the process continued. When the depilation was complete, she was bathed and painted with almond to whiten her already pale skin, and rouged on cheeks and lips and nipples. Sarah stared balefully into a gilt mirror as Memtaz carefully outlined her eyes with kohl and darkened her brows with India ink, completing the process. When she stood and Memtaz added a sky-blue caftan embroidered with gold thread to her tunic of cotton gauze, the Circassian slave clapped her hands delightedly.

"Very beautiful," she pronounced.

"How do I get out of here?" Sarah asked.

"You cannot. Best to make yourself the favorite and enjoy the position for as long as it lasts."

"Then what? Do I get handed over to the guardsmen when the pasha tires of me?"

"It is your job to make sure he does not tire of you."

Sarah sighed and surrendered. All of her conversations with Memtaz went the same way: in a circle.

"Why doesn't he just rape me and get it over with?" Sarah muttered despairingly. "He's toying with me, leaving me alone to imagine all sorts of horrible things. Then when he *does* send for me, I have to go through this ridiculous preparation process."

"Are you missing him?" Memtaz asked slyly.

"Are you kidding?" Sarah countered.

"You look like . . . *jinni*. An angel."

"I feel like General Custer's mare, braided hair and all."

"Beg pardon?" Memtaz said.

"Never mind. Am I ready?"

"You are ready."

Sarah tugged at the elaborate plaits in her

hair, which were giving her a headache, and Memtaz slapped her wrist.

"Leave alone, please."

"All this headgear hurts, Memtaz. These bodkins alone must weigh a pound," Sarah complained, indicating the carved ivory hairpins skewering her braids. The ornaments were heavy with pearls and other precious gems.

Memtaz pressed her lips together, but said nothing. She was beginning to lose patience with her recalcitrant charge, who could not seem to understand that thousands of women in the empire would be eager to take her place.

Sarah finally met her eyes.

"Ready to go?" Memtaz asked.

Sarah hesitated, then nodded.

Memtaz clapped her hands and the doors of the dressing chamber opened immediately, as if by magic. Two eunuchs stood waiting, then fell into place beside the women as they walked down the marble-floored corridor.

The Orchid Palace was smaller and less elaborate than Topkapi, but more tasteful in its way, the sandstone walls, hung with rich tapestries, casting a warm glow over the gleaming floors. The harem was located between the *mabeyn*, the pasha's apartments, and the quarters of the chief black eunuch. The valide pashana, Kalid Shah's grandmother, had the most ornate suite in the harem, but as Sarah was now the favorite, her chamber was almost as luxurious, with Memtaz's anteroom adjoining it. The Carriage House and Bird House connected the harem to outside world, both guarded from within by the eunuchs and outside by the corps of halberdiers. Sarah and Memtaz turned the corner for the mabeyn and paused before the carved double doors, waiting as the captain of the guards banged on them with his truncheon.

"Come," Kalid's voice called from within, and Sarah reacted to the very sound of it, her heart beating faster.

They entered Kalid's audience chamber, walking across a huge Kirman carpet embroidered with birds of paradise, passing marble columns hung with golden wall sconces containing flaming tapers. At one end of the chamber was a small sitting room hung with orchid silk draperies; there Kalid reclined on a brocade divan, the inlaid table before him covered with an assortment of delicacies. He examined the women as they approached, then gestured to the empty divan opposite him.

"For you," he said to Sarah, who sat on its edge gingerly.

"You may go," Kalid said to Memtaz.

The little servant hesitated.

"I will serve Miss Woolcott myself," Kalid said smoothly, causing the guardsmen to exchange startled glances. The pasha never served anyone himself.

"You all may go," Kalid said in a louder voice, and Sarah watched nervously as the chamber emptied, leaving her alone with the Pasha of Bursa.

"Sherbet?" Kalid said politely, extending a crystal dish rimmed with silver to Sarah.

She shook her head.

"You should have some, it's very good. You don't have to be afraid. It's already been tested for poison at the Bird House."

The possibility of poison had not occurred to Sarah, whose expression must have mirrored her alarm.

"You should think of this. You're the favorite now and a likely target of jealousy," Kalid said mildly, sampling the sherbet from a highly polished spoon.

"I don't want to be the favorite," Sarah said.

Kalid shrugged. "You have no choice in the matter."

"It appears I have no choice about anything," Sarah said tersely, staring at him.

Kalid shook his head. "Not true. You can have lime or peach or orange sherbet; preserves made with gardenia, linden flower, or chamomile; coffee flavored with cloves or cinnamon or rose petals. You have many choices. The food produced in my *gulhane* is the finest in the Empire. You will not be disappointed."

Sarah merely glared at him, letting him see what she thought of this witty repartee.

"Boza?" he said, lifting a silver pitcher of the

fermented barley drink invitingly. "Sprinkled with roasted chick peas and cinnamon. It's very good."

"No, thank you."

"Raki?" he said, pointing to the jug of liquor at his elbow.

"No."

He sat back. "I cannot tempt you with any of these delights?" he said, gesturing to the table laden with halvah, Turkish delight, and various types of pastries, as well as the glittering rainbow dishes of sherbet.

"All I want is for you to let me go."

Kalid sighed. "That I cannot do."

"Why not?"

"Because I want you."

His face changed as he said the words, and Sarah was riveted by his eyes. So they were back to it; this chatty mood was just a diversion, a tactic to cause her to lower her guard while he moved in for the kill. She drew her breath in sharply.

Kalid looked back at her steadily, his dark gaze penetrating. He was wearing a white linen tunic embroidered with gold that exposed the slender muscles of his throat and the top of his dense mat of chest hair. A purple silk caftan with gold tassels set off his dark looks to perfection; he had dressed carefully for this interview. His thick black hair caught and reflected the light from the tapers and the oil lamp on the serving table. He was gorgeous, but he was also her captor, and she could never forget that.

"We don't always get what we want," Sarah said.

"I do."

She smiled and looked away.

"What is amusing?" he said in his elegant accent, sounding like an Oxford don.

"You are so appallingly arrogant. That's amusing."

He made a dismissive gesture, reminding her of Roxalena's father. "I went to school for some years among the British. In my view, they are the most arrogant of men, thinking themselves above every other people on earth. They are very polite, and never say what they mean. Why then is my directness interpreted as arrogance?"

Sarah had no reply, and made none.

"Is this not so?"

"I'm not going to discuss the British with you."

"What will you discuss with me?"

"Nothing."

"Ah, and I thought you were a teacher."

"I am a teacher."

"Then teach me." He reclined on one elbow, his caftan falling open to the golden cord serving as a sash at his waist. His torso was clearly defined beneath the gauzy material of his tunic. Sarah looked away deliberately.

"Teach you what?" she said.

"Anything. Teach me about the United States of America, I have never been there."

"You wouldn't like America. It's a democracy."

"I know about democracy. It sounds very slow."

"I suppose it is slow, but we much prefer it to speedier types of government, like dictatorship."

"Meaning that I am a dictator?"

"I'm not here because I volunteered."

"But you will be very glad that you are here. One day."

"May I go now?" Sarah asked, tiring of the fencing.

"You may not," he said crisply, standing.

Sarah watched him warily, on her guard, stiffening as he approached her.

"What did my women do to your hair?" he asked, pronouncing the last word in the British fashion, "hay-uh."

"It wasn't my idea," Sarah replied darkly.

She flinched as he touched her head, removing one of the ivory combs gently.

"Don't be alarmed," he said drily. "I'm only trying to make you more comfortable. This looks very painful."

"It's nothing by comparison with the ada treatment," Sarah muttered, closing her eyes as he undid the first braid deftly and the pressure on her scalp eased.

"Better?" he said.

She had to admit that it was, nodding.

He removed the second comb and unplaited

the rest of her hair, combing it with his fingers, and Sarah relaxed, her eyes closing as he kneaded her scalp with strong fingers. He sat next to her and turned her away from him, her back against his shoulder.

"Why would anyone want to torture such beautiful hair into complicated knots?" he murmured, running the golden strands over the backs of his hands.

Sarah didn't answer, her scalp tingling with the renewed flow of blood. When his arm encircled her waist, she unthinkingly allowed him to support her. He was so close, and so warm, and his soft voice so comforting. . . .

He swept her fall of hair away from her nape and pressed his lips to the back of her neck. She started, but he held her, bringing his hands up from her waist to close over her breasts.

"Let me go," she said fiercely, struggling.

"My touch was not so repugnant a moment ago," he whispered in her ear, sliding one hand inside her caftan, seeking the open neck of her gossamer tunic.

"I'll scream," she said, panicking because his mouth sliding along the curve of her shoulder was evoking a response she didn't want to feel, dared not admit to feeling.

"No one will care," he muttered, his searching hand closing over her naked breast, kneading the nipple.

"Let me go," Sarah moaned, arching against him.

"You don't want me to let you go," he said hoarsely, spinning her around and under him in one smooth motion, pulling her tunic open to bare her rouged breasts. His mouth closed over one rosy nipple as Sarah struggled at first, then sighed helplessly, turning her head from side to side. He sucked gently, then rasped her with his teeth, stimulating the sensitive flesh until she was gasping helplessly. He lifted his head slightly, withdrawing the pressure, and Sarah clutched at his hair, pulling his mouth back against her.

When his lips touched her again, she whimpered, drowning in the syrupy warmth, the changing texture of his expert caress. His hair was like raw silk under her fingers, and when his free hand closed over her other breast she moaned softly, arching toward his touch.

He rose immediately, letting her fall back against the divan. Sarah's eyes flew open in bewilderment.

"That's all," he said silkily. "I was just waiting for you to make that sound." He turned away, his clothing rustling as he adjusted it.

Sarah gasped, stunned, staring at his back.

"I suggest you cover yourself. You wouldn't want the guardsmen to get the wrong idea," he added archly.

"Why, you—you—" Sarah sputtered.

He clapped his hands loudly, and the door flew open as Sarah pulled her tunic closed and folded her arms across her caftan.

77

"Take this woman back to the harem gate," he said in Turkish to the halberdiers, who stood at attention, waiting.

Sarah rose with as much dignity as she could muster and said, "I'll make you pay for this." Her voice was shaking with humiliation; she was almost crying, but too proud to let him see it.

"No, you won't, Sarah," he answered smoothly. "You'll come back for more." He waved his hand, and the guardsmen banged their truncheons on the floor.

Sarah strode from the audience chamber without looking at Kalid, amazed that her legs were able to support her.

At the harem entrance, she was met by the eunuchs assigned to her, and they escorted her to her room.

Kalid waited until Sarah was out of sight, then sat heavily, running trembling fingers through his hair.

His composure as he dismissed Sarah was pure pretense; he had never wanted a woman so much in his life, and forcing himself to stop was more difficult than he could have imagined. But he had managed to do it, and he was glad.

The American woman had to be shown who was in charge of this situation. He would bring her along, a little at a time, and eventually she would be clay in his hands, soft and yielding, to be molded according to his desire.

But he had to maintain control until then, and that would be difficult. She was ripe, succulent, waiting to be plucked, and holding back would not be easy. He wanted to sink into her flesh, get so deep into her that neither would be able to tell where the one left off and the other began.

He seized the bottle of raki and drank straight from it, wiping his mouth with the back of his hand.

Patience, he counseled himself.

You will have everything you want, in time.

"A summons from the valide pashana," Memtaz said, shaking Sarah's shoulder.

"Who?" Sarah inquired, sitting up and rubbing her eyes, thinking that another summons was just what she didn't need.

"The grandmother of Kalid Shah. She wishes you to attend upon her at her apartments."

Wonderful, Sarah thought. Still smarting from her recent encounter with Kalid, the last thing she needed was an interview with one of his relatives.

"Can I refuse?" Sarah asked wearily.

"It would not be wise. Kosem has great influence with her grandson and is very powerful in the harem. You should try to make a friend of her, mistress."

"Do I have to go through the hamman routine to see her?" Sarah asked, standing and brushing back her hair.

"Of course not. She is a woman."

"That's a relief. What do I wear?"

Sarah bathed quickly and donned the clothes Memtaz selected, loose white cashmere trousers and a fitted blouse of crimson silk with voluminous white sleeves slashed with crimson satin. She let her hair hang down her back and stepped into the high-heeled pattens worn by harem women indoors, then added the earbobs Memtaz insisted upon at the last minute. They were of gold with large rubies at the lobe and a string of pearls below, almost touching the shoulders.

"Am I presentable?" Sarah asked sarcastically, when she was finally dressed.

"To see a woman," Memtaz shrugged. "Come with me."

Kosem's apartment was just down the hall from the one Sarah occupied; its doors were almost as ornate as those leading to Kalid's audience chamber, and above them the imperial crest was carved into the wood and painted with gold. The eunuchs who accompanied the women everywhere stood aside as Memtaz knocked at Kosem's door.

"Enter," the old lady called, and Sarah looked around in amazement as they walked into another world.

The whole of the Orchid Palace could certainly be called luxurious, but the valide pashana's home was lush beyond description. Illuminated cages filled with exotic birds stood everywhere, along with gilt-edged mirrors and carved and inlaid furniture of every description. The carpets were bright and varied, some silk, some wool, all rich and soft underfoot. The walls were draped with hangings of the finest fabrics, and painted wardrobes filled with clothing and jewels stood lined up like sentinels around the main salon, which had a ceiling decorated with lapis and gold. Inside a sitting room similar to Kalid's, the old lady sat on an overstuffed plush couch, puffing on a pipe. She gestured for Sarah to come forward, then clapped to dismiss the group of servants standing at attendance, including Memtaz. They all vanished silently, like a mist at sunrise.

Sarah stood in front of Kalid's grandmother, wondering how much this wizened creature knew of her relationship with the young Pasha.

Kosem looked back at her, the black gaze so like her grandson's measuring Sarah intelligently. The pashana was dressed elaborately even by harem standards, in rose damask trousers embroidered with silver flowers, worn with an ivory silk smock fastened with diamond buttons and a waistcoat of the same material. Over this she had fastened a girdle encrusted with diamonds and pearls, and a *curdee* of magenta brocade lined with ermine was draped over her thin shoulders. Her cap was of ivory silk embroidered with more diamonds and pearls and held in place a wealth of graying hair which had once been as black as Kalid's. Eighty-two and tiny, she was still an impressive sight, and

Sarah knew that Kalid had inherited some of his startling physical presence from this woman.

"You are very skinny," Kosem finally offered in greeting.

"I'm sorry," Sarah said in reply, almost laughing.

"My grandson has strange tastes. It has always been so. He gets them from his mother. Too much schooling in England, that's my opinion, but nobody listens to an old woman, least of all the Pasha of Bursa. You may sit down."

Sarah sat.

"Please excuse my poor English. I learned it from my daughter-in-law but have not had much chance to practice since she died, except when the fancy strikes Kalid to speak it. I imagine the fancy will be striking him more often, now that you are here."

"Your English is very good."

"The rumor of the harem is that Kalid is infatuated with you," Kosem announced bluntly.

Sarah didn't know what to say.

"Oh, come. Speak up. Is this true?"

"You would have to ask him that," Sarah replied.

"I'm asking you. Has he made love to you?" Kosem asked, puffing on her *chuklib*.

Sarah could feel herself blushing furiously. "No, not really," Sarah heard herself replying, wondering why she didn't tell this nosy old lady to mind her own business.

"What does that mean?"

Sarah closed her eyes in an agony of embarrassment.

"Ah, I see. You are shy. Maybe that's why he wants you. With all the women in Bursa throwing themselves at him, reluctance must be quite a challenge."

Sarah remembered her fevered response to Kalid's last embrace and couldn't qualify it as reluctance, even to herself, but she said, "I imagine he will tire of this game soon enough, pashana. You have only to wait, and he will move on to someone else."

"I'm not so sure," Kosem said thoughtfully. "You have the manner, and the pale skin, and the yellow hair. He pines for his mother's people, you see. He likes the spirit of Western women, as well as their looks, though I'm not sure he will admit this. Consequently, these docile beauties here hold no charm for him."

Sarah listened, an attentive audience.

The old lady put down her pipe, setting it on the rim of an enameled dish at her side, and sat forward. "I will be direct," she said, as if she had been anything else. "I desire a grandchild, a legitimate grandchild born of a legitimate marriage, not some harem by-blow who will never take the throne of Bursa. I want you to marry my grandson and provide an heir for the house of Shah."

Sarah sat in stunned silence, wondering how this byzantine turn of events had happened to her so quickly. Two months ago she had been teaching school in Boston!

"Well?" Kosem said.

"I think you should talk to your grandson about that," Sarah finally said lamely.

"I have talked to him about it, talked until my tongue was about to drop from my head. He would have no one until he saw you at Topkapi. He parted with his father's jeweled sword, long desired by the Sultan, to get you."

"He bought me, your highness. You must understand that in my culture such a practice is offensive. I cannot marry a man who purchased me as he would a pet animal."

"Why not?" Kosem asked reasonably, shrugging gracefully. "You do not desire him?"

"I desire to go home!" Sarah replied heatedly. Why were all these people so dense on this subject?

"You have a man there?"

"No, but—"

"A man as handsome as my grandson?" Kosem went on insistently. "As rich and powerful?"

Sarah sighed and did not answer.

"There, you see? You do not."

"That is not the point."

"What is the point?" Kosem asked reasonably.

"I should be able to choose for myself," Sarah said in exasperation. "I don't want to be held against my will."

"You are not unwilling. The blood comes up in your face when you speak of Kalid. He knows how to please a woman, of this I have heard many tales. If he turns his attention to you, Sarah from Boston, you will find yourself in his bed before long."

Sarah looked away unhappily, aware that there was an element of truth in what the old lady said.

"Do you know what will happen to you if you do not marry Kalid?" Kosem asked.

Sarah looked back at her.

"He will use you as he pleases and then pass you along to his men when he has had his fill. Marriage is much preferable; when you are the mother of the pasha's heir you will be a pashana, a valide in your time, with a life of secure luxury even when you no longer share Kalid's bed. Without this protection, life for a woman in the harem as she ages can be very hard."

"Are you threatening me?" Sarah asked softly, a dangerous light in her eyes.

Kosem laughed and clapped her hands. "Ah, I see what draws my grandson to you. You have courage. This is a good thing."

Sarah waited tensely, sure that there was more to come.

Kosem leaned forward, her bright, dark eyes like raisins in her wrinkled face.

"You would not be my choice for my grandson, Sarah. I'm sure that you can understand why. A woman raised with our customs and traditions would be far more suitable, but if Kalid's blood cries out for your frail body, it is *kismet,* and I accept it. I am only saying that you should not fight your destiny."

"I do not accept that Kalid's whim is my destiny," Sarah countered evenly.

"It is not a whim. He has waited a long time for you. It is written on your forehead that you shall be his bride. In time you will come to know this."

Sarah didn't answer; there was no arguing with the old lady's relentless determination to see a Shah grandchild in line for the throne of Bursa.

"Now we will have some refreshments," Kosem said, as if they had been discussing the weather. She clapped her hands loudly and a servant appeared with a laden tray.

"And you can tell me all about the United States of America," Kosem added eagerly, picking up her pipe.

Sarah resigned herself to another discussion on the debits of democracy.

"Well, what did you think of her?" Kalid said to his grandmother, watching the old lady's face.

"Think of whom?" Kosem said innocently, lighting her pipe and puffing elaborately.

"Sarah Woolcott, grandmother. I know you sent for her, so stop pretending. Is she not beautiful?"

Kosem shrugged. "If you like milky Western women with no meat on their bones. Are you sure she is capable of childbearing?"

"Don't you ever think about anything else?" Kalid demanded in exasperation.

"No, and neither should you! It is your duty to—"

"Don't talk to me about my duty! I have been administering this kingdom since my father's death, fighting off the Arabs and the bedouins, paying duties to the Sultan and keeping the peace, preserving what your son left to me as if it were sacred ground! I have put the welfare of my people before everything and everybody, and you know this very well. Now I want this woman, and by all the prophets I will have her!" Kalid stood abruptly and began to pace about his audience chamber, his expression grim.

"I was not objecting to your choice, Kalid. She could have a hump and a harelip as far as I am concerned," Kosem said mildly. "I merely want you to marry her and get her pregnant as quickly as possible."

"I need time," Kalid said obstinately.

"Why?"

"She must come to me willingly."

"You are too proud, Kalid. Force her now, and she will become willing later. Many marriages are begun that way."

"Not mine."

"So she must desire you as much as you desire her."

"More."

Kosem smiled. "I do not think that is possible."

Her grandson smiled back at her confidently. "Yes it is, and you will see it happen."

Roxalena walked carefully along the cracked and weed-strewn path toward the abandoned bathhouse once used by the Sultan's harem, now overgrown with creepers and vines and inhabited by spiders and nesting birds. Abdul Hammid had built a new bathhouse on the Bosporus for his favorite, Roxalena's mother Nakshedil, and this one had fallen to ruin. Now no one came to the gardens except harem children wandering at play and the occasional groundskeeper assigned to cut away the undergrowth.

And a pair of clandestine lovers whose fate it was to meet in secret and risk death with every embrace.

"Osman?" Roxalena whispered, peering through the unrelieved blackness of the moonless night.

"Here," her lover said, and stepped out of the darkness to reveal himself.

Roxalena ran straight into his arms and he lifted her against him, kissing her deeply. Roxalena clung to him, and they began to undress each other with the harried urgency of forbidden passion. Osman carried the naked princess to the stone seat of the hamman inside the bathouse and set her there, tearing off his remaining clothes and then stretching out next to her, entering her in almost the same motion. Roxalena gasped and buried her face against his broad shoulder, crying out his name as she took her pleasure from him and then went limp, falling back with her arm across her eyes. He bent to kiss her damp brow.

"Did you miss me?" Osman said, and she laughed. She lowered her arm and looked up into his beloved face, touching his cheek. Osman was dark and stocky, his black curly hair, blunt features and peasant body a powerful aphrodisiac to a woman raised with eunuchs and overmanicured courtesans. She loved him with a childishly fierce devotion, part defiance of her imperious father and part pleased recognition of her earthy instincts.

Osman was the best part of her life.

"Did you find out about Sarah?" Roxalena asked, sitting up and looking around for her clothes. "Shirza told me you had heard something."

"Yes."

"Well?"

"You're not going to like it."

"Tell me."

"Your father sold her to Kalid Shah."

Roxalena stared at him.

"It's true," Osman said, nodding. "I had it straight from the body slave to the khislar. Do you remember that sword studded with

89

cabochon rubies your father always coveted? It was in the Shah family for long years, a souvenir of the Suleiman campaign against the Armenians."

Roxalena nodded.

"Kalid Shah traded it for your friend. And threw fifty thousand kurush into the bargain."

"Kalid kept that sword in the Orchid Palace vault. He wouldn't let anyone touch it but himself!"

"He must have wanted your Sarah very much."

"No wonder my father wouldn't talk to me about it. He's probably taking that sword to bed with him. Oh, he's such a liar. I can't bear him, Osman."

Osman stroked her arm silently. He had heard many such outbursts before, and he knew that a large part of his attraction for Roxalena was that he was the last person on earth the Sultan would have chosen for his daughter. It didn't matter; he loved the little princess so much that her reasons for loving him back didn't concern him.

"We must get word to Sarah's cousin. He has the same name, Woolcott, and owns a rug business in the city. I'm sure his government could do something to help," Roxalena said.

Osman was silent. He was not so sure. American businesses in Ottoman Turkey traded by the sufferance of the Sultan, and the embassy was notoriously reluctant to upset him.

Roxalena stirred, and it took him a moment to realize that she was laughing.

"What is it?" he said.

"I told Sarah that she had caught Kalid's eye, and she dismissed it. Now she is in his harem, purchased at an exorbitant price."

"And?"

Roxalena grinned. "And the Pasha of Bursa cannot guess just how much trouble his prize will be."

Chapter Four

"It is time for you to attend the justice hearing, mistress," Memtaz said.

"I'm not going," Sarah said, looking up from her book.

"It is a direct summons from the pasha."

"Tell him I died and cannot be disturbed."

Memtaz looked at Sarah sadly. "It will not go well with me if you ignore the request, mistress."

"That's blackmail, Memtaz."

"Why should you not go? You just spent three hours preparing in the hamman, and your clothes are all ready."

"Don't remind me about the hamman. I have endured enough hostile stares to last me for the rest of my life. Who is that tall woman with the russet hair who's always getting a skin treatment or a massage? She keeps looking daggers at me every time I appear."

"Looking daggers?"

"Staring at me with hatred. Not that any of the harem women seem particularly glad to see me."

"The red-haired woman is Fatma. She was the favorite before you came here."

That gave Sarah a moment's pause. "The favorite? She was sleeping with Kalid?"

Memtaz nodded. "Up until about six months before you arrived. I think he became bored."

"Then it was over before he ever met me."

"Yes."

"So why am I the object of her anger?"

Memtaz shrugged. "It is one thing to fall out of favor. It is another to be replaced."

"She has not been replaced, Memtaz. I am not going to bed with Kalid Shah."

Memtaz said nothing.

"It's the truth, Memtaz."

Memtaz handed her a pair of tissue-linen shalwar and Sarah stepped into the trousers automatically.

"No one will believe it," Memtaz said philosophically.

"Why on earth not? Is everybody in the empire ruled by a runaway sex drive?"

"They will not believe it because you are both young and beautiful, and the pasha purchased you at a high price and has made you his favorite. Why else would he behave so?"

"Maybe he wants to discuss international politics with me," Sarah said dryly.

Memtaz handed her a *yelek*, a loose blouse with immense hanging sleeves, and Sarah donned the garment and the matching girdle resentfully. Both pieces were of lilac silk and the girdle was embroidered with silver thread and marquise amethysts.

"Very pretty," Memtaz said approvingly, proffering a purple gauze drapery with a silver border to be worn as a shawl and then lifted over the head as a veil. Sarah tossed it over her shoulders and looked at Memtaz with finality.

"Am I ready?" she asked.

"You will be very satisfactory in those clothes, mistress," Memtaz said serenely.

"Please stop calling me 'mistress.' You are not my slave."

"I am your slave."

"Then I release you."

"You cannot release me. Only the pasha can do that, and he has assigned me to you to wait upon your every need."

"Then call me Sarah."

"I could never do that, mistress. It would not be seemly."

"Well, I've got a news bulletin for you, Memtaz. In my country it is not 'seemly' for people to go down on their knees bowing and scraping before other people. It makes me very nervous to see it here. So if you want to please me, you will stop throwing yourself on the floor every time I look at you."

Memtaz dropped her eyes, but said nothing.

After a few moments Sarah sighed and put her hand on the little slave's shoulder. "Memtaz, I'm sorry. It's not fair for me to take my irritation out on you."

"Irritation?"

"Annoyance, unhappiness at my situation. I don't want to see Kalid again. Our last meeting ended . . . badly. And here I am gilding the lily to answer another summons from the great man."

"You will see him in a group, mistress, not alone. The hearings are public. He merely wants you in attendance."

"And what happens at a hearing?"

"The pasha metes out justice."

"I'd pay good money to see that," Sarah muttered bitterly, holding out her wrists as Memtaz adorned them with silver bangles.

"Beg pardon?" Memtaz said.

"I don't see how an unjust man can mete out justice."

"The pasha is known as a very fair prince, and his people consider themselves fortunate to be governed by such a ruler."

"Hmmph," Sarah said, and then pushed away the silver diadem Memtaz was trying to drape across her forehead.

"I can't wear that, Memtaz, it makes me cross-eyed."

"What is that?"

"I can't see! Look, I'm decked out like a Christmas tree as it is. Let's just go."

"What is a Christmas tree?"

"A fir tree decorated with baubles. In my country we cut them down and bring them into our houses in celebration of a holiday."

Memtaz raised her brows. "And you say that our customs are strange?"

Two eunuchs appeared in the doorway expectantly.

"It is time," Memtaz said.

Sarah glanced around briefly at the lavish apartment. The ikbal's chamber was only slightly smaller than Kosem's, and Sarah did not have quite the extensive collection of jewelry and clothing that littered the valide pashana's rooms, but in other respects the two apartments were similar. Mirrors and gilt furniture and colorful rugs abounded, and the sandstone walls cast a rosy lavender glow over every luxurious appointment.

Sarah looked away wearily.

She was truly a bird in a gilded cage.

"I'm ready," she said, and the eunuchs parted to let her pass.

Kalid entered his throne room behind the procession of functionaries and saw immediately that Sarah was missing. The seat next to Kosem was empty.

Kalid walked across the immense bird of

paradise rug that covered the pink marble floor and ascended the red-carpeted steps leading to his throne. The chair itself, of rich dark mahogany and contrasting balsa wood, was carved with intricate arabesques painted in gold and lapis, and the high latticed back was studded with precious gems. He turned and faced his audience, and all of the people in it bowed with one motion, arms folded at midsection, heads inclining toward the floor. He waited until they looked up again and then sat regally, extending his hand to a scribe who gave him the list of cases to be decided.

The men were seated on his right, his chief clerks and accountants and the procurator of each district in Bursa, as well as his khislar and the captain of his guards. To his left were the women, all veiled, his grandmother and lesser relatives from the harem, present to witness the dispensing of his legendary wisdom. A selected audience of common people were also admitted to this ceremony once a month, and they rustled their clothing fitfully, awed to be in the presence of the pasha.

Only Sarah was absent.

Kalid looked over the sheet of paper in his hand and then glanced up again. Everyone waited for him to begin.

At that moment a side door opened, and two eunuchs came through it, followed by Sarah and Memtaz. Kalid held up his hand, and they stopped moving.

Sarah looked around the packed room, then at the dais, where an empty seat loomed next to Kosem.

Sarah had a sinking feeling that it was for her.

Kalid said something in Turkish and gestured pointedly toward the dais.

"Go up and sit next to the valide pashana," Memtaz whispered fiercely. "Hurry, you are already late."

It seemed to take an eternity for Sarah to cross the ocean of carpeting that led to the dais, and she could feel all eyes on her back as she stepped up to take her seat. She avoided Kalid's gaze as she folded her hands in her lap and looked at a point on the far wall above his khislar's turbaned head.

Kalid clapped his hands and the hearing began. The procurator of each district had selected a case appropriate for the pasha's review, and Sarah became interested in spite of herself as the event progressed. She could not understand most of what was being said, but Kosem gave a running, sotto voce translation of the proceedings that enabled Sarah to follow each judgment as it was rendered.

The first man complained that a neighbor had stolen his wife, and it evolved during the testimony that the deserted husband had beaten his spouse. Kalid dissolved the first marriage and awarded the wife to the neighbor, explaining that any man who mistreated his wife deserved to lose her.

Kosem nodded vigorously. "Very sound," she commented to Sarah, who studied her captor over the veil covering her nose and mouth as he listened to each petitioner in turn and then rendered his opinion.

Kalid was wearing a dark blue military uniform with a gold sash draped with medals. He gave a full hearing to each person who spoke, then replied thoughtfully, in a carefully modulated voice that commanded attention as well as respect. By the time he reached the fourth case, a boundary dispute between two sheepherders over grazing land, Sarah knew why he had insisted on her presence at this hearing. He obviously wanted her to see him in a role other than sexual predator, and his plan was working.

She *was* impressed.

"My grandson is very wise, is he not?" said the valide pashana, as if she had read Sarah's mind.

Sarah turned to look at the old lady, who was watching her with a sly smile, her eyes full of knowledge above her silken veil.

"I suppose he's doing well," Sarah conceded.

"Well! There is no fairer pasha in the Sultanate, and everyone says so. And none more handsome, surely you would agree?"

Sarah had to smile. Kosem was relentless.

"He shaved his beard for you, did you know that?" Kosem hissed. "He thought you would find him more attractive without it, since it is the Western custom to go clean-shaven."

Kalid was enormously attractive to Sarah with or without the beard, and doubtless he knew it. "Actually, beards are in style in the West now, especially in my country and England. The Prince of Wales has a full beard," Sarah replied perversely.

"But why cover such a beautiful face with hair?" Kosem said. "Kalid favors his mother. She was a gavur, but she was a lovely creature. Too pale, of course, like you, but he has her compelling features. Except for the nose. He has his father's nose."

Kalid's khislar, a tall Sudanese named Achmed, turned and threw Kosem a dirty look.

Kosem shot him a rude gesture in return. "He wants me to be quiet," Kosem muttered to Sarah. "The man is overbearing. Kalid indulges him too much. I'll be dead soon enough, and then he'll hear nothing further from me."

Sarah turned away and bit her lip to keep from laughing.

For somebody who talked about dying all the time, Kosem was remarkably full of life.

The hearing went on for more than two hours, with Kalid disposing of some twenty cases before he was done. Then he concluded the proceedings and left the throne room without looking at Sarah once.

The khislar stood in front of the gathering and said something in Turkish. Then the harem ladies and their advisors filed out of the room through doors leading to the interior of the palace as the people thronged out the courtyard gate.

"Is that it?" Sarah said.

"Justice has been done," Kosem said.

But not for me, Sarah thought.

Memtaz approached with a member of the pasha's guard, and Sarah knew from the look on her face that she had received another 'come hither' from on high.

The servant brought her hands together and bowed from the waist. "My lord Kalid requires your presence in the stables," she said.

"The stables?" Sarah said.

"You are to receive your first riding lesson."

In a pig's eye, Sarah thought. "Will you please tell your lord Kalid that I have no desire to learn how to ride or to see him. I will be resting in my room." She stalked down the corridor, the eunuchs falling into step behind her as Memtaz turned unhappily to convey the message to Kalid's man.

Sarah returned to the ikbal's apartment and flung herself face-down on her sleeping couch. She lay immobile, like a sullen child, for several minutes, her cheek pressed to the muslin cover of the feather bed, then stood and methodically stripped off her finery, item by item. She was left standing barefoot in her linen shift, which was sleeveless and gossamer thin, clinging to her body like a second skin. She lay back down and stared at the ornate plaster ceiling, painted with a pastoral scene of nymphs and shepherds, wondering how long she would be able to stand this captivity before she went insane.

After a couple of minutes, she heard a commotion in the corridor—feminine screams and thuds and the sound of excited voices. She sat up to see Kalid storming through the entrance to her outer chamber as the tirewomen working there started up and then fell prostrate to the floor in fright.

Memtaz scurried in his wake, wringing her hands, in tears. She was followed by Sarah's two eunuchs, wide-eyed with alarm.

"Out," Kalid shouted in Turkish. "Everybody out! Clear the room right now."

The wardrobers scrambled to their feet and fled, followed by two terrified servants who had been trimming the lamps. The eunuchs looked at one another and withdrew to the hall, while Memtaz stood rooted, weeping loudly.

"Stop that noise!" Kalid flung at her.

Memtaz stuffed her fist into her mouth and sobbed around it as she ran out the door.

"Leave her alone, you bully," Sarah said to Kalid. "Whatever you're throwing a fit about is not her fault."

"No, it is yours," Kalid said, his hands on his hips, his eyes locked with hers.

"What are you talking about?" Sarah said disdainfully.

"I gave you a direct order and you disregarded it."

"Go to hell." Sarah turned her back on him.

Kalid reached around her and grabbed the neck of her shift; it bunched in his hand as he pulled her around to face him.

"You still do not seem to appreciate your situation here," he said softly, his dark eyes inches from hers. "When I summon you, you come to me."

"The old order changes, yielding forth to new," Sarah said, holding his gaze.

His eyes narrowed. "What is that?"

"You people are always quoting your ancient books, I thought I'd throw in one of mine."

"You will learn to obey me," he said softly, ignoring the quip, still holding her.

"Or what? You'll kill me? I think we've been through that one before, haven't we?"

"Or I will order that your servant Memtaz be given twenty lashes," Kalid said smoothly.

Sarah's mouth fell open in shock.

He smiled down at her triumphantly.

"You wouldn't," she whispered.

He stepped back from her and folded his arms, still wearing that superior smile.

Sarah was stunned. She couldn't comprehend such staggering unfairness, especially from someone who had just demonstrated exquisite judgment in dealing with legal cases from all over his kingdom.

"Is this what you learned at Oxford College,

donme pasha?" Sarah said quietly.

"This is what I learned from my father. I could have you whipped and you would endure it, cursing me with every kiss of the lash, but if I threaten a dependent, you will spring to her defense and do what I want in order to spare her. You are such an American."

"I take that as a compliment," Sarah said flatly.

"It was not intended as one. Your Yankee sensibilities are allowing me to win. You are out-maneuvered, kourista." As he said the last word he extended a slender forefinger and slipped it inside the scoop neck of her shift, tracing the valley between her breasts.

Sarah flinched away from him.

"Ah. You were not so reluctant the other night."

Sarah's face flamed as she remembered the way she had clung to him, pressing his mouth eagerly to her swollen nipple.

"Aren't you breaking your own rules, coming into the harem?" she retorted, saying the first thing that came into her head. "I thought men were forbidden to enter it."

"I do as I please," he replied. "You would profit by remembering that. Now I will expect you in one quarter of an hour at the stables, dressed for riding, or your servant will suffer the consequences." He turned on his heel and strode from the room.

Sarah sat heavily on the sleeping couch,

clenching and unclenching her fists.

She had to get out of this place.

She bit her thumbnail, tortured by questions. Where was James, and why wasn't he doing anything to help her? Was it possible he didn't even know where she was? Did Roxalena know what her father had done, and would she confront him about it if she did? And wasn't there any way at all to slip out of the palace? The harem women were so well guarded that escape seemed impossible, but Memtaz often spoke of bathing outings to the Bosporus and shopping trips to the Kahouli bazaar. The women were heavily veiled and closely watched whenever they ventured beyond the walls, but at least then it would not be necessary to negotiate the labyrinth of the palace to reach the outside world.

She would already be there.

Memtaz came bustling through the anteroom with a stack of clothes in her hands.

"Are you all right?" Sarah asked, standing and putting her hand on the other woman's shoulder.

"I am fine, mistress. I was only upset that I had displeased my master."

Sarah sighed. "I take it those are for me."

"Yes. You will please to put these on and then join Pasha Kalid in the stables."

"Why not?" Sarah said. "Sounds like a peachy idea." She sighed again and donned the long-sleeved, button-front silk blouse, along with the split suede riding skirt and lace-up boots. When she was ready, she marched out of the ikbal's chamber and picked up her escort, the two eunuchs who, as usual, already had their orders. They led Sarah through the Boxwood Gardens and past the Open Pool and through the Bird House Gate.

Once on the other side of the kushane, they entered an equestrian world, complete with paddock and jumping rings and a long series of stables. The eunuchs stopped at the first stable, and Sarah walked inside, where Kalid was waiting, grooming a splendid white Arabian with a braided forelock and tail.

"Good, you're here," he said, when he looked up and saw her. "I'm going to teach you to ride."

He was wearing tight twill trousers with a loose cotton shirt and highly polished riding boots. The shirt had dolman sleeves and a lace-up V neck, and it was tucked into a rawhide belt. This was the first time Sarah had ever seen Kalid in Western dress, and the impact on her was considerable.

She came to the reluctant conclusion that he would look good in anything.

"How can you be sure that I don't know how to ride already?" she asked, to cover her reaction.

"Schoolteachers from Boston do not ride horses."

"You might be surprised at what this schoolteacher from Boston can do," Sarah said darkly.

He smiled. "No doubt, but today we will concentrate on getting you astride and maintaining the proper stance."

"Why is it so important that I learn to ride a horse?" Sarah asked wearily.

"I want you to accompany me when I make tours of my lands," he replied, slipping a bridle over the Arabian's head.

"I don't want to accompany you anywhere."

"That is immaterial." Often he sounded like the British solicitors who had once been his classmates, and it was almost possible to forget that he was really an Eastern potentate who was holding her against her will. But then he became the pasha again, shouting orders and ruling her life, and she remembered.

A stableman came forward leading a mare and Kalid said, "Ah, here is Ousta, for you. A sorrel, very gentle." He took the horse's lead and dismissed the attendant.

"And what is your horse's name?" Sarah asked.

"Khan."

"As in Genghis Khan?"

"The very same."

Sarah nodded wearily.

Kalid led Khan outside and put him into the paddock, where he trotted around happily, stopping every so often to munch some grass.

"We won't be needing Khan for the moment," Kalid said, as he brought Ousta out onto the first trail and gave Sarah the reins. She held them as

Kalid saddled the horse and said, "Ousta will be able to tell that you're inexperienced, so once you're seated, I'll lead you around for a while so that she doesn't run away with you."

"That's comforting."

He cupped his hands and gave her a leg up onto the horse's back. He was very close as he lifted her swiftly, and she had a blunt impression of masculine strength that made her swallow and turn her head. He kept his hands on her waist a few seconds longer than was necessary, and Sarah knew that this lesson was going to be even more trying than she had anticipated.

Ousta whinnied and reared slightly. Sarah clung to the pommel desperately.

"Get me down off this thing," she gasped. "I feel as if I'm forty feet in the air."

Kalid laughed. "Now take the reins," he said, as he handed her the leather straps. "And don't pull too much or you'll hurt her. The bit will cut into her mouth."

"Hurt her! What about me?"

"You'll be just fine. I am here. Now sit up very straight and don't slouch."

Sarah tried.

"Relax your back muscles," Kalid said.

"Stop barking at me. I'm doing the best I can."

He reached up and ran one hand down her spine, then positioned her shoulders. "Better?" he said.

"Yes," she replied grudgingly.

"Good. Now hold the reins tightly enough to maintain control but not enough to pull the horse's head back. Try it."

Sarah did.

"That's fine. Now I'm going to slap her and she'll walk forward. I'll walk beside you."

"She'll run away," Sarah said anxiously.

"No, she won't, she's very well trained." He smacked the horse's rump and she took a few steps, then stopped.

Sarah looked down at him.

"Well? Nudge her with your knees," Kalid said.

Sarah obeyed, and the horse trotted forward. Sarah hung on warily, jouncing.

"I'm going to fall off," she said wildly.

"Grip with your knees," Kalid instructed her patiently. "She'll respond."

Sarah obeyed his directions and was able to control the horse, which trotted around at a leisurely pace as Kalid followed on foot, telling Sarah what to do. Then he took hold of the horse's bridle and led the animal in a circle as Sarah hung on, improving her grip and seat as Kalid talked. Finally he said, "All right. That's enough for now. We'll try again in a few days."

"Can't I stay on a little longer?" Sarah asked.

Kalid laughed. "I thought you wanted no part of this."

"Well, I think I'm getting the hang of it."

"Indeed you are, but an inexperienced rider is

stressful for the animal. She needs a rest. Down you come." He lifted her off Ousta's back and set her down before him. She looked up into his sparkling brown eyes and saw approval there as he said, "You did very well."

Sarah didn't want to react, to be warmed by the compliment, but she was.

"May I go now?" she said briskly, to dismiss the unwelcome emotion she felt.

"Certainly not. We're going for a ride."

"I just went for a ride."

"We. The two of us. On Khan." He got the big Arabian and vaulted into the saddle, then took Sarah's hand and pulled her up behind him with one movement.

"Hang on tight," he called, then kicked the animal, which shot forward instantly. Sarah almost fell off as she seized Kalid in a convulsive grip and then shut her eyes as they approached the paddock fence. The horse soared over it and took off down a cobbled lane leading to the open countryside.

It was several minutes before Sarah could open her eyes. When she did, she saw that they were galloping through a wide field carpeted by wildflowers in the full sun, with the distant blue sparkle of the Bosporus as a backdrop. Kalid was leaning forward, riding hard, and Sarah could feel the play of his muscles under her hands as he controlled the charging animal. Strands of Kalid's hair blew back into her face; it smelled clean and peppery, like grass. She clung to his lean waist, forgetting their circumstances, forgetting everything but the sensual pleasure of speed and safety. Finally she leaned forward to put her cheek against his back and closed her eyes again, not in fear this time but in surrender to the magic of the moment.

It was a long time before they slowed and finally stopped. When Sarah raised her head, she saw that they were at an oasis, with numerous shade trees and a clear stream running through green grass. Kalid jumped down and then took her hand to help her off. This time when she stood before him, she could not meet his eyes.

"Did you like that?" he asked quietly, and she could tell by his tone that he knew the answer.

She turned aside, pulling a handkerchief from her sleeve and kneeling to dip it into the stream.

"It's so hot," she said, as she wrung out the cloth and then wiped her face and neck with it.

Kalid loosened the laces at the neck of his shirt and drew it over his head. "You'll feel better after a few minutes in the shade," he said, tossing the shirt aside. He bent and splashed his torso with the water, and Sarah watched as the rivulets ran down the hard muscles of his arms, the taut biceps and triceps flexing as he moved. His chest hair glistened with droplets, and his ribs were visible beneath the satiny skin of his back as he turned and caught her watching him.

111

Sarah looked away quickly, but she could feel the warmth creeping up her neck as blood seeped into her face.

He came and sat next to her on the grass, using his shirt to blot the moisture from his body.

"Why are you so obstinate, Sarah?" he said softly. "Give in to your feelings. I know what you want, and I can make sure you have it. Today and any day."

Sarah studied her hands in her lap, saying nothing.

"We could bring each other so much pleasure, kourista," he murmured huskily.

"Pleasure is not the most important thing in life," Sarah replied, not trusting herself to look at him.

"What is?"

"Freedom," she shot back defiantly.

He shook his head. "Freedom is the excuse you bring up because it allows you to lie to yourself. You're afraid of me, aren't you? Afraid of what you might become with me, afraid of passing the limits you have always set for your life."

Sarah swallowed with difficulty and twisted the damp handkerchief in her lap. It was obvious that he knew women very well, and she wondered about his past lovers—Fatma and probably many others—who had taught him so much.

"I can't allow myself to forget how I got here and what you did to me," she said quietly.

"Why? Why can't you forget? Does it really matter now, when we are alone?" he said silkily, reaching out to stroke her throat with his fingers. Sarah closed her eyes and arched her neck, and in the next instant she was in his arms.

His bare skin was a shock; he was hot, hot, despite his recent ablution, and his scent, a mixture of soap and sweat, was overpowering, an aphrodisiac. Her arms went around his neck almost involuntarily as he pulled her across his knees and his mouth came down on hers.

He had never kissed her before, and Sarah had never been kissed like this. Her memory of all previous embraces vanished as her lips parted to admit his probing tongue; she reciprocated, tasting the pungent wine he had drunk earlier in the day and the slick hardness of his teeth. As he moved his lips to her cheek, then to the shell of her ear, he pulled her blouse loose from her skirt and lifted her shift, seeking the soft flesh beneath her clothes.

"You are mine," he said against her hair. "I knew you were mine from the first moment I saw you." He turned and laid her flat against the ground, stretching out next to her and kissing her forehead, her nose, then her mouth again, more deeply this time.

When he reached for the buttons of her blouse, Sarah sat up abruptly and pushed him away.

"What is it?" he said, panting, his flushed face inches away from hers.

"Do I have to give a reason? You didn't. Two can play at that game." She stalked over to the stream, tucking her blouse back into her skirt.

She heard him come up behind her and then he grabbed her arm, whirling her to face him. His face was like thunder.

"I should leave you out here. It would be days before anyone found you," he said furiously.

"You won't do that. And do you know why? It's too important to the great pasha to prove that he can break me."

"I could break you in half with my bare hands, and it wouldn't change a single mulish thought in that stubborn head," he said wearily, letting her go.

"That's right. So why don't you just give me up? I'm sure you can find more compliant women in the harem."

His face took on a hard, set cast and he said, "Understand this, kourista. I will never give you up. If you refuse to bed me, I will not force you, but you will grow old in the harem, old and dried-up and unused, so old and withered that no man will ever again be driven to the foolishness I have demonstrated. Now get over to that horse before I follow my first instinct and leave you here to rot."

Sarah obeyed, because she was tired, tired of fighting this beautiful monolith who looked like a man, tired of hatching escape plans she knew would never come to fruition, tired of wondering why no one was coming to help her. Was it true that she was really and finally alone here, so far from her home?

Kalid helped her onto the horse behind him and kicked it into action immediately. The return ride was nothing like the ride out; Kalid was silent and his back was rigid all the way. When they got to the stables, he dismounted and handed her down without looking at her. The eunuchs were waiting to escort her back to her room.

Chapter Five

James and Beatrice Woolcott were eating dinner when their servant, Listak, came into the dining room and said, "Visitor, madam. Shall I say to come back?"

James rose and blotted his lips with his napkin. "No, no, I'll take it. You go on with your dinner, Beatrice, it's probably just the warehouse manager. I told him to come here and give me a report when he was finished with the inventory. I just didn't think he would be done so soon. You can clear my place away, Listak, and bring some coffee to the sitting room. With two cups."

The servant bowed and retreated as James left his table and walked down the hall to his parlor. The small room, decorated in the height of fussy

Victorian fashion, featured his best Afghan rug on the polished floor and Tiffany lamps on the Chippendale tables.

In the midst of all this display of Western taste, Osman Bey was a particularly large and Eastern odd note. He rose to his feet as James entered.

James took in the halberdier's uniform, the breadth of the Anatolian's shoulders, and the serious expression on his face.

"Has something happened to Sarah?" James said.

Beatrice Woolcott was finishing her dessert when her husband rejoined her. She knew by the grim lines around his mouth that something was wrong.

"James, what is it?" she said.

James was ashen. He sat across from her and put his arms on the table, his head bent.

"For heaven's sake, James, tell me!" Beatrice said, getting up and coming around to his side.

"Sarah has been sold," he said.

Beatrice looked as if she were going to faint. "Wh—what?" she finally said weakly.

"The Sultan sold her to the Pasha of Bursa. The Captain of the Guards at Topkapi was my visitor just now. He told me that the pasha took a fancy to Sarah, and the Sultan traded her for some family heirloom and a lot of money."

"Oh, my God," Beatrice said, going as white as her husband and clenching her hands.

"Apparently, under Turkish law any woman in the harem is the Sultan's property and he can do with her as he pleases."

"Did you know this when you arranged for her to go there?" Beatrice asked.

"Of course I didn't, what do you take me for?" James answered heatedly, staring at his wife.

"I don't know, James—you were very anxious to send her there. You thought it would help your business."

"Beatrice, please, recriminations are not going to serve this situation now. I have to find a way to get her back."

"Go to the embassy. Surely an American citizen can't be treated this way!"

James sighed. "We're living in Turkey, and here we're under the Sultan's jurisdiction. Local law applies. I will certainly try, but I'm not sure how much the United States representatives can do."

Beatrice reached over and patted his hand. "Why did this guardsman come to you with the story? I'm sure there was some risk involved, if he works for the Sultan."

"Princess Roxalena sent him. She befriended Sarah and is worried about her, but we both know there is little the Princess can do against her father."

"What will happen to Sarah?" Beatrice asked softly.

James looked away. "There is only one reason the Pasha would want her, and I'm afraid everyone is clear about what that is."

Beatrice was silent for a long time. "He wouldn't kill her?" she finally said feebly.

"I doubt it. She might be discarded when he loses interest, but by that time she could wish she were dead."

"James, I'm so sorry," Beatrice said, her compassion for his situation overcoming her natural tendency to carp.

"You're right, Bea, I know you are. I should have never let her go into that harem."

"Don't despair. You'll go to the embassy tomorrow and see what can be done."

James nodded bleakly, not comforted at all.

"Did you talk to Sarah's brother?" Roxalena hissed, stepping back into the shadows as a kitchen skivvy passed them carrying a basket of ruby-colored pomegranates on her head.

Osman nodded. "I talked to him, and I know he will try, but I'm not sure there's anything he can do."

"Kalid will keep her. He won't be persuaded by government officials or anybody else. He's very determined when he wants something. Or somebody."

"What do you think she will do?" Osman asked.

"Try to escape."

Osman sighed. "I don't see how she can be successful at that. Where would she go, who would help her? She knows no one in Bursa. She has no friends."

119

"She has friends at Topkapi," Roxalena said firmly. "I have to think, Osman, there must be a way for me to help."

"Us. For us to help."

The muezzin in the tower began the call to evening prayer.

"I must go," Osman said. "At midnight, in the boathouse?"

"At midnight," Roxalena answered, slipping behind a screen, then out the kushane door.

The pool in the hamman was filled with misting water, rose petals afloat on its surface. It was surrounded by marble columns and screened off from the rest of the harem by a film of gauzy drapes. The ceiling of the bathing area was crenelated and painted with gold arabesques; the floor was of glazed lapis tiles. The pool itself was pink marble with an orchid pattern visible on its bottom, crafted of contrasting tiles and inlaid mother-of-pearl. Surrounding the pool were tall plants and trees of various types, interspersed with stone benches where the harem women took their ease when not splashing or soaking in the water. Trays laden with sweetmeats and refreshing drinks, as well as ointments and lotions for the care of the skin, stood waiting for the masseuses and servants who used them. The ladies of the harem must always be maintained in a state of contentment and constant readiness for the pleasure of the pasha.

Sarah lowered herself into the water, which seemed hot at first but gradually had a soothing effect. She was an object of ridicule in the harem because she insisted on bathing in her shift, while the other women ran about as naked as newborns, donning the silk robes that lay draped about the hamman only when they were chilled. Some made little fires in the marble bowls that held potpourri and fed the embers sticks of sandalwood and myrrh, holding their caftans aloft to capture the fumes, which would then perfume their clothing as well as their bodies. And if a dispute arose, as sometimes happened, sturdy eunuchs selected for the purpose seized the offenders and tossed them out of the hamman to cool their tempers in private.

Sarah soaked for a few minutes and then climbed out of the pool, donning her pattens, the clogs that protected delicate feet from the heated bath marble as well as the wet floor. She walked into the adjoining tepidarium, past a splashing fountain, and toward the couches where the harem women reclined and drank coffee, dressed each other's hair and told each other stories. Servants were in attendance to fold the women in warm cloaks, perfume their hair and skin, and bring them treats. Sarah waved away the slaves and picked up a book; written in Turkish, it nevertheless had pictures and was more interesting than watching a group of grown women behaving like, and being treated like, children.

Sarah was not popular in the harem. As the new favorite, she had been given the ikbal's apartment which had formerly belonged to Fatma. The other women all assumed that she was enjoying a wild sexual relationship with Kalid, which might have had its amusing side if only Sarah hadn't completely lost her sense of humor.

Kalid had not sent for Sarah for two weeks.

Sarah used the time to formulate escape plans, insisting to herself that she did not miss Kalid. Or if she did, it was only because talking to him posed a challenge, a battle of wits that was completely missing with Memtaz and the other women.

Sarah was bored.

She watched Fatma light a jeweled chibuk and then expel a long stream of smoke. The tepidarium was almost empty today; only Fatma and Sarah and couple of others were present, along with the inevitable servants and eunuchs. Sarah studied Fatma, a gorgeous Russian from the Caucasus with flawless ivory skin and waist-length wavy auburn hair. She couldn't imagine why Kalid didn't concentrate on this woman and leave Sarah alone.

Fatma was certainly much more willing.

Sarah sighed and went back to her book. For some reason, Kalid did not want everyone to know that they were not sleeping together. Maybe he didn't want Sarah's rebellion to give the other women ideas. Each night, she was taken by Memtaz to the men's quarters and left in the music room adjoining the pasha's apartments. There she spent the evening alone, amidst standing harps and timbrels and a Bullock's grand piano, reading the English books that had thoughtfully been provided for her and teaching herself mah jongg.

Yes, she was very bored.

A servant appeared at her side with a dish of sherbet, rich burgundy in color, topped with a sauce of raspberry preserves. Sarah looked up to see Fatma smiling and nodding at her, gesturing for her to eat it.

Now this was a switch. A peace offering from the woman who had made no secret of her silent animosity up to this point? While Sarah puzzled over what to do, Memtaz appeared from the hamman and bent to straighten Sarah's pattens under her couch.

"Do not eat that, mistress," she said under her breath, her hands moving busily.

Sarah glanced at her, startled.

"A gift from such a one is not to be trusted," Memtaz added in a louder whisper.

Sarah looked over at Fatma, who was watching her closely, immobile as a statue.

Sarah stood abruptly, stumbling ostentatiously and sending the dish of sherbet crashing to the floor. The crystal shattered, and the gooey confection splattered on the tiles.

"Oh, how clumsy of me, I'm so sorry," Sarah said, glancing over at Fatma and shrugging helplessly. "Memtaz, please tell Fatma that I appreciate her thoughtfulness."

Then she fled, not looking back, as Memtaz conveyed the message and then patiently began to clean up the mess.

"Pasha Kalid requires your presence in the music room again tonight," Memtaz announced.

Sarah stood obediently, anticipating another boring evening of reading *A Hiker's Guide to the Cotswolds* or *A Thousand Years of British Monarchy,* obviously relics of the pasha's Oxford days.

If this was the punishment Kalid had devised for her, it was certainly effective.

Sarah was shocked to enter the music room and find Kalid waiting for her.

Her heart began to pound the moment she saw him. He was once again in Western dress, this time silk chamois trousers and an embroidered cotton shirt. The pale colors complemented his vivid looks and made him seem deceptively like the young accountants and clerks and teachers she had known in Boston. If it weren't for the Roman nose and the golden honey hue of his skin, he might have been attending a concert at the Conservatory of Music.

"You seem surprised to see me," he greeted her.

"I didn't go through the half-day hamman ritual, so I thought I would be alone."

"Memtaz told me that you objected to the elaborate preparation, so I gave her permission to dispense with it."

"So you have been keeping tabs on me."

"Certainly." He was standing next to a large map of the United States set up on an easel.

"Will this be a geography lesson?" Sarah asked.

"I wish to learn more about your country," he said.

"Where did you get the map?"

"Almost everything is available to me, kourista. At the right price, of course."

"Including people," she said sarcastically.

He held up his hand. "I do not wish to argue this evening. I want you to show me the various places about which I inquire."

"Fine," Sarah said. Whatever he wanted. It would keep him happy and it had to be more interesting than the Cotswolds.

"Where is your government in Washington, D.C.?"

Sarah pointed to the capital between Virginia and Maryland on the Potomac River.

"I thought it was in the center of the country," Kalid said.

Sarah shook her head.

"And where is Boston?"

Sarah raised her hand north and showed him her home town on the edge of the Atlantic Ocean.

"And that is in what district?"

"State. We call them states. Massachusetts."

"Massa—bah, I cannot say it."

"Mass-a-too-setts," Sarah said, enunciating carefully.

Kalid imitated her, with creditable success.

"And your parents? Where did they come from?"

"My father was from Boston. My mother came from New Hampshire, here."

He peered at her finger on the map. "And all of this," he said, gesturing west. "What is out here?"

"The rest of the country. It's big—three thousand miles from coast to coast, between two oceans. How could you have gone to Oxford and be so ignorant about it?"

"In Oxford I learned about England, not the United States. What did you know about the Ottoman Empire before you came here?"

He had a point.

"And your work, where was that?" he asked.

"In Boston. I taught school there."

"School?"

"Elementary school. Fourth grade."

He raised an inquiring eyebrow.

"The children were about ten years old."

"And did you never wish to have children of your own?" he asked, his dark eyes fixed on hers.

"Some day. When the time is right."

"And the man is right?"

"Yes," Sarah said cautiously. What was all this chit-chat? In the past, he had gone in more for direct assault than polite conversation. Was he changing his methods? He was so tricky that she was almost afraid to look away from him.

A servant entered with coffee on a tray and set it on a carved mahogany table in front of Kalid. The pasha dismissed the girl with a wave of his hand.

"Sit," he said, and Sarah joined him on a damask couch.

"Coffee?" Kalid said to Sarah.

"Is it drugged?" she countered, holding his gaze.

He was gracious enough to smile. "Let me ask you a question. If I had taken you aside at Topkapi and asked you if you would come here with me, would you have agreed?"

"Of course not."

"Then what choice did you leave me but to drug you?"

"Kalid, didn't it ever occur to you that you might not get what you wanted?"

"No," he said ingenuously, and poured a stream of coffee into a delicate china cup.

"So your only alternative was to kidnap me?"

"Yes."

Sarah sighed. "England obviously didn't make much of an impression on you."

"On the contrary," he said in his clipped

127

accent, sounding very English indeed. "My grandmother tells me that I am entirely too Western. She finds my intense need to have my desire for you reciprocated a quaint and curious English notion."

Sarah looked away, feeling herself go weak in the knees. Hearing him talk about his obsession with her in such a detached fashion had more of an impact than his most ardent embrace; she was glad she was sitting down.

He handed her the cup of coffee. "Perhaps I did stay too long in England. I seem to fit nowhere now," he observed.

"I think you fit here very well."

He smiled dryly. "You say that because you are not Turkish. To the Turks, I am too lenient. They admire a strong hand. And the women are puzzled by my . . . discrimination. Here the number of women a man beds is proof of virility, and I am sorely lacking in that regard."

Sarah almost choked on her coffee. "I wouldn't agree," she finally said, coughing.

"Kosem is very worried about me," he said sadly.

Kosem didn't witness our last two wrestling matches, Sarah thought. Aloud she said, "Why?"

"She does not share my taste."

"Beg pardon?"

"She thinks you are too skinny and doubts whether you will be able to bear children."

Sarah put down her cup. "Kalid—" she began.

He held up his hand. "Don't worry. I have

reassured her on both counts."

Sarah opened her mouth to frame a tart retort and then saw the smile in his eyes. Was he teasing her?

"Now," he said, leaning forward to put his cup on the table, "let us continue my lesson."

They talked for another two hours, about many different things, and then Kalid let her go.

It was only when she was walking back to her room between the two eunuchs that Sarah realized that this was the first time she had seen him that he had not touched her.

It was another week before Kalid summoned Sarah again.

She tried not to admit to herself that she was disappointed. She knew that he was deliberately keeping her off balance; each day she didn't know whether he would send for her, or if he would touch her when he did, so she was in a constant state of anxious anticipation.

She was, in short, leading the life of a harem woman.

When Memtaz bustled into her room in a state of high excitement, Sarah knew that the pasha had spoken.

"You will attend upon my master this evening, but first, this afternoon, you are going on an outing to the Kahouli Bazaar," Memtaz said. She clapped her hands delightedly.

"Oh, is that fun?"

"The most fun. And you will bring sweetmeats and drinks and stop on the way back for a . . ." Memtaz paused.

"Picnic?" Sarah supplied.

"Yes, yes! A picnic."

"Whose idea was this?" Sarah asked suspiciously.

"The valide pashana thought you needed an outing."

Sarah filed that away. If she knew her valide pashanas, Kosem had an ulterior motive for this excursion.

"You are not going?" Sarah asked Memtaz.

"Not this time. But I have been there before and I will go again sometime."

"Memtaz," Sarah said thoughtfully, "you knew Kalid's mother, is that right?"

"Yes, mistress. Very well."

"What was she like?"

"Like you," Memtaz replied, and smiled.

"Like me?" Sarah said. "Really?"

"Oh, yes. She came here against her will, too. She was a captive, as I told you. But she came to love the old pasha very much and lived out the rest of her life in happiness here."

"She never wanted to go home again?"

"I think she had a longing, yes, a longing she passed on to her son. He wanted to go to England very much, to see it for her."

"What did she look like?"

"Oh, *gulbeyaz*. Most beautiful. Once the pasha saw her, he was lost to all others. He had no other kadin for the rest of his life."

"Was she blonde?"

"Not so much as you—darker, the color of amber. With the dimples, and the cleft in the chin, that my master has now." Memtaz looked around the room. "Where is your *feradge?*"

"My what?"

"Your cloak. You must be completely veiled, covered up to the eyes in order to go out in a carriage."

"Memtaz, I don't think I have a feradge. I've never been out of the palace since I got here."

"Oh, yes, I see. I'll find you one. You must get ready—the carriages will be here at one o'clock."

The feradge turned out to be a sort of wrap, like a blanket, which went over the shoulders and the head and concealed everything but the eyes of the wearer. As the harem women assembled by the Gates of Felicity with the khislar, Achmed, the little procession looked like a line of mummies or ghosts.

Achmed assigned two eunuchs to walk beside each carriage and a halberdier to drive it. The carriages had canopies of ivory silk fringed with gold tassels, and the seats were padded with plush and strewn with embroidered cushions. Twin lanterns sat on either side of the driver's bench, and each coach was pulled by a matched team of horses. Kosem's carriage was in the lead, the pasha's crest emblazoned on the doors, and the valide pashana gestured for

Sarah to join her for the drive down the hill into town.

The sea gleamed below them as the carriages proceeded at a walking pace, the khislar in the lead, down the dusty, winding road that led from the Orchid Palace to the bazaar in Bursa. This was the first time Sarah had seen the route she'd traveled the night she was kidnapped, and she craned her neck to peer over the side of the coach, trying to memorize landmarks and get her bearings.

"Planning your escape route?" Kosem's voice interrupted her reverie. Sarah turned to look at the old lady; her black eyes were the only thing visible above her cloak.

"You look startled," Kosem added serenely, smiling. "Was I reading your mind?"

"It always startles me to hear you speaking English," Sarah said mildly.

"Nonsense. You were plotting, as usual."

"If you think that, why did you invite me to come on this excursion?" Sarah asked.

"Because I wanted to talk to you, and my grandson gets suspicious if I request too many audiences with you. He thinks I'm—how do you say it? Up to something."

Sarah suppressed a smile. "Are you?"

"Definitely. I know you want to get out of here, and I have a plan, one that doesn't involve escaping from the palace in the dead of night and swimming the Bosporus."

She now had Sarah's full attention.

"I want you to marry my grandson and give him an heir. If you do, I will make sure that as soon as you wish to leave, you will have safe passage from the palace and back home to the United States. I have my own retainers, my own sources, people that I can bribe. Kalid will know nothing of it."

Sarah was so dumbfounded that she was silent for a full minute. The carriage wheels creaked on the unpaved road, and the coach weaved as her thoughts raced wildly.

"Are you talking about my leaving the child behind when I go?" Sarah finally managed to say. She had to make some reply to this preposterous suggestion.

"Of course. He would take over from my grandson when he dies; the child must remain here."

Sarah didn't know whether to hit her or burst out laughing. When she had her emotions under control she said, "Valide pashana, I thank you for your kind offer, but I could never leave a child of mine under any circumstances."

"But my grandson will have no other woman but you! What am I to do? If he dies without an heir, the pashadom will be plunged into chaos. There will be civil war!"

"How old is Kalid?" Sarah asked.

Kosem thought about it.

"Thirty?" she said at length.

"I think he has a few years left to father children," Sarah observed dryly.

133

"But I will not live to see it! I must know the line is secure before I die, don't you understand?"

Sarah sighed. "Your highness, I can't help you. I think you should talk to your advisors about this, it's really family business."

"I have done so," Kosem said morosely, staring out the window of the coach. "Nothing comes of it."

The sounds of the bazaar were filtering into the carriage, getting louder and more insistent as they approached the center of the town. Sarah turned to look out the window and was overwhelmed by the sights and sounds and smells.

Striped stalls were set up so close to one another that they seemed to be one, the alleys between them hardly wide enough for a person to walk. The wares displayed were so varied as to dazzle the eye: reed baskets, richly colored blankets and shawls, wool rugs and countless woven items, lengths of silk and other fine cloth, silver and metalwork, jewelry and other finery, herbs and roots for charms and potions, perfumes and lotions and scented oils. And the food! Hanging bunches of dried fish, sweetmeats to be tied in napkins, kebobs heated over braziers, roasted nuts and vegetables, all of it sending out a delicious scent that mingled with the smell of heat and dust and humanity. And over all of it was the din: the cries of the vendors hawking their wares and the babble of voices speaking diverse languages.

Sarah stared, fascinated. She had never seen so many different types of people in one place. There were men in caftans and in Western clothes but wearing red fezzes; halberdiers and eunuchs in their white pants and black and gold short jackets; janissaries, the Sultan's paid military, in dark blue uniforms; veiled women of all shapes and sizes; blacks from Nubia and Abyssinia and the upper reaches of the Nile in their colorful native dress; and European traders of every skin hue and country, all mingled in the crowd like varicolored pebbles on a beach.

"You may have anything you wish from the bazaar, upon my grandson's instruction," Kosem said to Sarah. "Just gesture for it and the eunuchs will buy it."

The pashana's carriage stopped in a cobbled street at the edge of the bazaar, and the other harem coaches lined up behind it. Sarah and Kosem alighted from the vehicle by means of a set of drop stairs, assisted by the khislar. As they walked forward, Kosem took Sarah's arm, Achmed fell into step beside them, and the eunuchs took up the rear.

They had obviously been well instructed by the pasha.

"What do you think of this?" Kosem asked, holding up a length of poppy silk as they passed a stall displaying bolts of the luxurious cloth dyed every color of the spectrum.

"Very pretty," Sarah said, and Kosem signaled one of the eunuchs to purchase it. Sarah realized that she had to be careful; she would wind up with half the bazaar if she approved of everything she saw.

"Do you need anything?" Sarah asked.

Kosem looked at her. "Need?" she said.

Sarah realized that it had been a foolish question. The pashana's purchases were matters of whim, not necessity.

They turned down an alley and Kosem stooped to admire a silver urn engraved with twining grape leaves around its rim. Sarah bent her head and scanned the rear of the alley covertly. All she could see was the dirt-packed road continuing to either side and a stone building with an arched entrance facing her.

It didn't look very promising.

Kosem said something in Turkish, and the merchant answered in a flowery speech.

Kosem shook her head.

"Are you buying it?" Sarah asked.

"He wants too much."

"Don't you bargain with him?" Sarah asked, remembering the infamous negotiations regarding a purchase in the Middle East. This bartering was almost an art form.

"Certainly not," Kosem replied. "He should be honored to sell to the valide pashana."

Sarah looked away, her lips twitching.

The merchant ran after them as they walked

on, and Kosem wound up with the urn, at her price.

After about an hour of this process, the eunuchs were so laden with booty that Achmed sent them back to the carriage with it. As the khislar stood directing them, Kosem stopped to admire a pair of cast bronze earbobs inlaid with turquoise, and Sarah saw her chance.

She grabbed two trays of jewelry and upset them, scattering rings and bracelets and diadems on the ground. The stall owner shrieked, and other shoppers jumped back out of the way as Sarah ripped two hanging rugs in a neighboring stall from their hooks and flung them in the faces of those nearest her. Then she turned and ran for her life as Kosem turned to see the source of the commotion and the khislar looked over his shoulder and shouted in alarm.

The eunuchs dropped their burdens and dashed after Sarah with the khislar hot on their heels. Sarah wrapped her feradge over her arm to allow her legs more freedom of movement and ran headlong around a corner, where she crashed into a man leading a donkey laden with boxes of green figs. She whirled and headed in the other direction, where people cleared out of her way as she dashed past them. She ran until she was out of the bazaar and the houses were farther apart, with courtyards between them and splashing fountains surrounded by flowering gardens. This was obviously a residential section, but Sarah ran on until the stitch in her side was so painful that she slumped against the side of a stucco house, gasping for breath. She was wiping her perspiring face with the edge of her cloak when the door to the street opened and a woman came out of it, wearing the face veil, dumping a pail of water into the street.

She turned and saw Sarah, who shrank back against the wall. It was several seconds before Sarah realized that the woman was gesturing for Sarah to come inside the house. Not believing her luck, Sarah scanned the street quickly for her pursuers and then followed her hostess into the house.

The main room was furnished with a handwoven rug and a large table and chairs set before an open hearth that took up most of one stone wall. Despite the heat, a small fire was burning and a cooking pot hung over it. A baby was sleeping in a hand-carved cradle in the corner, and an oil lamp hung from a chain overhead.

The woman unpinned her face veil and offered Sarah a seat. Sarah collapsed into it, removing her feradge and yashmak, sighing gratefully. The woman lifted the pot from its hook and raised her brows, asking if Sarah wanted something to eat. Sarah shook her head and mimed drinking, asking for water. The woman produced a jug and poured watered wine from it into a cup and handed it to Sarah.

Sarah downed half of it in one gulp, grimacing at its bitterness, but it quenched her thirst. She rested and then finished the drink, sitting back and closing her eyes.

A man came in from the back room, and the woman signaled to him with her eyes, indicating Sarah. The man nodded and withdrew quickly, dropping the beaded curtain between the two rooms.

It was several minutes before Sarah opened her eyes again; she had almost fallen asleep. Her benefactor was sitting in a chair opposite her, stitching on a piece of needlework confined in a hoop. Sarah tried to remember what Turkish she knew.

"*Tessekur ederim*," she said, thanking the woman for her spontaneous hospitality.

The woman nodded and smiled.

"Can I get a carriage from here to the docks?" Sarah asked in elementary Turkish. James lived near the docks.

The woman shrugged incomprehension.

Sarah stared at her, puzzled. She had just understood when Sarah thanked her. Maybe she spoke only a few words of Turkish. Maybe she was Armenian or Circassian; they had their own sections in the city where their native languages were spoken.

Sarah tried again, asking how far she was from the sea. She had no idea whether she had run away from it or toward it, she had changed direction so many times.

The woman shrugged again, then rose and dished up a bowl of stew from the hanging pot, placing it before Sarah together with a wooden spoon.

Sarah realized that she was famished; she had eaten nothing since her breakfast of feta cheese and honey, and her recent exercise had given her an appetite. She was eating heartily when the door to the street opened, and both women looked up to see Achmed, khislar to Kalid Shah, framed in the arched entrance.

Chapter Six

James Woolcott sat fidgeting in the outer office of the Under Secretary to the American Ambassador in Constantinople, holding his fedora in his hands. He was wearing a dark blue, double-breasted frock coat with a matching vest and striped gray trousers. His standing collar was teamed with a four-in-hand tie, and a pair of dove-gray gloves was folded into his waistcoat pocket.

He believed that in order to be taken seriously, he must dress for the occasion.

Minor functionaries bustled past him, stacks of paper in hand, and a large American flag stood in a corner to his left, its wide border decorated with gold braid. He was staring at the portrait of President Chester A. Arthur on the facing wall when the door to the secretary's office opened and a young diplomat-in-training said, "Secretary Danforth will see you now."

James rose and entered the inner office, which was well furnished in teak and oak, with a local Kirman carpet on the floor. Heavy red drapes with gold tassels partially concealed the grilled windows and a bust of the late President Lincoln stood on a pedestal by the door.

Secretary Danforth came out from behind his massive desk and extended his hand. James shook it and then sat in the guest chair indicated by Danforth as he resumed his seat.

"A pleasure to meet you, Mr. Woolcott. I understand that you have a thriving business here. I'm always proud to make the acquaintance of successful Americans abroad. Their prosperity improves the image of our country to the natives. Now how can we here at the embassy be of service to you?"

Danforth was a portly man in his forties with a florid face and the hail-fellow-well-met air of a career diplomat. He was also something of a dandy, sporting a cutaway coat with checked trousers and a trim, waxed moustache.

James cleared his throat. "Well, Mr. Danforth, about six weeks ago my cousin Sarah came from Boston to visit me here. She spent some time seeing the local churches and sights and became fascinated with the harem at Topkapi."

"Shocking practice," Danforth said, frowning.

"Yes, of course. But I knew Sarah wanted to see it, and when I became aware that the Sultan was seeking a teacher for his daughter, I arranged for my cousin to go into the harem as an English tutor for the Princess Roxalena."

Danforth raised his brows. "Was that wise?"

"Apparently not. I saw no harm in it at the time, as the Sultan had traditionally been tolerant of Western influences, but Sarah had only been inside the harem about three weeks when she disappeared."

"Disappeared?" Danforth echoed.

"Yes. I received a message from the Princess saying that Sarah had been sold into the harem of the Pasha of Bursa for a sum of money and an heirloom that the Sultan had been coveting for some time."

"The Pasha of Bursa?" Danforth said, smiling. "Well, that's no problem at all, Mr. Woolcott. The pasha's a reasonable fellow, has an Oxford education. I'll just get in touch with him and ask him to return your cousin to you."

James swallowed nervously. "I . . . ah, don't think you understand the situation, Secretary Danforth. The pasha bought Sarah for himself, to be kept for him personally. For his . . . pleasure."

Danforth's high color deepened even further. "Oh. That's rather a different matter. Under local law, women are chattels, you understand. Very unfortunate, but there's little influence we can bring to bear in such a situation. We cannot impose our values on a foreign culture. Embassy personnel are guests here."

James stared at him. "Are you telling me there's nothing we can do?" he asked incredulously.

Danforth coughed. "No, not exactly. It's just that no matter how westernized some of these people seem, they revert to their barbarism whenever the mood takes them, and the Sultan supports these regressions among his subordinates. He's a dictator and could throw all of us out at a whim. We have to tread carefully if we want to keep the profitable trade routes open and businesses like yours in operation."

James was silent. He did not want to lose his livelihood, nor did he want to be the cause of widespread bankruptcy among the American colonials in Constantinople.

Under Secretary Danforth painted a realistic but not very encouraging picture.

"Can we at least make inquiries?" James asked weakly.

"Of course, of course," Danforth said briskly, picking up his pen. "Just give me the details and I will talk to the Ambassador and see what can be arranged."

James sighed, reviewed the story in his mind, and then started at the beginning.

Roxalena surveyed the large array of items displayed on the floor of the tepidarium at Topkapi and then shrugged.

"I see nothing of unusual beauty or value here," she said to the anxious tradeswoman, who immediately launched into her set speech again, babbling about the quality of her Damask silks and Jersualem lace. Roxalena held up her hand.

"Bring these things down to my apartment," Roxalena said to the "bundle woman," so called because she came into the harem periodically with her wares concealed in cloth bundles. "I wish to consider them in private."

Shirza helped the merchant to gather up her fabrics and trinkets and carry them to Roxalena's suite, away from the prying eyes of the other harem women. Once they reached the princess sultana's rooms, Shirza closed the door to the corridor and Roxalena gestured for them to come into the inner chamber, where she slept.

"Display your wares here," Roxalena said, gesturing to her sleeping couch.

The bundle woman complied, and Roxalena quickly selected two marcasite-studded silver bangles and a *bornoze*, or bathrobe, of unbleached Egyptian cotton, which she gave to Shirza. Then she signaled to the servant with her eyes. Shirza scurried to the door and took up her position just inside it.

"Will you be stopping at the Orchid Palace in Bursa sometime soon?" Roxalena inquired of the bundle woman casually, paying her for the jewelry she had chosen.

The woman nodded. "It's part of my regular route, Princess. I should be there next week."

Roxalena looked at Shirza, who nodded encouragement.

Roxalena reached inside the capacious sleeve of her caftan and withdrew a two-hundred-kurush note. She ripped it in half as the peddler's eyes widened.

"There is a woman in the harem at the Orchid Palace, a Western woman with long yellow hair," Roxalena said. "Her name is Sarah. I want you to find her and give her the note I will write for you. When you come back to me with proof that you have seen her, I will give you the other half of this bill."

The bundle woman nodded vigorously. She would have to peddle her wares for six months to earn the sum Roxalena was dangling before her; she was more than eager to comply.

"Do you understand?" Roxalena asked.

"Yes, mistress. Yes."

"Very well." Roxalena went to her vanity table and wrote carefully, in elementary Turkish, "I have sent word to your kinsman where you are. He will work with your embassy to free you. Do not despair." She added in English, "I am yur frend. I will help." She did not sign it. She blew the note dry, folded it, and handed it to the peddler.

"And tell Sarah the letter came from me. Remember, I must have proof. A lock of hair, a personal item, something to show that you gave her this letter." Roxalena was well aware that the woman might resort to any deception in order to collect the bribe.

The woman snatched the letter and the first half of the two-hundred-kurush bill and stuffed them into her bodice.

"And if you report this to anyone, I will make sure that my father deals most harshly with you," Roxalena added.

The peddler looked suitably chastened.

"You may go," Roxalena said imperiously.

The woman scrambled to pack up her wares and fled to the door, where Shirza let her into the corridor to join the waiting eunuchs. When Shirza returned, Roxalena grasped her hand.

"Do you think it will work?" Roxalena asked.

Shirza squeezed Roxalena's fingers encouragingly. "I think it will, mistress."

"I miss Sarah," Roxalena said mistily, biting her lip.

"You'll see her again."

Roxalena nodded, but her expression indicated that she was not convinced.

Kalid paced back and forth in his audience chamber, raking his fingers through his hair. His jodphurs were splashed with mud; there was a rent in his sleeve and a streak of dirt on his cheek. Every time the door opened to admit a servant or a messenger, he whirled expectantly, then looked away, distracted.

"Where is my horse?" he shouted to the last

unfortunate who walked in on him, a groom who stopped dead in his tracks and said, "He is being saddled, master. Khan was so weary from your first run that we had to rub him down—"

"I don't want to hear excuses!" Kalid roared. "I have been here ten minutes and you have not produced a fresh horse! Now if I do not have—" he stopped in mid-sentence as the doors opened once more to admit his khislar, who had Sarah's arm in a steel grip.

Kalid stared. Her hands were tied before her and her veil was down around her shoulders, snagged in her hair; her eyes were swollen and tear-stained.

Kalid rushed forward and embraced her, folding her in his arms, murmuring something in Turkish. Sarah was so exhausted and defeated that she slumped against him wearily and allowed her head to fall to his shoulder.

"Are you all right?" he said into her ear, in English. "I just came back from looking for you myself." He kissed her cheeks, her forehead, her eyes, every place he could reach.

"I'm all right," Sarah whispered, wondering why she felt so comforted when this was the very person she was seeking to escape.

"Out, all of you," Kalid called in Turkish to the other people in the room, over Sarah's shoulder. And then, "Achmed, remain."

The khislar turned back and stood waiting, his arms folded, his expression blank.

Kalid stood cradling Sarah in his arms, as if afraid she might vanish again if he let go. He felt so good—solid, safe, and warm. Sarah clung to him without thought.

"Now tell me exactly what happened," Kalid said in Turkish to the khislar.

Achmed replied in the same language, and as the two men conversed Sarah felt Kalid's embrace relax. Finally Kalid looked down at her, then flung her away from him so furiously that Sarah stumbled.

"I see," he said tightly. "Now I understand. Apparently everyone, including my revered grandmother, has been afraid to inform me of the truth. I thought you had been kidnapped or lost your way at the bazaar. I just spent three hours flogging my horse through every alley in Bursa looking for you. What no one wanted to tell me was that you were running away from me."

Sarah said nothing, forcing herself to mime courage and meet his blazing eyes.

"I knew you were stubborn, and willful, and obstinate. I did not realize that you were also stupid," he said in a dangerously low tone.

Sarah's throat closed. She had never seen him this angry before, and she had seen him angry often.

"Have you any idea what might happen to you in this part of the world without my protection? If you think you have been ill-treated here, that's because you have never encountered

149

the bedouins. They would take turns raping you and then slit your throat and leave you by the side of the road for the hyenas."

Sarah looked away from him unresponsively, unable to bear the fury in his face.

"Or," he said, "they might offer you at the auctions in Medina or Beirut. Yellow hair and a pretty face would fetch a high price. How would you like being sold into slavery?"

"I am in slavery!" Sarah replied heatedly, holding up her bound hands defiantly.

He held his hand out to the khislar for his sword, and when Achmed gave it to him, he sliced through the rope that held her hands together with one stroke. Kalid threw the sword on the floor and seized the front of her feradge, holding her face up to his.

"You do not know what slavery is!" he said between his teeth. "You think you are in slavery here, where you soak in the hamman, eating sherbet and drinking boza while you dream up new ways to torture me? Is it slavery when you torment me with your refusals, reading travelogues while I lie awake at night, unable to sleep, tantalized by visions of making love to you? I am the one in slavery, not you! I could teach you what it really means to be a slave!"

He shoved her away from him, but this time she kept her footing. "I am not free to come and go," Sarah said quietly. "That's what it means to be a slave."

"Oh, and where would you go? Back into

Bursa, running through the streets like a wild dog? You're lucky that you stumbled into the home of a janissary who was loyal to the Sultan's pasha and so turned you back to me."

"For a price," Sarah said contemptuously. "I saw the payoff. Obviously you buy your military the way you buy your women. How did they know who I was, anyway?"

"My men went from house to house with the word as soon as you disappeared. How many blond women in harem finery dashing around without a male escort do you think there are in Bursa?"

"I had to try," Sarah said stubbornly.

"Why? Why did you have to try?" Kalid demanded, looking at her intently.

"Because I cannot stay here! I have a life back in Boston, friends, family, a job. I came here on a vacation to see my cousin, not to become the bed slave of some oversexed hybrid dictator!"

"Am I so repulsive to you, then?" he asked softly.

Sarah met his eyes and could feel herself growing warm.

He knew the answer to his question.

"That's not the point," she said miserably, looking away from him in dismay.

Kalid threw up his hands. He stood staring at the floor, thinking, for several seconds, then said to the khislar in Turkish, "Bring the *baltacilar* to me."

Achmed did not move.

Kalid looked at him. "Yes?" he said.

"She should be flogged, master," Achmed said. "As an example to the other women, if for no other reason."

Kalid looked at Sarah, who was obviously trying to understand their interchange, without much success.

"You will not mark that skin," Kalid said softly.

"A period of time in the dungeon on bread and water?" Achmed suggested.

Kalid shook his head.

Achmed bowed and left, returning almost instantly with the second halberdier, who wore a heavy belt around his middle which contained literally hundreds of keys.

"The ikbal is to be confined to her rooms until I rescind this order," Kalid said to him. "You will unlock her door for food to be brought in and on any other occasion you receive my express notice, but at no other time. Her servant Memtaz is to be confined with her. And you will post two armed guards outside her door at all times. They can take the same shift as the halberdiers. Are there any questions?"

The baltacilar bowed.

"You may go," Kalid said to him. The pasha then nodded to the khislar, who took Sarah's arm and dragged her away, struggling.

"What are you doing?" Sarah called over her shoulder to Kalid. "Where is he taking me?"

Kalid listened until he could no longer hear

her voice, then slumped into his chair, staring fixedly into space.

Kosem advanced gingerly into the audience room. When Kalid looked up and saw her, he groaned.

"No," he said wearily. "Not now."

"Kalid, I must talk to you."

"Take her away!" Kalid made a sweeping gesture to the eunuchs escorting his grandmother. Each one of them immediately seized a frail arm.

"Kalid, please!" Kosem said. "I will not be long. I have something important to say."

Kalid gestured for the servants to release the old lady. "I am furious with you," he said flatly, not looking at her. "It was your idea to take Sarah to the bazaar."

"Kalid, she would not have seized that opportunity to get away if she were happy here. Give up on this girl and get another."

He said nothing.

"She is running away from you! How long can you keep her under lock and key?"

"As long as it takes."

"And by then I will be dead."

"It will happen soon. She is powerfully attracted to me. I can build on that. She has all these Western notions of propriety and civilized behavior; I have to overcome those barriers with a passion so intense it will sweep all before it."

"How do you know you can do this?" Kosem asked.

"I know I can because my mother grew to love my father," he said simply.

Kosem relented, bending to kiss his cheek. "You always were a romantic, son of my son. I give you *keyf*." She gathered the hem of her caftan into her hand and tiptoed out of the audience room, keaving Kalid alone.

Kalid stared at the door long after she had left, not as confident as he pretended, wondering if he would ever find the fulfillment his grandmother had wished him.

If Sarah had been unhappy in the Orchid Palace before her brief escape, after three days of close confinement in the harem she was in complete despair. Denied the freedom of the palace, she saw no one but Memtaz, who brought in her meals and did her best to keep her mistress occupied. Sarah was allowed books but she had read most of them, and she had little interest in the intricate pastimes that amused harem women, strategic games involving tiles and colored marbles that she found childish and unabsorbing.

Her mood was not improved when Memtaz told her that Kalid had sent for Fatma every night since Sarah was recaptured.

For Sarah, there was no word from him at all. So when Memtaz announced that a bundle woman was visiting the harem with her wares,

154

Sarah asked permission to have the woman admitted to see her. Memtaz returned shortly with the peddler, and Sarah fell on her like a long-lost relative, so eager was she to relieve the tedium and abandonment of her imprisoned existence.

"Sarah?" the bundle woman said, as soon as she entered the ikbal's apartment.

Sarah stared at her. "Do you know me?"

The woman said something else, but her accent was so thick that Sarah could not understand her.

"Memtaz, what is she saying?" Sarah asked quickly.

"It is her dialect. She is from Pamphylia. She says that she has a message from the Princess at Topkapi," Memtaz whispered, glancing at the door.

Sarah held her finger to her lips, her heart beating faster. "Roxalena?" she said in an undertone.

The peddler nodded emphatically.

Sarah and Memtaz exchanged glances.

"Memtaz, go and listen at the door," Sarah muttered.

"Mistress, this is dangerous. If my master—"

"Go to the door!" Sarah hissed. Memtaz scurried to obey.

Sarah looked at the bundle woman, who withdrew Roxalena's note from her bosom and handed it to Sarah.

Sarah scanned it quickly and then held it to

her lips. She could feel the sting of tears behind her eyes.

God bless Roxalena. She *was* a friend.

"Let me give you something for your trouble," Sarah said to the peddler, looking around for a bauble.

The woman held up her hand and looked toward Memtaz. Sarah gestured for the servant to come back.

"What does she want?" Sarah asked.

Memtaz conferred with the visitor, then said, "She needs something to prove to the princess that she saw you. A lock of hair?"

Sarah ran to her vanity table and snipped off a curl of hair, then removed her father's gold signet ring from her pinky. Roxalena had often remarked on it.

"Give these to Roxalena," Sarah said, pressing the items into the bundle woman's hands.

The peddler nodded and thrust them inside her blouse, then bolted for the door, eager to leave and collect her reward now that her mission had been accomplished. Memtaz saw her out the door to meet her escort, but when the servant returned after a protracted period, her expression was clouded.

"What is it?" Sarah demanded anxiously. "Did someone stop that woman and question her?"

Memtaz shook her head. "I heard the eunuchs talking. Pasha Kalid has been badly injured in a bedouin raid. They think he might die."

Chapter Seven

Sarah felt faint; her hand shot out to steady herself on a table as she said, "Die?"

Memtaz nodded worriedly. "It's a pistol wound. The ball is still in his shoulder. The valide pashana has sent to Ankara for a doctor skilled in such matters, but it is a long trip to reach here. The pasha is bleeding badly."

Sarah did not know what to say. Kalid had been such a constant in her life since she came to the Orchid Palace, such a wall of solidity, that the idea of something happening to him had never entered her mind.

"Doesn't the pasha have his own doctor?" Sarah asked Memtaz, after a long pause.

"He is away, mistress. The pasha sent him

to tend a friend in Kucuksu, on the Asian side of the Bosporus."

"How do you know this?" Sarah asked.

"It is the talk of the palace, mistress. It just happened early this morning, but already there is much concern."

Sarah walked over to her sleeping couch and sat down on it heavily, her thoughts in turmoil. Memtaz waited patiently until Sarah looked up and said, "Memtaz, do you think I could get permission to see the valide pashana?"

Memtaz looked doubtful. "You are under house arrest, mistress. It took a great deal of talking to persuade the khislar to allow the bundle woman to visit you."

"But circumstances have changed! The pasha's life is in danger and I might be able to help him. If Kosem gives her permission for me to tend him, that is."

"Tend him? Oh, no, mistress, that would never be allowed. Only the khislar and members of the family—"

"Memtaz, will you talk to Achmed when you go to get my evening meal?" Sarah said, interrupting her. "Kosem will listen to him. I would do it myself, but I can't get out of here."

Memtaz bent her head in acquiescence. "I will do as you ask, mistress. But I am puzzled as to why you want to help the pasha. I thought it was your heartfelt desire to escape him. Are you afraid of what might happen to you if he dies?"

Sarah hadn't even thought about that aspect

of it. If Kalid died, her only value would be what she might bring at a slave auction, and she was sure the khislar would not hesitate to sell her. Or leave her in the harem for the next pasha, whoever that might be.

"I'm not thinking that far ahead, Memtaz. Just see if I can visit the valide pashana tonight. Please."

Memtaz bowed and withdrew. Sarah walked over to the window and gazed out over the tiled roof of the Bird House, praying that Kosem would see her.

Kosem's caramel skin was very pale as Sarah was ushered into her presence that evening. The valide pashana was composed, but the hand that held the chibuk was shaking as she raised the ornately carved pipe to her lips.

Sarah had dressed carefully for the interview, donning a silver tissue shalwar and a caftan of imperial purple shot with silver thread. She advanced on the pasha's grandmother, who was alone in her antechamber, surrounded by the finery that was the comfort of her old age.

"You may be seated," Kosem said, and Sarah obeyed, sitting on the edge of a damask couch opposite the one Kosem occupied.

"Thank you for seeing me," Sarah said.

"The khislar said your servant was most persistent. You seem to have won her allegiance in a short time."

"It is important that I have your permission to tend Kalid."

"Why?" Kosem's gaze was direct.

"My father was a doctor in Boston, valide pashana. Until he died two years ago, I used to assist him in his surgery all the time. I think I may be able to help."

"You misunderstood my question. Why do you want to help Kalid? I thought you saw him as your captor, your tormentor. Just the other day you abused my trust and fled through the bazaar to get away from him. I should think you would want to see him suffer. I do not understand your motives in coming to me."

Sarah sighed. "I'm not happy being held against my will, that is true. But Kalid has dealt with me . . . humanely, and I have never wanted revenge on him. I have always known that by his lights he was treating me very well."

"By his lights?" Kosem said, not familiar with the idiom.

"By his own standards."

Kosem puffed for several seconds and then said, "I do not think you are being honest with yourself, but I also know that self-deception is an honored Western tradition. Your feelings about my grandson are confused, and deeper than you will admit. But that concern is for another time. Right now we must get him well. Come with me."

Kosem rose and Sarah followed her. The two women left the valide pashana's chamber, and her escort of eunuchs fell in beside them. They walked quickly through the palace to the mabeyn, past a corps of janissaries and halberdiers, who parted automatically when they saw the pasha's grandmother.

Sarah had never seen Kalid's private apartment. The anteroom was surprisingly austere, sparsely decorated with trophies of war and family heirlooms, two of the walls lined with book-filled shelves. Inside the inner chamber, attended by the khislar and several retainers, Kalid lay unconscious on his sleeping couch, naked to the waist. The wound on his shoulder was red and angry and surrounded by a charcoal powder burn. His eyes were closed, his long lashes fanned on his cheeks, his breathing shallow. His abundant black hair had lost its sheen; now it was dull and stringy, matted with sweat. Beads of perspiration dotted his forehead and upper lip, and his color was bad, almost gray. A table by the bed held a basin and pitcher, soap and clean cloths, and a wastebasket under it was filled with bloodstained linen.

Sarah looked at Kosem, who was watching her closely. Careful not to let the older woman see her alarm, Sarah turned away and sat on the edge of the couch, touching the skin around Kalid's wound gently with trembling fingers. It was fiery hot.

"This is getting infected," Sarah said, with more authority than she felt, since she wasn't sure she was capable of handling this alone. But she knew that she could not leave Kalid to the barbaric practices of whatever witch doctors the khislar might summon. "The ball is still in his shoulder, and it must come out."

"What does that mean?" Kosem said, peering at Sarah anxiously.

"I have to remove it," Sarah replied.

"You!" the khislar said. His English was almost non-existent, but this much he understood.

"Can you think of anyone else?" Sarah said, switching to Turkish. "Kalid's doctor is away, and I have experience doing this sort of thing." She was exaggerating wildly, praying every minute that she would not do more harm than good.

"The Empire is full of medical men, surgeons and herbalists, Greeks and Cypriots with potions and curatives of every kind. Any one of them could be brought here in an instant at my command," Achmed said, outraged.

"Sarah will do it," Kosem said quietly.

The khislar shot her a mutinous glance, but they both knew her word was law in this situation.

"You may go," Kosem said to him. "Take up your post in the anteroom, outside the door. And take these others with you."

Achmed obeyed, the muscles in his jaw quivering, standing aside as the little procession preceded him out the door. Then it slammed shut behind him.

"I don't think it's a good idea to upset Achmed," Sarah said nervously, wiping Kalid's brow with a cloth from his bedside table.

"He is jealous of your influence," Kosem replied. "Before you came, Kalid listened only to him. Now there is another."

"I have not noticed Kalid listening to me," Sarah said dryly.

"You underestimate your power," Kosem said, watching as Sarah washed Kalid's shoulder with tallow and lye soap, rinsing it carefully with water from his bedside laver. The wound was beginning to suppurate, draining watery blood and serum, the skin around it tightening. Sarah would have to work fast.

"I'll need a small, sharp knife and the strongest liquor you have, something with a high alcohol content."

"Raki?" Kosem suggested.

Sarah shook her head. "Rum?" she said hopefully.

Kosem wrinkled her nose. "Rum can be purchased at the bazaar," she said disdainfully. It was obvious that her opinion of the drink favored by Europeans was not very high.

"Then send someone for it. Now. And I'll need green leaves from a broadleaf tree, like an oak or maple. When crushed and applied to the wound as a poultice, they have healing properties."

"What trees are these, oak and maple?" Kosem asked. The English names meant nothing to her.

163

"Tell Memtaz to get them. She'll know." Memtaz came from a Black Sea village where almost everyone studied natural cures. "And I'll need her help to remove the ball."

"You shall have everything you need," Kosem said firmly, and turned to go.

Sarah went back to wiping Kalid's forehead, taking his pulse with her free hand. It was rapid, his heart pumping more strongly to make up for the blood he had lost. Sarah tried to remain objective and remember everything she had learned observing her father, but she found herself staring down at Kalid as tears formed in her eyes and she choked back a sob.

When she was fighting with him, it was possible to dismiss how she really felt, to concentrate on the anger and let that block the other emotions she didn't want to experience. But seeing him like this, ill and defenseless, brought out all the tenderness and longing she'd managed to suppress since she met him. She picked up his limp hand and held it to her cheek as warm tears coursed over it and into her mouth.

What would she do if she couldn't save him?

She indulged in a combination of panic and self-pity for about five minutes, then let Kalid's hand fall to his side and searched in her sleeve for her handkerchief. She wiped her eyes and blew her nose, composing herself just as Kosem returned with a gleaming knife displayed on a silver salver.

Sarah picked it up and studied it. "I think this will be fine," she finally said. "What is it?"

"A craftsman's knife for carving wood," Kosem replied. "Achmed sharpened it on a whetstone."

Sarah nodded. It was hardly a surgical scalpel, but it would have to do.

"How is he?" Kosem asked.

"The same."

By the time the rum arrived and Memtaz came in with the leaves Sarah had requested, Kalid was beginning to toss and mutter with fever. Sarah uncorked the bottle of liquor and dribbled some of the liquid between his parted lips. He choked and turned his head.

"Hold his head, Memtaz," Sarah said quickly. "He has to take a good bit of this, or the pain will cause him to buck too much for me to keep a steady hand."

Memtaz held Kalid as Sarah opened his mouth and poured the liquor down his throat. He gasped and sputtered but swallowed most of it, lapsing back into semi-consciousness as soon as the women let his head slip back onto the pillow.

"I think we should let Achmed come in and hold him down when I cut him," Sarah said to Kosem. "The liquor is not enough to put him out completely, and he will react. I just don't know how much."

Kosem nodded, gesturing to Memtaz to summon the khislar.

"Do you have a strong stomach?" Sarah asked the valide pashana. "Maybe you should go."

"I will stay," Kosem replied flatly.

Sarah sighed. Arguing the point would waste time, and Kalid's fever was getting worse every minute. "Then you must be quiet," she said, and Kosem did not protest.

Memtaz returned with the khislar, and Sarah positioned him to keep Kalid's torso as immobile as possible. Then she poured the rest of the bottle of rum over the wound, ignoring the others as they exchanged doubtful glances.

"Are you ready?" Sarah said to Achmed.

He nodded.

"Hold him tight," she said warningly.

His supple hands gripped Kalid more closely.

Sarah placed the knife at the edge of the wound and inserted it carefully. As she began to probe Kalid moaned and tossed from side to side. Achmed increased his pressure on Kalid's arms, pinning him to the couch.

"Have you found it?" Memtaz said urgently, wiping Kalid's brow briskly.

Sarah shook her head, biting her lip. She changed direction with the knife and encountered something solid as Kalid groaned and tried to lift himself off the couch. She slipped the knife under it and extracted a flattened bit of metal about the size of a Buffalo nickel.

"Got it," she said triumphantly, tossing the spent ball on a tray. The wound was now pouring blood and she stanched it, then opened another bottle of rum and doused it with liquor again.

"You can let him go," she said to Achmed, who relaxed his hold. Kalid subsided, muttering unintelligibly, tossing his head on the pillow.

"Now we have to dress it," Sarah said to Memtaz, who nodded and rose, returning with the leaves she had gathered. She crushed them with a pestle to release the green sap as Kosem watched, looking somewhat strained but in control.

Sarah selected the largest leaves and placed them against the open wound, then covered the poultice with a cotton cloth and tied it in place. When she was finished, her hands were aching and she was blinking from the perspiration running into her eyes, but she was smiling.

"Done," she said, and Memtaz sighed gratefully.

Kosem rose and kissed Sarah's cheek wordlessly, then quickly left the room.

Achmed bowed and said, *"Afiyet seker olsun."* It was a blessing, and Sarah inclined her head in thanks.

"Is there anything else I can do for you?" Achmed asked.

"You can bring a sleeping couch into this room. I'll be staying here tonight."

"As you wish, mistress."

It was the first time he had ever called her that, and Sarah smiled. It had certainly taken an extreme circumstance to win his respect.

When he returned with the couch Sarah sank onto it gratefully, drying her hands and ignoring her bloodstained clothes.

"Wake me in two hours," she said.

"As you wish, mistress," he said again, and took up his stance by the door.

Sarah changed Kalid's dressing several times that night, and by morning the wound looked less angry. She tended him all the next day, and in the evening he opened his eyes and looked at her.

"Kalid," she said, "do you know me?"

He reached for her hand and squeezed it weakly; then his eyes closed again. He was bathed in sweat; his fever had broken.

"Tell the valide pashana that her grandson will recover," Sarah said to Achmed, unable to conceal the delight in her voice.

Achmed bowed and left to convey the message, returning shortly with Kosem, who put the back of her hand to Kalid's forehead and said, "The heat has passed."

Sarah nodded.

"Did he say anything?"

"Not yet. But he looked at me with understanding, and I think he knew who I was."

"He knew." Kosem studied the American girl, then added, "I wanted you to tend him because no matter how much you may protest, I know you care for him. Loving hands make the best cure. You were better for him than any doctor we could have found."

Sarah looked away, touched.

"How can I help you now?" Kosem asked.

"He has to drink a lot of fluids to replace his lost blood volume. Water, juices, sherbets, anything like that. It's better that he doesn't take solid food for a couple of days yet, but a meat broth or a clear soup is fine."

"I'll give the order to the kitchen. Memtaz will bring you something as soon as it's ready."

Sarah nodded.

"Thank you," Kosem said. "You will have my thanks forever, Sarah Woolcott of Boston, U.S.A."

Kalid was lying in a lake of fire, with a throbbing pain in his shoulder that would not stop. He heard voices from a distance, and people touched him and moved him, but he was detached from all of it, as if it were happening to somebody else. Gradually the pain receded to a more tolerable level, and he became aware of his surroundings. He knew he was alive, but injured, and he remembered the bedouin raid in which he had been shot.

A woman was bending over him. He knew it was a woman because she smelled so good. It was a scent he recognized—not the powerful Oriental perfumes of the Eastern women but the light, delicate lemon verbena Sarah got from the kitchen help and crushed into a powder herself. But he knew it couldn't be Sarah; she was locked up, on his order. How could she be here? Was he dreaming?

He opened his eyes; even that much took an effort. Sarah was tightening the bandage against his shoulder, and when she saw that he was looking at her she froze, then smiled at him.

She said something he couldn't understand. Her free hand was lying against his chest. He reached for it and closed his fingers over it briefly.

She smiled broadly.

He couldn't keep his eyes open any longer, but he retained the image of her face before him as he drifted back into sleep.

"Gah," Kalid said, as Sarah held a bowl of broth to his lips.

"Come on, you have to drink this, it will help to restore your strength," Sarah said.

He closed his lips and turned his head to the side.

"All right. I thought you were interested in getting up off this couch," Sarah said airily.

He sighed and gestured for her to give him the bowl. When she did, he took it in both hands and drained it.

"You are a tyrant," he said wearily, letting his head fall back against his pillow.

"It takes one to know one," she replied, and laughed, pleased with herself.

170

"You're in a wonderful mood," he said irritably, rubbing his sore shoulder. "I think you're enjoying this role reversal."

Sarah snatched his hand away from the healing wound. "Maybe I am. I know I'm enjoying seeing you recover so quickly."

"Why?" he asked, watching her face.

"It's a testament to my nursing skills," she replied, and he smiled archly.

"Maybe it's a testament to my spectacular stamina," he countered, closing his eyes.

"That too. Would you like to try some solid food?"

"I would like to try a bath."

"Tomorrow."

"You said that yesterday."

Sarah shook her head. "Wait another day."

"Achmed will take me to the hamman in the mabeyn as soon as you go to sleep."

Sarah looked down at him. He had several days' growth of beard stubbling his cheeks, and he still looked somewhat tired, but the fire was back in his eyes and the purple shadows under them had vanished.

"You won't do that," she said.

"Why not?"

"Because you may be as willful as a two-year-old, but you are not an idiot. I've brought you this far, and you will listen to what I say if you want to make a complete recovery."

"You're feeling very smug, aren't you?" he said.

"Yes, I am. And I must say I'm a little baffled, too. How could this have happened to you? Aren't you guarded all the time when you're out of the palace?"

He stared at her. "You know I'm not. Were there guards with us when we rode to the oasis?"

"No."

He shrugged. "I dismiss them when they are not necessary for ceremonial occasions."

"That's not very smart, is it?"

He looked away. "Would you want a posse following you everywhere you went?"

"I guess not."

The khislar entered and bowed. "The valide pashana requests permission to enter," Achmed said.

"She's requesting permission again. She must think I'm getting better," Kalid said dryly.

Sarah laughed.

"Tell my grandmother she may come in," Kalid said to Achmed, who bowed again. The khislar went out to speak to Kosem and then stood aside as she swept into the room, beaming.

"Look at you, son of my son!" Kosem said joyfully. "You will be out hunting again soon!"

Sarah stood as Kosem entered. Suddenly the room spun, and she sat down again, hard.

"Are you all right?" Kalid said sharply, sitting up quickly and reaching for her.

"What is it, my dear?" Kosem said, rushing across the room to bend over her.

The Panther and the Pearl

"I don't know. I felt a little dizzy."

"Of course you feel dizzy—you have not left my grandson's side for five days. When was the last time you had something to eat?"

"I don't know. Can't remember."

"How could you let her go without something to eat?" Kalid shouted at his grandmother.

Kosem took Sarah's arm and helped her to stand. "Kalid is right, this is my fault. I was so concerned about him that I forgot about his nurse. Did you sleep at all last night?"

"I slept here on the couch."

"How much?"

"On and off."

Kosem turned to the khislar. "Take Sarah back to the ikbal's chamber and tell Memtaz to bring her a meal. And then leave word that Sarah is not to be disturbed until tomorrow morning. I will keep watch with the pasha tonight."

"But . . ." Sarah said, looking back at Kalid.

"Go," he said. "I will be fine."

Sarah was too exhausted to fight both of them. "All right," she conceded. "But call me if he spikes a fever again."

"Spikes?" Kosem said.

"If he gets hot, delirious."

Kosem nodded, and Sarah was led away by Achmed, who closed the door behind them.

"How could you do this to me?" Kalid said furiously to his grandmother, as soon as they were alone.

"Do what?"

"Let Sarah tend me this way!"

"She saved your life!"

"She has seen me weak and puling like an infant, helpless and dependent. She will never love me now."

Kosem sat on the couch Sarah had vacated and patted his hand. "No wonder Sarah won't sleep with you, Kalid. You have no understanding of women."

"Oh, be quiet," he said wearily. "Your advice is worthless. She will despise me now. She feels sorry for me."

"She loves you."

"Don't be ridiculous."

"She never left your side. She insisted on caring for you herself when Achmed wanted to bring in outside experts."

"What does that prove? Maybe she just wanted to keep me alive so she wouldn't fall into worse hands than mine. Anyway, she is soft-hearted. She would have done the same if you had brought her a dog that was run over in the road."

Kosem shook her head. "I know devotion when I see it."

"Devotion to a patient! Her father was a doctor, and she learned to nurse the sick at his knee. Her reaction doesn't mean she cares for me. She was only following the tradition of her family to aid others. Besides, she is an American. They are all like that."

"Like what?"

"Helpers, tenders, what the British call do-gooders. Americans are famous for it all over the world. They have more charities than people in her country."

"Kalid, listen to yourself. You are finding every excuse for her concern but the obvious one."

"It's not obvious to me. You don't understand her background the way I do. I met Americans at Oxford; they are not like us or anyone else. Bad circumstances bring out the best in them, and that is what you saw with Sarah during this past week. Once I am well, her pity will vanish and she will be cursing me again, hatching plots and hurling insults and trying to run away."

The khislar returned and took up his post inside the door.

"Is Sarah asleep?" Kosem asked him.

He nodded. "She ate and then went to bed."

"Good." Kosem rose and kissed her grandson's forehead. "I think you are wrong," she said. "But we shall see."

Kalid watched her leave his apartment, then said to Achmed, "Bring me a jug of raki."

"Sarah said—"

"I don't care what Sarah said! Bring me the liquor. Now."

Achmed bowed and left the room.

When Sarah saw Kalid the next morning, he had bathed and shaved and looked almost like his old self. Which put her on her guard once again, and he sensed it immediately.

"I didn't say you could take a bath," she greeted him. He was lying on a divan in the sun in the courtyard of the mabeyn. A fountain splashed pleasantly in the background.

"You are not giving orders any more."

"That's gratitude for you," Sarah said, sitting on the stone balustrade of the fountain.

"Is that what I am supposed to feel? Gratitude?"

"Don't bait me, Kalid. I'm just concerned that you might have a relapse."

He ignored her, bending forward to examine a chessboard on the table before him.

"Who's playing you?" she asked.

"Achmed."

"Who's winning?"

"I am," he replied.

Of course, she thought. "Are you black?" she asked.

He nodded.

"King's bishop to knight four," she said.

He studied the board and then shot her a sharp glance. "You play chess?"

"My father taught me."

He sighed and pushed the board away from him disgustedly. "I should have known."

"I'm surprised that you play," she said.

"Why?"

"I didn't think the game was known in this country."

Kalid stared at her and then burst out laughing.

"What's so funny?"

"Chess originated in Asia. The word 'chess' comes from my name, Shah, which means 'king' in Persian."

"I'm sorry I'm so ignorant of your culture," she said tartly.

"Then I shall inform you. Chess originated in India. The first form of it was called *chaturanga*. It spread to Persia about thirteen hundred years ago, and the Arabs adopted it when they conquered Persia. The Arabs brought it with them to Spain and thus to Europe. Your country received it from the European settlers—and very late, I'm afraid."

"Well, I guess you told me," Sarah mumbled, peeling back the bandage on his shoulder to examine his wound. It was cool and dry, the healing skin pink and puckering.

"You can leave this off now," Sarah said, discarding the bandage. "The fresh air will be good for it."

"What did you use to pack the wound?" Kalid asked curiously. "Kosem said something about leaves from a tree."

"That's right. The Indians in the United States discovered a long time ago that the green sap has healing properties. It seems to kill the infection."

"The Indians were the original people there?"

"Yes."

"And the Europeans stole their land from them?" he added.

Sarah hesitated, then nodded.

"I seem to remember hearing something about this at school. Why are these people called Indians? Surely they are not from India?"

"No, the European explorers who discovered North America were looking for a passage to India, one that would not involve sailing around the continent of Africa to get there. When they landed, they thought they had already reached India, and so they called the people they found there Indians. The name stuck."

"I see."

"Of course, this problem was solved by the construction of the Suez Canal."

He nodded. "You know many things," he said, unable to keep the admiration out of his voice.

"Except about chess," she said, and they both laughed.

"It's what comes of being a schoolteacher," Sarah added dryly. "You teach the lessons to the children and they stay with you." She saw that a book was lying open-faced on the couch at his side.

"What are you reading?" she asked.

"Mr. Mark Twain, whose real name, it appears, is Samuel Clemens," Kalid replied, watching her face.

Sarah stared at him.

He nodded. "Yes, I remembered that you said your favorite American author was this man

Twain, so I ordered some of his books from an English language bookstore in Constantinople frequented by tourists."

"Why didn't you give them to me?"

"When they arrived, I had you sequestered in the harem. I was very angry with you, so I kept them to myself."

Sarah bit her lip to keep from smiling. "That was very childish, don't you think?"

"Yes," he said, sighing. "You do seem to bring out the worst in me, kourista."

He hadn't called her by that name since he was hurt, and the sound of it on his lips was very winning.

"Which one is that?" Sarah asked with interest, leaning forward to read the title.

"His latest. *Huckleberry Finn.* It's all about a homeless boy and a black slave traveling down a big river in your country."

"The Mississippi."

"How did you know?"

"Twain always writes about that river. The time he spent on it was the seminal experience of his life. He even got his pen name from the river."

"How is that?"

"He was a riverboat pilot when he was young, and the term 'mark twain' means two fathoms. It's the minimum depth for most boats to pass through at low tide without getting stuck on the riverbed."

"Oh. Well, anyway, it's a difficult book. Most

of it is written in some regional dialect that I can hardly follow at all. My English is not good enough."

"I'll take it, then," Sarah said quickly.

"You may have it," Kalid said, grinning at her eagerness.

"What else did you order?" Sarah asked.

"*Tom Sawyer, The Prince and the Pauper, The Innocents Abroad,*" he replied, reciting titles. "They're all in my room. I'll have Achmed bring them to you."

"You should get *Life on the Mississippi.* It deals with Twain's days as a student river pilot. It's very funny."

"I'll get it for you," he said quietly.

"Thank you." Sarah glanced away for a moment, and when she looked back, Kalid had dropped his head back against the pillow on the divan and closed his eyes. His newly washed hair shone like polished ebony in the full sun. His lean torso, bare to the waist above his tight trousers, was like a sculpture cast in gleaming bronze, balanced in proportion, perfect but for the single blemish of the wound on his shoulder.

Sarah felt a lump growing in her throat. She stood and whispered, "I should go and let you get some rest."

He didn't answer. She leaned closer and saw that his breathing was deep and even.

He was asleep.

Sarah brushed his hair back from his forehead, then walked across the courtyard to the entrance of the mabeyn, where the eunuchs were waiting to escort her back to the harem.

When Sarah arrived at Kalid's apartment the next day, Kalid was not there. Achmed announced that the pasha was at the stables, preparing to ride.

Sarah flew out of the mabeyn and into the hall, where two halberdiers blocked her path. Achmed followed more slowly.

"Achmed, tell them I must be allowed to go to the stables. Kalid can't ride yet. The exercise will be too much for him."

The khislar gave the order and the coterie of servants looked after Sarah as she ran through the palace, past the Boxwood Gardens, and through the Kushane Gate to the riding stables, where Kalid was just saddling Khan.

"Kalid, please. You can't go riding—the jouncing might open up your shoulder," Sarah said breathlessly from the entrance, leaning against the doorway.

"I'm just going to canter around the paddock," he replied. "Khan needs the exercise."

"Let one of the grooms exercise him," Sarah said.

Kalid turned to face her. He was wearing the loose cotton shirt and twill trousers he used for riding; with the knee-high boots, the clothing gave him a vaguely piratical air.

"Why don't you come with me?" he said reasonably. "You can ride Ousta and make sure I don't overdo it. The head groom tells me you've been out here practicing riding while I was ill, so you should be able to keep up with me by now. The shalwar are just like pants, so you can ride astride without having to change."

Sarah knew he was humoring her, but she was concerned enough to go along with his suggestion. By the time they were riding slowly around the huge ring of the paddock, she was glad she had accompanied him; it was a beautiful day, cooler than usual with a crisp breeze, and the fresh air would do them both good.

"How am I doing?" Kalid asked, teasing her.

"You seem to be all right," Sarah conceded, cantering slowly at his side.

"If I fall out of the saddle, be sure to call for help. I don't think you can lift me by yourself."

"I lifted you many times when you were injured," Sara replied, looking at him.

He looked away diffidently. Clearly this was a subject he did not wish to pursue.

"Everyone falls ill at some time or other, Kalid," Sarah said gently. "I never thought you were superhuman."

"You don't think I'm human at all," he retorted, pulling up on Kahn's bridle.

"What is that supposed to mean?" Sarah inquired, slowing her horse also.

"You think I can be around you all the time without wanting to make love to you," he said bluntly.

Sarah said nothing.

"Come on back to the stables," he said, dropping the subject. "Khan's had enough, and I ordered lunch for us in my quarters."

"You were pretty sure I'd show up when I heard you were going riding," she said.

"Yes."

"I'm sorry I'm so predictable."

"You're not predictable at all, kourista. You are just an excellent nurse."

They returned the horses, and as they walked past the gardens, Kalid said to her abruptly, "I don't think I ever thanked you for saving my life, Sarah."

"I didn't save your life, Kalid, I just—"

He stopped walking and took hold of her shoulders, spinning her around to face him.

"Kosem told me what you did," he said. "You saved my life. It's not easy for me to express gratitude . . ."

"Yes, I know," she said quietly.

He sighed and pulled her toward him. "But I am grateful, and I want you to know that," he said, enfolding her. She rested her cheek against his chest and heard his heart beating under her ear.

"My little American," he said tenderly, stroking her hair. "How could I know when I saw you at the Sultan's palace that you would become so important to me?"

Sarah wrapped her arms around his waist as she felt the burning of tears forming in her eyes. He was so many people; she didn't get to see this gentle side of him very often.

"You fit against me very well," he said, a smile in his voice. "Just shoulder-high." She felt his fingers moving through the mass of her hair, settling on the nape of her neck, caressing.

She buried her face against his shirt, inhaling the piney fragrance of his soap, and clutched him tighter.

"What is it?" he said, holding her off to look at her.

"I was just thinking what might have happened to you if I hadn't been here when you were shot," she said.

"Don't think about it," he said briskly, taking her hand. "Now let's go. I'm hungry."

When they reached his apartment, a gilt table in his inner chamber was laid with dishes of lamb cutlets, goat cheese borek, and rice pilav, as well as eggplant and other vegetables roasted slowly in olive oil. Kalid dismissed the servants and then poured them glasses of wine. Sarah left her goblet of bright yellow liquor untouched while they ate until he said, "Taste the retsina. You might like it."

Sarah took a sip and made a face. "It tastes oily."

He nodded. "It's resin wine, from Greece. An acquired taste, but now I like it."

"I don't think I want to acquire that taste."

He smiled. "More lamb?" he said.

She shook her head.

"You don't eat very much," he said.

"I'm still trying to get used to the food here," Sarah replied. "I think I take in just enough to keep going."

He reached across the table and encircled her upper arm, visible through her sheer sleeve, with his fingers. "I could snap you like a dry twig," he said musingly.

"Sometimes you have wanted to," she replied.

He left his couch and came around to hers, kneeling before her. "No longer," he said quietly. "Now I just want to caress every part of your body and make it mine."

Sarah watched, entranced, as he unbuttoned her blouse and then leaned forward to kiss the skin he had exposed, his eyes closed, his arm slipping around her waist deftly. When he drew her to him, she hesitated, aware that she should stop him, but then gave in and went willingly, gasping as he ripped open the gauze waistcoat she wore beneath the blouse. His mouth searched hungrily for one nipple as his free hand closed over the other breast. She did not resist as he moved again, pulling her sleeves off and dropping her blouse, then removing her vest, leaving her naked to the waist.

Kalid buried his face between her breasts and locked his hands behind her, his soft hair and his soft mouth brushing her lightly, tantalizingly. She lay back as he turned his head and placed his burning cheek against her belly, her eyes closing again in luxurious abandonment. When he sat back to stand, she reached for him and he lifted her bodily, carrying her to a rug strewn with cushions and setting her on it. Then he flung himself down next to her and embraced her immediately, kissing her tenderly, moving his mouth surely over hers, pressing, then drawing away, until Sarah reacted as he intended, clutching him closer. She pressed against him and kissed him back urgently, parting her lips to admit his tongue, responding to his increasingly ardent caresses until she was weak and enervated in his arms. Then he dragged his open mouth along the supple line of her throat down to her breast again, sucking, nipping, laving her with his tongue as she dug her nails into his scalp, feeling the dense, wavy hair curling around her fingers as her pleasure increased to the point of near pain.

Sarah gazed down at him as he made love to her, at the thick, blue-black hair disarranged from her caresses, the deep flush staining his dusky cheeks, his red-lipped mouth moist and swollen from her kisses. His teeth were stark white against his dusky skin. He moved his head, and his tongue found her navel, exposed by the low waist of her trousers. Then she sighed her loss as he moved back, standing quickly to pull off his shirt, not bothering to unbutton it but yanking it over his head.

When Sarah saw him naked to the waist she reached up for him with a small, helpless sound, overcome by the need to feel his bare skin against hers. He dropped to his knees and embraced her again, letting her take the lead as she kissed his neck, his chest, the pink and shiny skin of his healed wound, then took his flat nipple in her mouth, imitating him. He moaned and pushed her flat on her back, looming over her, his dark eyes filling the world.

"I knew you didn't hate me when you saved my life," he said hoarsely. "Why would you save the life of a hated captor?"

"I don't hate you," she whispered. "I never did."

He slipped his arm under her and she rolled against him, twining her legs with his. The strength and force of his whole body pressing hers was a shock; she felt him rigid against her thighs, and she stiffened. Sensing her reaction, he ran his hand down her spine, gentling her, and she relaxed as he kissed her again, stroking her breasts, rasping the nipples with his thumbs until she arched her back and moaned, returning the pressure. Then he worked his fingers under the waistband of her trousers, tugging them down toward her feet.

She lifted her hips to help him; she was far too excited to resist. The harem women wore no underwear, and as her golden triangle was revealed, he drew the flat of his hand across her abdomen, seeking the soft mound below it. Her skin was dewed with perspiration, her eyes half closed, her breathing audible; she was more than ready. As he drew his seeking fingers over her slim thigh she arched herself toward him, anticipating his touch.

He gave her what she desired, slipping his hand between her legs. She started, gasping, but then sighed and her legs fell apart to admit him. He caressed her repeatedly, expertly, and she moaned deeply, flushing, turning her face away from him to hide her helpless pleasure.

Kalid was lost; he could hold back no longer. Her response was more abandoned than he could have imagined, more sensuous than he had anticipated in his most feverish dreams. He had to have what he most wanted, what he had longed for from the first time he touched her. He put his arms around her hips and lifted her to his mouth.

Sarah went rigid, shocked, and tried to push him away. But then the pleasure began again, even more intense than before, and she went limp, unable to resist. His mouth was relentless, hot and wet, his lips soft and caressing, his tongue hard and thrusting, as he stroked her toward a peak that she never seemed to reach. She felt the pleasure climb and climb and was helpless before its rushing warmth. She dragged her fingers through his hair, writhing silently, incapable of making a sound. His fiery skin seared her inner thighs and his powerful hands held her steady as he played her, slowly, deliciously, like an instrument.

Sarah was almost swooning; she had never felt like this before in her life, melting, so connected to a man as the source of her pleasure.

She finally shuddered to a powerful climax, then lay spent, her eyes closed, as he tore off his trousers and then moved over her again, pulling her legs around him.

Sarah wound her arms about his neck, lifting up to meet him. His nakedness was welcome now, the texture of his skin and hair against her a joy. She felt him, stallion-ready between her thighs, as she shifted position instinctively to accommodate him. He groaned, and she heard for the first time that unique, helpless growl of full male arousal. She reached down and touched him, tentatively, curiously, opening her eyes to see him as he dropped his face to her shoulder in mute gratification and pulled her to him more tightly. Sarah looked past his head dazedly, her lids falling, and saw the table where they had dined, and next to it, his sleeping couch.

And draped across the back of it was a brocade undervest that she recognized.

It was Fatma's.

Sarah's eyes flew open and she stiffened, but he thought it was timidity and held her down, murmuring soothingly.

Sarah's mind, drugged with sexual lassitude, tried to deal with what she had seen. In seconds he would be inside her, and although she wanted him desperately, could almost feel him there, she knew that all would be lost if she let it happen. She was nothing to him, no more than a sexual toy like Fatma and the other harem women. And if she gave in to her craving to be joined with him, she might get pregnant with the child of a man who did not love her, who thought of her as chattel.

"Kalid, no!" she said urgently, pulling back from him suddenly, trying to throw him off her.

He was almost too far gone to stop; he raised his head and looked down into her face, disbelieving, a pulse pounding in his throat. Then his expression tightened and he pinned her arms, letting her take his full weight. He was going to ignore her.

"Kalid, please. Don't force me. I'm a virgin," Sarah gasped, turning her face away from his.

He paused for an eternal second, then vaulted off her so abruptly that his sudden absence was a shock. Sarah scrambled to cover herself with a cashmere shawl from his sleeping couch; when she was able to steal a look at him, he was sitting on the divan where he had eaten lunch, bent double, his head in his hands.

"Kalid . . ." she began.

He held up one hand to quiet her, otherwise maintaining the same position. It was several minutes of total, drumming silence before he stood and pulled on his pants, then threw her a silk robe, hitting her in the face with it.

"Get out of my sight," he said tersely, as she belted the robe around her. "Now."

Sarah tried to run out of the room, but his fragile control snapped and he seized her as she shot past him, shaking her roughly.

"I should beat you within an inch of your life," he said, through gritted teeth. "In my language we have a word for a woman who leads a man to the brink and then refuses him. It is not a nice word." He was so enraged that the tendons stood out on his neck like cords of rope.

"I didn't mean to do that," Sarah replied, trying futilely to pull away from him. His arms were like steel; no one would believe that he had been ill so recently.

"What are you saying?" he demanded.

"I meant to stop you right at the beginning, but . . ."

"But?" he said, searching her face.

She looked at him with such naked longing that he felt himself begin to respond sexually again, in spite of his fury.

"I want you," she said softly. "You've proved that, and it must give you a great deal of satisfaction. When you touch me, I find it impossible to resist you."

"Not completely," he said darkly, "or we wouldn't be having this conversation."

"I'm sure I'm not the first woman you've affected that way," she went on, as if he hadn't spoken. "It's your trump card, isn't it?"

"Trump?" he said, puzzled.

"It doesn't matter," she said. "I'm not giving in to it." She was near tears, fighting a losing battle to hold them back.

"Why won't you relent and give us what we both want?" he said in exasperation, his hands still on her shoulders. It was the eternal question he always asked; was self-denial for a principle so unexpected in a woman?

"Because you don't love me, Kalid!" she answered, crying openly now. "You want to overcome my resistance with your seductive powers, prove to me that you can make me give in to my baser desires. You simply want to *win*."

He said nothing, his hands falling away from her.

"That's all this is for you, a contest of wills," she added, wiping her eyes with her fingers like a child.

He turned his back deliberately, so she couldn't see his reaction to her words.

"And if I did love you?" he said quietly.

"If you did love me, you would know that I have to be the only lover in your life. If I sleep with you, I must see that you value me as much as I value you. I will not be used interchangeably with any other woman who happens to take your fancy."

He whirled to face her. "What the devil are you talking about?" he said sharply.

"I know that you summoned Fatma every night while I was confined to the harem," she said quietly, pointing to the delicate undervest draped on his couch.

Kalid guarded his expression, his face blank, feeling a secret surge of hard-earned triumph.

GET YOUR 4 FREE BOOKS NOW—A $19.96 Value!

Mail the Free Book Certificate Today!

Get Four Books Totally FREE— A $19.96 Value!

PLEASE RUSH
MY FOUR FREE
BOOKS TO ME
RIGHT AWAY!

Leisure Romance Book Club
65 Commerce Road
Stamford CT 06902-4563

AFFIX
STAMP
HERE

So that was why she had refused him. She was jealous!

He smiled insinuatingly. "Fatma knows how to please a man," he said, driving the knife in deeper.

He saw the thrust reach its target as she flinched.

"Wonderful," Sarah said icily. "I hope you'll be deliriously happy together. In the meantime, what happens to me? Are you going to lock me up again?"

"I don't want to lock you up," he said in a tired voice, running his fingers through his hair. "I would have you go or stay as you please, but I fear you would go, so . . ." He spread his hands.

"Why is it so important to seduce me?" Sarah said, equally wearily. They were both worn out from this struggle. "Am I the only woman who has ever resisted you this long?"

"You are the only woman who has ever resisted me at all," he said flatly, his arms folded belligerently, the newly formed scar on his shoulder standing out in stark contrast with the smooth, amber-toned skin surrounding it.

"I suppose that's because you bought all of them, right?" Sarah said bitterly. "Like dogs, they want to please their master."

"I bought you, that doesn't seem to be influencing the outcome with us," he shot back.

"I was not for sale, donme pasha. You still seem to be confused about that."

Doreen Owens Malek

"Nevertheless, you are here. And I could stop a passing gypsy caravan at any moment and trade you for a more compliant bedmate. Bear it in mind."

He strode to the outer door and pounded on it. Achmed appeared instantly, with two other eunuchs hovering in the background.

"Take the ikbal back to the harem," Kalid said shortly.

Achmed bowed and ushered Sarah, still dressed in Kalid's robe, out the door.

Chapter Eight

"The Sultan will see us shortly," Danforth said to James Woolcott, who didn't look very happy.

"I don't understand why we're wasting time here when we know that Sarah is in Bursa!" James said heatedly.

"It's protocol, Mr. Woolcott. You must trust me on this. It would be considered a grave insult if we contacted the Pasha of Bursa without seeing Sultan Hammid first."

"I'm not interested in protocol. I just want Sarah back," James said, annoyed.

"Well, the embassy is interested in protocol, and we do it this way or not at all," Danforth replied, beginning to show a little pique himself. This was a messy business, women being carried off into harems; it offended his Puritan sensibilities. Danforth privately thought that Woolcott and his foolish cousin were the architects of their own misfortune; anyone who got involved with the locals usually lived to regret it. The Under Secretary considered the Ottoman Empire barbaric and the embassy an oasis of sanity in the midst of a desert of turbaned savages. But it was a choice posting, since there was little to do except attend teas and entertain visiting dignitaries on their way to India or the Far East, and he was next in line for Europe if he could only acquit himself handsomely here.

He had to handle this matter efficiently and delicately. The Sarah Woolcott affair was not going to stand in the way of his getting to Paris or Vienna.

The doors of the Topkapi audience room were opened by the khislar. James and Danforth advanced inside it, to find the room crowded with janissaries and halberdiers lined up on either side of the throne. Osman Bey was standing on the Sultan's left, and the khislar moved to his right. The Sultan himself was seated, wearing the midnight-blue uniform of Chief Janissary, a fez with a half moon and a gold tassel perched on his head.

Danforth gave a ceremonial greeting in Turkish, and the Sultan bowed his head. They talked back and forth, with James straining to follow the conversation, for about a minute. James had learned quite a bit of Turkish in connection with his business, but this ceremonial language, filled with flowery phrases, was a little beyond him. Finally Danforth turned to him and said, "Just what is it that you want me to ask the Sultan?"

"Ask him what has happened to Sarah," James said in exasperation.

Danforth translated the question, and they both listened as the Sultan replied.

"He says he has no knowledge of this woman," Danforth said, avoiding James's eyes.

"What is he talking about? I arranged for Sarah to come here through that man right there," James said, outraged, pointing to the khislar.

Danforth spoke again, and the Sultan shrugged before saying something that left Danforth speechless with amazement for several seconds.

"What did he say?" James demanded, watching Danforth's face closely.

"The Sultan says that the woman may have been here. He takes little notice of such things. You would have to question the khislar about the arrangements for the harem."

"Then question him! What the devil is going on here, Danforth? It's obvious the Sultan is lying, and you're not even challenging him about it!"

"Be quiet!" Danforth replied, keeping a smile on his face with an effort. "You don't know how much English some of them may understand."

James fell silent, frustrated, as Danforth turned to the khislar and asked him a series of questions, which resulted in several terse replies. They were simple enough for James to understand, and he looked from one to the other as they talked, growing more incensed as it became obvious that Danforth wasn't getting anywhere.

"The khislar says there was such a woman here for a short while, tutoring the princess sultana, but he does not know what became of her."

James's face was turning redder by the second. "I gathered that much myself. Danforth, this is utterly preposterous! You cannot mean to let these people get away with this!"

Osman Bey had been avoiding James's gaze, but now he looked at him meaningfully, turning slightly and signing with his eyes toward the hall. James subsided immediately, gaining control of himself after a few moments of difficulty.

"Thank the Sultan for the courtesy of this audience, and ask him if we have his permission to visit his Pasha at Bursa," James said, in as reasonable a tone as he could muster.

Danforth, relieved that James wasn't going to make a scene, communicated the message. The Sultan shrugged and said something in a mild tone, dismissively.

"He says that we may go to Bursa if we wish," Danforth translated.

James nodded. "Then let's get out of here," James said briskly. "Our mission has been accomplished."

Danforth gave a concluding speech, and they bowed their way out toward the hall. Osman Bey seized his chance when the Sultan turned to speak to the khislar. He walked forward briskly and held the door for James, saying under his breath in simple Turkish, "She is still at Bursa. She tried to run away but was given back to the pasha by a janissary. She is in good health and unhurt."

"How do you know?" James muttered, glancing at the throne, where the Sultan was still talking, not looking at them.

"The Princess Roxalena has been bribing people for information. Good luck. I must go." Osman turned away and walked back into the throne room, as James and Danforth made their exit.

"Did you hear that?" James said to Danforth.

Danforth nodded. "I'll send word as soon as possible that we want to see the pasha."

"I hope he will be more cooperative."

"Oh, he's a different type altogether from the Sultan. The Sultan just lies, stonewalls, and evades, all the while daring you to make an international incident of his unresponsiveness. Kalid Shah is very sophisticated, well educated, but even more dangerous in his way than the Sultan could ever be."

"What do you mean?" James asked, as they

199

walked toward the Bird House Gate, led by an escort of halberdiers.

"The pasha has been abroad. He understands Western culture. I doubt that he will lie about Sarah's presence in his harem, but he may challenge you to take her back from him."

"What?" James said, aghast.

"I don't know for sure, I'm only guessing. But from the stories I've heard about this fellow, we can expect anything. He's said to be very . . . resourceful."

They approached their carriage as James removed his handkerchief from his pocket and blotted his brow.

"On days like this, I wish I had never left Boston," he said to Danforth.

The secretary nodded.

He had those days, too.

Sarah sat on the edge of the bathing pool and dangled her feet in the water. Behind her, Memtaz was combing her hair, and across from her, Fatma was sitting on a bench, smoking a nargileh with two of the other women. The sweetish smoke drifted toward Sarah, causing her to wrinkle her nose.

"I hate the smell of that stuff," she said to Memtaz. "It makes me sick."

"Fatma is very fond of hashish."

"So I've noticed."

"It helps to pass the time," Memtaz said.

"I think it clouds the judgment," Sarah said.

"That may be so, but there is little need to make decisions in the harem. All decisions are made for us."

Sarah let that pass. Fatma looked up and said something to Memtaz in Turkish that Sarah could barely understand.

"What was that?" Sarah asked Memtaz. "Something about a necklace?"

"She asked that I put aside the amethyst-and-citrine necklace for her. If the pasha sends for her again this evening, she would like to wear it."

"Tell Fatma she can have it," Sarah said darkly, realizing that the question had been meant to convey a message, not to Memtaz, but to her. She wanted to feed the necklace to Fatma bead by bead, but she kept her expression carefully blank. She had been torturing herself with visions of Kalid and Fatma in passionate communion ever since the pasha had thrown her out of his apartment, but she certainly didn't want Fatma to know that.

It would give the redhead far too much satisfaction to know that Sarah was jealous.

Sarah winced as Memtaz tugged at a knot, pinching her scalp. Sarah was going stir-crazy again, thinking back on her last meeting with Kalid and almost wishing that she had given in to him. She would be enjoying an ardent interlude with the pasha instead of swishing her feet in the hamman and wishing she could strangle her rival.

But *almost* was the operative word. She had stuck to her guns and she was proud of it, even if she was now lying awake at night imagining Kalid caressing Fatma in the intimate way he had caressed her.

It wasn't a pleasant picture.

Memtaz finished her task and Sarah rose, picking up her pattens and walking over to the tepidarium. Fatma rose also, and as Sarah went past her she stuck out one slender foot.

Sarah tripped, slid wildly on the slick hamman floor, and shot fully dressed into the pool.

Fatma shrieked with laughter, crying helplessly, falling into her companions in an excess of mirth. Sarah climbed slowly out of the pool, pushing her plastered hair back from her eyes, as everyone stopped to watch the confrontation that had been building silently between the two women for some time.

Sarah walked over to Fatma, who watched her slyly, waiting to see what she would do.

Sarah smiled at her sweetly, then hauled off and punched her squarely in the nose.

Fatma gasped, putting her hand to her face as blood spurted between her fingers. Then she let out a bloodcurdling yell and lunged forward, grabbing for Sarah's neck.

Memtaz screamed and scuttled for the door, yelling for the eunuchs. Two of them appeared magically and dashed for the struggling women, separating them with difficulty and then carrying them off to different rooms.

"Get the khislar," Memtaz shouted to the guard at the door, who abandoned his post as Fatma was carried past them, kicking and squirming. The sound effects were piercing, emanating from opposite ends of the bathing suite, until Achmed finally rushed in, adjusting his turban.

"What is the meaning of all this caterwauling?" he demanded of Memtaz, as the other harem women gathered around to witness the spectacle.

"There was a fight between my mistress and Fatma," Memtaz said quietly, lowering her eyes.

Achmed sighed and nodded. Finally.

"And where is your mistress?" Achmed asked.

Memtaz nodded at an adjoining room. Achmed stalked toward it as the women parted ranks to let him pass.

"Go back to what you were doing," he barked at them, and they obeyed reluctantly, still trying to follow the action. An event like this broke up the tedium of harem life and was eagerly anticipated and recounted afterward with relish.

Achmed entered the dressing room and found Sarah there, detained by a eunuch, dripping wet and spitting mad.

"Release her," Achmed said to the eunuch, who obeyed. Sarah rubbed her arm where the man had held her.

"I understand you have been fighting," Achmed said to Sarah, hands on hips, like a school principal with a recalcitrant student

203

who had been called on the carpet.

"Talk to Fatma. She started it," Sarah replied sullenly in kind, aware that she sounded like a ten-year-old after a recess brawl and not caring at all.

"At the moment I am talking to you. What happened?"

"Fatma tripped me as I walked past her, and I fell into the pool. So I punched her."

"You punched her?" Achmed said, staring at her. Sarah spoke Turkish with a heavy accent, and he was not sure he had understood correctly.

"That's right."

"Do you think that was an appropriate response to a prank?" Achmed inquired.

"It wasn't a prank."

"No? How would you describe it?"

"An attempt to humiliate me and make me the object of ridicule," Sarah replied evenly.

"I see. And why would she want to do that?"

Sarah looked at him in disbelief to see if he were serious. He was.

"I replaced her as the favorite," Sarah said shortly, "and now she sees her chance to regain her former glory."

"You listen too much to harem gossip," Achmed said, and Sarah wasn't sure what he meant. Before she could ask, he went on to say, "We cannot have brawling in the harem. One more incident like this, and you will be confined to your apartment again."

"I don't see why I should be punished because Fatma is behaving like an hysterical teenager," Sarah retorted, behaving like one herself. This whole experience was causing her to lose any maturity she thought she possessed.

Achmed held up his hands, weary of the exchange. "You heard me. I have nothing more to say. Stay away from Fatma or you will suffer the consequences."

Achmed strode briskly from the room, his back rigid with righteous indignation. Sarah picked up one of her pattens from the floor and threw it at the closing door.

Kalid was sitting in his audience room, listening to a farming report that was less than riveting, when Achmed tapped on the door and then pulled it open cautiously.

"Come in," Kalid said to him.

The khislar advanced into the room and waited, his arms folded across his chest.

"We'll continue this in the afternoon at one o'clock," Kalid said to his minister of agriculture. The man rose, gathered up his papers and bowed his way out of the room.

"What is it?" Kalid said to Achmed.

"You asked me to report to you on Sarah's activities in the harem," Achmed replied.

"And?"

"And she just had a tussle with Fatma."

Kalid stared at him, then began to smile. "Tell me what happened," he said.

Doreen Owens Malek

By the time the khislar was finished relating the story, Kalid was laughing openly.

"I can't believe Sarah punched Fatma in the nose," he said, chuckling.

"I saw the evidence myself. Fatma's nose is already swelling. It may be broken."

"Have Doctor Shakoz look at it. He's back from his trip." Kalid was still smiling, but the khislar was stone-faced.

"I see that you don't find this incident amusing," Kalid added to Achmed.

"No, master. I must maintain order in the harem. If these women are allowed to go unchastised, I don't know what mayhem will result in the future."

"All right. Send Sarah to me."

It was only a few minutes before Sarah arrived, dressed simply in a shift with a gold-trimmed caftan belted at the waist, her hair still damp. They had not seen each other since their last altercation, and Kalid drank in the sight of his favorite hungrily, noting that her face, bare of the harem's usual makeup, made her look like a little girl. He shooed away her escort and then sat back in his chair as she stood mutely before him.

"Achmed is very upset with you," he began.

Sarah said nothing.

"He told me that you punched Fatma in the nose."

"After she tripped me."

"That's very mature."

"Are you going to instruct me about maturity now?"

"I'm going to instruct you about decorous behavior. It was my former impression that this sort of tiff was beneath you."

"Well, maybe I'm learning how to get along around here. I'll reduce myself to whatever level is necessary to survive."

"Fiery words from a proper Boston miss."

"I don't think I'm so proper any more. You've seen to that. And I'd like to know what you're planning to say to Fatma. Is she going to receive a lecture too?"

"I'll deal with Fatma in my own way."

"I can just imagine what that might be. Please tell your paramour that if she tries anything like this morning's stunt again, she'll wind up with a shiner."

"What is a shiner?"

"A black eye. What do they call it in England?"

"A poke," he said.

"Well, if you don't want your Titian-haired trollop to wind up with a poke, tell her to leave me alone."

"My Titian-haired trollop?" he whispered, wide-eyed.

Sarah stared at him balefully. "Oh, you *are* a snake. You're enjoying this, aren't you? Throwing me in with Fatma, on her home territory, and letting her toy with me."

"Territory?" he said inquiringly.

"You know exactly what I mean. Well, you

might be surprised by the results. Be sure to check your local newspaper for the next installment in the serial." Sarah whirled and stomped angrily toward the door.

"You have not been dismissed," he called after her.

She turned to face him again. "May I have your imperial majesty's permission to withdraw?" she asked sarcastically.

He looked at her with what could only be described as sadness. "Do we have to be enemies, Sarah?" he said quietly.

"That wasn't my choice, donme pasha," she replied neutrally, not looking at him.

"All right," he said, sighing. "You may go."

Sarah walked out, and her escort fell in behind her. The khislar passed her on his way into the audience room.

"Back again so soon?" Kalid said to him testily. "What is it this time?"

"I have received a message from Turhan Aga."

"And what does the captain of my halberdiers have to say?" Kalid asked, tapping his fingers on the arm of his chair.

"He requests an audience. He was given a letter for you from a messenger who came to the Carriage House gate."

"Why didn't he just pass the letter on to you?" Kalid asked, wondering at the excess of ceremony.

"He promised to deliver it personally."

Kalid made an expansive gesture. "Send him in."

208

Turhan Aga, Osman Bey's counterpart at the Orchid Palace, was a middle-aged native of Izmir whose loyalty to his pasha was unquestioned and had led to a series of promotions resulting in his present position. He hustled into the room when admitted and dropped to one knee, a form of genuflection learned from the Christian Turks in his native city that he had never abandoned.

"What do you have for me?" said Kalid, who was fond of the captain.

Turhan withdrew the envelope from his jacket and handed it to his sovereign.

Kalid saw the American Embassy crest on the back of the envelope and tucked it into his shirt.

"Thank you, Turhan. You may go."

The captain bowed and withdrew from the audience room. As the khislar followed him, Kalid said, "Achmed, stay here."

The khislar turned back immediately, waiting.

Kalid watched the doors close behind Turhan Aga and then said, "The letter is from the American Embassy."

Achmed watched impassively as Kalid opened it and scanned the lines quickly. There were two paragraphs in English followed by a Turkish translation under it.

"The Under Secretary, somebody named Danforth, requests an audience as soon as possible in connection with the disappearance of an

American woman, Margaret Sarah Woolcott."

"Margaret?" the khislar said.

Kalid shrugged. "It's the first I've heard the name. Anyway, I cannot ignore it. I must reply."

Achmed snorted. "What are they going to do? Declare war on Turkey?"

"Ah, my friend, you are not a diplomat. You don't understand the game. I will merely say that I am occupied with domestic matters at present, which is true, and that I will not have time to grant an audience for several weeks."

"Which is not true."

"This man Danforth isn't going to call me a liar. He will wait until the appointed time."

"What do you hope to gain by the delay?"

"Sarah," Kalid said simply.

Achmed knew when to remain silent, so he did not offer an opinion on his pasha's obsession with the American woman.

"I'll write the letter today, and you can send Turhan Aga, or one of the janissaries, to the embassy with it."

Achmed bowed.

"We will see how well the Americans handle this," Kalid said musingly. "We Easterners are ancient hands at such intricacies, but they are novices. Their country is only one hundred years old."

"But very powerful," Achmed reminded him.

"Do you think the President of the United States will travel to Constantinople in search of one little schoolteacher?" Kalid asked, amused.

Achmed said nothing. He didn't know what the Americans would do.

But then, if Kalid Shah was afraid of anything, Achmed hadn't yet seen it.

"That will be all, Achmed. I wish to be left alone until the minister of agriculture returns."

Achmed bowed again and left as Kalid went back to studying the letter in his hand.

Roxalena stepped out from behind a large bush in the Garden of the Kadins at Topkapi and gestured for Osman Bey to come to her side. He looked around furtively and then covered the ground between them in four steps. Roxalena seized his arm.

"Did you talk to Sarah's cousin?" she hissed.

"Just for a moment. The Sultan was present the whole time, and I was only able to say a few words to him as he left."

"Did you tell him that she had tried to escape from the Orchid Palace?"

Osman nodded.

"Good. That will make him more intent on getting her out of there," Roxalena said. "I wish I had been able to go to the audience, but my father forbade it."

"He probably knew why you wanted to attend."

Roxalena sighed. "I saw the Embassy carriage arrive, but there was no way for me to get a message to Mr. Woolcott. If I keep on bribing people, I will have no jewelry left and the Sultan will find out eventually. Someone will betray me to an agent of my father's who can pay better."

"You are doing everything that you can, Roxalena," Osman said, squeezing her hand.

"But is it enough to help Sarah?"

Osman shrugged.

Who could say?

Sarah did not know what Kalid had said to Fatma about their "disagreement," but the redhead virtually disappeared from her life after that day. If Sarah entered the hamman, Fatma left it; if Sarah was reclining in the tepidarium and Fatma wandered in, she turned around and went somewhere else. It really wasn't that difficult for them to avoid one another; there were many women in the harem and many places to go, both within the harem itself and in the unrestricted areas of the Orchid Palace. Sarah was relieved that her problem was solved but almost disappointed that she didn't get another crack at Fatma.

As days went by and she heard nothing from Kalid, she was mean-spirited enough to want one.

Memtaz came into her sleeping chamber one morning about ten days after Sarah last saw the pasha and said solemnly, "Mistress, I believe there has been a theft."

"A theft of what?"

"Your amethyst necklace."

"It was never *my* necklace, Memtaz, it was in the ikbal's jewel box when I got here."

"You are the ikbal now; therefore it is yours."

"All right, fine. What do you think happened to it?"

"Fatma had it last. She borrowed it, do you remember?"

How could I forget? Sarah thought. Well, if Fatma had it, she could keep it. It had once been hers anyway.

"I don't care about the necklace, Memtaz. It isn't important to me that it be returned."

"I should report any incidents of stealing to the khislar," Memtaz said stubbornly.

Sarah sighed. "Maybe Fatma forgot to bring it back. Why don't you ask her where it is?"

"I have already done so. Fatma says that she brought it back, but that is not so, mistress. I take great care of your things, and I would know if the necklace had been returned."

Sarah rubbed the bridge of her nose wearily. She might not mind responding in kind to Fatma's aggressive taunts, but this petty squabbling over trinkets was beneath both of them.

"I don't want you to tell the khislar about it," Sarah said firmly to Memtaz.

"Is that an order, mistress?" Memtaz said primly.

"Yes, it is."

"Very well." Memtaz picked up Sarah's discarded clothing and said, "Will you be having

213

the evening meal in the tepidarium, mistress?"

"No. In here. Alone."

Memtaz bowed.

Sarah was reading when Memtaz returned with a silver tray. She had a light meal of feta cheese, olive compote, and *rahat lokum*, or Turkish delight. She went to bed early, before Memtaz retired.

Sarah woke again, abruptly, in the middle of the night, doubled up with pain.

She reached for the bell beside her sleeping couch and knocked over a water glass instead. The crash brought Memtaz running into her room.

"What is it, mistress?" Memtaz said, gasping when she saw Sarah's distressed expression, the beads of perspiration on her forehead.

"I don't know . . . my stomach hurts," Sarah moaned. It was an effort to get the words out; each breath sent a bolt of agony slicing through her midsection.

"I'll get the khislar," Memtaz said, and ran headlong out of the room. She was back in seconds with Achmed, who took one look at Sarah and said to Memtaz, "Send for Doctor Shakoz."

Sarah looked up at Achmed and said haltingly, "What's wrong . . . with me?"

"I don't know," Achmed said, but he exchanged a glance with Memtaz that said he suspected something.

"Give me water," Sarah said, and Memtaz

moved to obey. Achmed blocked her hand.

"Don't let her take anything by mouth until the doctor sees her," he said.

Time seemed to pass very slowly for Sarah, in a haze of pain, until the doctor finally bustled into the room. He adjusted his pince nez and knelt next to Sarah, probing her abdomen with stiff fingers.

Sarah screamed.

He said something in Greek, and Achmed translated, saying to Memtaz, "Is she pregnant?"

"No!" Sarah moaned.

Memtaz shook her head.

"Has she had an abortion?" Achmed went on, translating the doctor's Greek again.

"For God's sake, no!" Sarah gasped.

The doctor muttered to Achmed and the khislar said, "Doctor Shakoz says that women sometimes do these things to themselves, with knitting needles and such, and tell no one about it until the damage must be repaired."

"Will you inform this . . . idiot that I've not had . . . an abortion?" Sarah panted, grabbing Achmed's tunic. "Can't he see I'm not bleeding? What's . . . wrong with him?"

Achmed conferred with Shakoz and then took Memtaz aside as the doctor continued his examination.

"Did you bring her dinner?" Achmed asked Memtaz.

The servant nodded.

"Did she eat alone?"

Memtaz nodded again.

"Did you get the tray from the marble shelves beside the harem doors?"

Memtaz said, "Yes, of course."

"Who made up the tray and carried the food to you?"

"Nesime, the kitchen skivvy. She always brings the ikbal's food separate from the others."

"What was on it?"

"Cheese, an olive compote. Some Turkish delight for a sweet." Memtaz leaned in closer to him and said, "Why are you asking these questions? Do you think my mistress has been poisoned?"

Chapter Nine

Achmed's silence was eloquent.

"All of her food is tasted in the Bird House, along with the pasha's!" Memtaz said.

"What else but poison could cause such a sudden attack?" Achmed countered. "She was fine earlier today, wasn't she?"

"She seemed fine," Memtaz replied, glancing at the couch where Sarah lay moaning.

"I want a list of exactly what she had to eat all day yesterday and today," Achmed said grimly, walking toward the door.

"Where are you going?" Memtaz asked fearfully. She did not want to be left alone with this problem.

"To tell the pasha what has happened," Achmed replied. "He would want to know

Doreen Owens Malek

immediately if Sarah is in danger."

Memtaz looked after him unhappily and then went back into Sarah's bed chamber, where Doctor Shakoz was now peeling back Sarah's eyelids, then looking inside her mouth at her gums and down into her throat. The doctor's wiry salt-and-pepper hair, prominent nose, and scientific air looked out of place in the feminine bower of the harem.

He was the only man other than the Pasha and the eunuchs permitted to see the harem women unveiled.

"What can I do?" Memtaz asked him in Greek, which she spoke sparingly.

"Get me a better light," he grunted.

Memtaz complied, and Sarah winced at the glare of the oil lamp the servant handed to the doctor. By the time he had adjusted it to his satisfaction, Kalid had burst into the room.

The servants present bowed as Doctor Shakoz continued his work.

"What's wrong with her?" Kalid demanded, falling to his knees next to Sarah's couch. "Has she caught a fever?" He put his hand to her brow.

Sarah closed her eyes and sighed with relief when Kalid touched her.

"I think not," the doctor replied, switching to Turkish.

"Then what? Tell me!"

"Perhaps we should discuss this alone," the doctor said circumspectly, moving to the other

218

side of the room, out of Sarah's earshot.

"You can speak in front of these servants," Kalid said impatiently. "What is it?"

"I think this woman has been poisoned."

Kalid looked as if he had been slapped. He murmured a curse in Turkish under his breath. "With what?" he finally said aloud, raking his hair back distractedly with his hand.

The doctor shrugged. "Some alkaloid toxin. Mercury, lye mixed with ash, one of the arsenicals. It's difficult to say. But from the color of her mouth and the severe intestinal spasms she is suffering, I would say arsenic."

"*Arzenig,*" Memtaz whispered, horrified.

"Arsenopyrite," the doctor went on pedantically. "Usually gray, brittle flakes. It has a bitter taste when ingested."

"I don't need a chemistry lesson, man. What is the antidote?" Kalid demanded, seizing the doctor's shoulders.

"Egg white and milk to coat the digestive tract and hinder absorption," the doctor replied, staring up at Kalid. "But she has already absorbed some part of it, or she wouldn't be having this reaction."

"Run to the kitchen and get the egg whites and milk," Kalid said to Memtaz, who shot out of the room. He turned to Achmed. "What did she eat most recently?"

Achmed repeated what Memtaz had told him.

"The olives would disguise the bitter taste," Doctor Shakoz offered.

"Is it safe for her to be moved?" Kalid asked Doctor Shakoz urgently.

"It wouldn't hurt. Fresh air would even help. She needs as much oxygen as possible."

"Have her carried on a litter to my apartment," Kalid said to the khislar, who went into the hall to give the order to the eunuchs on duty. "And send a servant after Memtaz to tell her to come to my quarters in the mabeyn at once with the antidote," Kalid called after him.

"Why are you taking her there?" the doctor asked.

"I have the northeast corner of the palace. There is a cross breeze almost all the time," Kalid replied.

The doctor nodded, not fooled for a minute. He had heard about the pasha's ardor for his American ikbal.

"Someone had to plan this very well," Kalid said grimly, shooting a glance at Sarah, who was quieter now, but only half-conscious. "They had to get the poison, pass it into the hands of a confederate who could taint the food, and then wait for the right dish to be served that would cover the taste." His eyes became narrow and hard. "Someone wanted to harm Sarah very badly."

He watched lingeringly as she was carried past him, then he followed the litter out of the room.

"Could she die?" he asked the doctor, who was walking hurriedly at his side, trying to keep up with the taller man. Kalid had delayed asking the question, afraid to hear the answer.

The doctor shrugged. "Impossible to say. It would depend on how much of the poison she has ingested."

"She never eats much," Kalid said.

"That is good," Doctor Shakoz said, nodding. "If she ate only a little of the olive dish, she probably didn't get much of the poison, just enough to produce the malaise and the spasms you saw. She is young and healthy, no? There is a strong chance that she can throw this off and recover."

"But if she had consumed the whole dish, she would be dead," Kalid said flatly.

"Most likely."

Kalid considered that.

Whoever had poisoned Sarah did not know that she was a light eater.

Once they got Sarah settled in Kalid's antechamber and Dr. Shakoz had administered the first dose of the antidote, the pasha turned to Achmed and said, "I want the entire kitchen staff assembled in my audience room immediately."

Achmed stared at him.

"They are all sleeping, master."

Kalid gazed back at him as if the khislar were deranged. "I know they are all sleeping, Achmed. Wake them up! And get Turhan Aga in here and the captain of the janissaries as well. I want the kitchen staff's living quarters searched from top to bottom while the workers are away from their rooms and anything unusual or suspicious reported to me immediately. Is that understood?"

"It may not have been a kitchen worker, master. Quite a few other slaves handle the food, cooking it and transporting it and serving it."

"I know that," Kalid said. "I'm just starting with the kitchen staff. I intend to take this palace apart bit by bit until I find the person responsible for Sarah's illness. And I want reports on Sarah's condition brought to me every thirty minutes from the doctor, and several pots of strong coffee brewed and sent here to me as soon as possible." He looked around him grimly. "I think it will be a long night."

Nesime was terrified. She was so terrified that she was hardly able to answer the questions the pasha put to her, despite his best efforts to calm her.

"I did nothing wrong," she sobbed, looking at Memtaz, hoping that the senior servant would come to her aid. "I took the ikbal's food to the harem as I always do. There was nothing different about last night."

"There was no one else in the kitchen when you left?" Kalid asked her.

"Just the cooks."

"Which cooks?"

"Selim the Armenian and Kemal Murad."

Kalid nodded, satisfied that this girl was guiltless.

"Send in the Armenian," he said to the khislar. To the kitchen skivvy he said, "You may go."

Nesime fled in floods of relieved tears, blotting her face with the edge of her sleeve, pushing her way past the crowd lined up in the hall. They were waiting to be interviewed one by one.

The cook came into the pasha's presence, his white hat in his hand, looking around at Memtaz and Achmed, the only other occupants of the audience room. The sky beyond the leaded windows was just beginning to get light; Kalid had been conducting this interrogation for hours.

"Did you prepare the harem food last night for the evening meal?" Kalid asked him.

"Some of it, master."

"An olive compote brought to the ikbal's chamber?"

The Armenian shook his head.

"Who made that dish?"

"Kemal Murad."

"Send him to me. You may go."

Selim left, wiping his brow with his forearm, and seconds later Kemal Murad entered the room and bowed.

"I understand you prepared an olive compote that was served to the ikbal last evening," the pasha said.

Murad stared at him, silent.

"Is this true?" Kalid barked.

Murad nodded.

"And did you put poison in it?" Kalid asked quietly.

"No, master."

"Did anyone ask you to add a grayish, flaky substance to it, perhaps saying that it was a spice?"

"No, master."

Kalid stared at him a few seconds more and then waved his hand dismissively.

"Amazing," he said sarcastically to Achmed, when the cook had left. "The woman is given arsenic in her food, and nobody knows how it got there. I suppose an evil jinni slipped into the kitchens and spat into the dish."

Turhan Aga appeared in the doorway, and Kalid waved him into the room.

"What have you found?" Kalid said.

The captain of the halberdiers held up a necklace, sparkling indigo and amber in the light of the oil lamps.

"What is it?" Kalid asked.

"The ikbal's necklace," Memtaz interjected. "I told Sarah that it was missing. I thought it had been stolen."

"Why wasn't I told of this?" Achmed inquired.

"I thought I should have told you, but Sarah said not to bother you with it, so I obeyed my mistress."

"Where did you find it?" Kalid asked Turhan.

"One of my men found it inside the straw mattress on Kemal Murad's bed."

"The cook who was just here?" Kalid said.

Turhan nodded.

"How would he have gotten it?" Achmed asked.

"Perhaps he received it as a bribe," Turhan suggested. "It's very valuable, isn't it?"

"A bribe from whom?" Kalid said impatiently. "If it was stolen, anyone could have given it to him."

"I know who had it last," Memtaz piped up quickly.

All eyes turned to her.

"Fatma," she said.

Kalid looked at her, and they all saw the impact of that piece of information in his face.

"And there's something else," Memtaz said. "Some time ago, Fatma offered my mistress a dish of raspberry sherbet in the tepidarium. I told her not to eat it, and Sarah pretended to drop it, smashing the dish."

Kalid studied her, realizing with horror that the olive compote may not have been Fatma's first attempt on Sarah's life. The sugary syrup of the sherbet would have disguised the bitterness of the arsenic just as well as olives.

"You should have informed me!" Achmed said sternly. "All such incidents should be reported at once. We could have tested the sherbet on an animal to see if it was poisoned."

"It doesn't matter now," Kalid said wearily. "Memtaz, you did well in telling Sarah not to eat the dessert. Go and rest in the bedchamber with your mistress. If your loyalty to Sarah caused

225

you to shirk your duty to the khislar, I will not fault you for it."

Memtaz left as Achmed folded his arms disgustedly.

"Don't pout, my friend," Kalid said to him. "I need you for what's to come." He sat back and said softly, "Fatma. I should have guessed it, I suppose, but I thought she was too much in love with herself to risk her life this way. She had to know that it would be death for her if she were caught."

"Jealousy does strange things," Turhan said.

Kalid sat forward again. "Get Murad back in here," he said quietly to the khislar. "And bring Fatma from the harem. Now."

The pasha and Turhan Aga exchanged glances as Achmed strode briskly from the room.

"So she should make a complete recovery," Kalid said to the doctor, who nodded.

"She's out of danger now. I will administer a purgative once she's strong enough to tolerate it, and that will eliminate the rest of the poison from her system."

"Can I see her now?" Kalid asked.

"Not yet. She should rest. Soon, perhaps this evening."

Kalid nodded. "Thank you, doctor. You may go back to your patient."

When the doctor had gone, Kalid looked at his grandmother and said, "I want a public execution, to take place tomorrow."

They were sitting in the inner chamber of his apartment; Sarah and Memtaz were in the next room. Kosem raised her pipe to her lips and said, "Has the cook confessed?"

Kalid nodded. "To looking the other way as Fatma doctored the dish of olives."

"And what does Fatma say?"

"She screams and cries and denies everything. She is a coward and will die like one."

Kosem sighed. "I wish you had awakened me when this first happened. I had many experiences dealing with poisons when I was a young girl. The harem then was a very dangerous place, not like it is now, all games and sweets and smoking the nargileh, with just the occasional incident like this one to liven things up a bit. In the old days, favorites fell like leaves from trees, and rivals were eliminated with one tainted cup of coffee."

"The harem was dangerous enough for Sarah. And I thought you needed your sleep. You're always telling me you're going to die any minute."

Kosem made a disgusted sound. "You picked a strange time to start paying attention to me." She puffed on her pipe reflectively. "Are the prisoners both in the dungeon?"

"Murad is chained in the dungeon. Fatma is confined in the storeroom of the Bird House."

"What kind of execution do you have planned?"

"I'd like to kill them both with my bare hands," he said, in a tone that left no doubt that he meant it.

"But of course you won't do that," Kosem said, watching his face anxiously. Would she be able to control him, convince him that his government would lose all appearance of civilization if he carried out these executions? The Western powers might recall their embassies, and the Sultan would be infuriated that his pasha had usurped the power of personal execution, a right that traditionally was the Sultan's alone. It would be a disaster beyond all reason.

But Kosem knew that where Sarah was concerned, Kalid did not listen to reason.

"What does the khislar recommend?" Kosem asked.

"Hanging for the cook, ritual drowning in the Bosporus for the woman."

"A sensible plan."

Kalid snorted and looked past her with an expression she remembered seeing on his father's face. It convinced her that she had better speak her mind.

"But there is a danger in killing those two, Kalid," she said quickly.

"What danger? It will be a pleasure."

"And what will Sarah think of you when she recovers and hears, as she surely will, that you executed the people who tried to kill her?" Kosem asked.

"She will think that justice was done!"

"Will she? Or will she think that you are a brutal tyrant? She will judge you by the standards of her own country and find you sorely lacking in humanity."

Kalid leaped from his seat and began to pace the room. "And what will happen if I do nothing?" he countered. "We'll have a poisoning every week around here—any scullery maid who resents a slight will be lacing the eggplant with strychnine!"

"I am not suggesting that you do nothing," Kosem said mildly. "Punishment is in order. Certainly everyone will understand that. But something less than death might be appropriate."

"My father would have killed them both the same day he caught them," Kalid said.

"That is true, but let us all hope that you are more enlightened than your father. He once hanged a tailor for making him a suit of clothes that fit badly. People have come to expect more progressive behavior from you. We are only fifteen years away from the twentieth century, after all."

"They wanted Sarah dead. I want them to die," he said flatly, his face set.

"Son of my son, I know what happened when the cook Murad admitted his complicity in this matter," Kosem said. "Rumors move faster than thieves in the night through the harem. You attacked the man and would have killed him if Achmed had not intervened and pulled you off him."

"Achmed should be disciplined for putting his hands on me," Kalid said stonily.

"What nonsense! He was quite correct, and you know it. Do you want to acquire a reputation like your father's? Everyone feared him, but no one respected him. The Western powers would not send embassies here, and we were regarded throughout the world as barefoot barbarians. Do you want to destroy everything that you have accomplished in the years since you took the throne with one act of savagery? And all over this American woman!"

Kalid turned to stare at her.

Kosem held up her hand. "Don't look at me that way. I have grown fond of Sarah, and you know this. She saved your life when you were wounded, and for that alone she has my undying gratitude. But don't let your feelings for a concubine allow you to make a bad political decision."

Kalid sat again and stared at the floor for a long time. Finally he said, "I could banish them both from the district, put them outside the walls of the palace with only the clothes they stand in as armor against the future."

Kosem turned her head, smiling secretly. Kalid was just as passionate as his father, but there was an intelligence there, a sophistication, that her husband had always lacked. Did it come from Kalid's English mother or from his Western education, his exposure to a different way of life than that found in the pashadom? Kosem herself had never been out of the Empire; in fact she'd rarely been out of Bursa, but she could see the difference between the two men and was thankful for it.

"An excellent idea," Kosem said.

"I could also cut the cook's hand off and shave Fatma's head before I banished them," he said thoughtfully.

Kosem closed her eyes. "And what would Sarah think of those measures?" Kosem said quietly.

Kalid stood abruptly. "I know what I think of you!" he said. "You are a nosy, interfering old woman, and I don't know why I listen to you at all. Now go back to the harem before I lose patience with your interference."

Kosem left, wearing a smug expression. As soon as the door closed behind her, Kalid called for the halberdier who always stood outside his door.

"Send the khislar to me," he said shortly. "I have orders for the disposition of the prisoners."

Kalid slipped into the room where Sarah was resting, holding up his hand for silence. Memtaz looked up from her needlework and inclined her head.

Kalid sat next to Sarah and took her hand. Her eyes opened, and she smiled when she saw him.

"How are you feeling?" he asked.

"Much better." She blinked and then tightened the grip of her fingers. "Kalid, what happened to me? All that the doctor will tell me is that I've been sick. This much I know."

"What do you remember?"

"I remember waking up in the middle of the night with terrible stomach pains. The rest is hazy. I remember your voice, and seeing Memtaz, and you, and the doctor. Until I woke up this morning, I really didn't know what was going on for sure."

"Fatma poisoned you."

Sarah stared up at him, absorbing the enormity of it. Then she turned her head away from him.

"Is Fatma dead?" she asked quietly.

"No."

Sarah looked back at him. "She's not?"

"I didn't execute her."

Sarah's gaze softened. "Why not?"

"Maybe you have been a good influence on me."

Sarah laughed.

"I don't understand why you should be worried about her. She tried to kill you," Kalid said.

"I'm not worried about her. I detested her, and obviously the feeling was mutual," Sarah said in a tired voice.

"You wouldn't have poisoned her."

"I might have beat her up once or twice."

Kalid grinned. "So why were you concerned that she might be dead?"

"I was concerned about *you*, Kalid."

He looked away from her thoughtfully, then nodded.

"What have you done with her?" Sarah asked.

"She's been banished, along with the cook who helped her get to your food."

"Banished? Like the ancient Greeks? Did you stick her on a mountaintop or something?"

"Or something."

Dr. Shakoz tapped on the door, which was ajar, and entered when Kalid nodded at him.

"How is my patient?" he said cheerfully in Turkish.

"Fine," Sarah replied.

"Ah, you look very well. Your color is back, your eyes are clear, and I think later you may eat something."

Sarah smiled. "Thank you, doctor."

"No, no. It is I who should be thanking you. I understand you tended the pasha when he was wounded and I was away. I owe you a great debt."

"I think you can consider it repaid."

"I would like to take Sarah out for an excursion today, doctor. Is that permissible?" Kalid asked.

"Where?"

"Just to the Sweet Waters."

"I don't see why not," Dr. Shakoz said amiably. "Not for too long, of course. But a change of scene can't hurt. I'll be back tonight to check on you again, young lady."

"Thank you, doctor."

After Shakoz left, Sarah asked Kalid, "What are the Sweet Waters?"

"What you call 'the beach' in the United States."

"Good. I love the beach."

"Memtaz will help you dress, and I'll have my carriage brought around to the Bird House gate at two o'clock."

"Do we have to have guards coming along with us?" Sarah asked. She felt a strong need to be alone with him.

"I will drive the carriage myself," he replied.

Sarah smiled at him as he left, and he stopped and regarded her silently, with a strange expression on his face.

"What is it?" Sarah asked.

"Nothing," he said. "I'll see you soon." He closed the door quietly behind him.

"Oh, mistress, this is so exciting," Memtaz said, as Sarah sat up on her couch. "The Sweet Waters is such a lovely spot. You will have a fine time. What would you like to wear?"

"Anything simple, Memtaz." Sarah swung her legs over the side of the sleeping couch, and the room spun around her. She put her hands to her temples as Memtaz rushed to her side.

"Are you all right, mistress?" Memtaz said anxiously.

"Yes, I'm fine. I just haven't walked for several days, and I need to get myself . . . oriented." Sarah put her feet on the floor deliberately, one at a time.

"Perhaps you should not go," Memtaz said.

"I'm going," Sarah replied firmly. "Just bring me the clothes I need and point me in the right direction."

"You can wear just a shift and a caftan, mistress, but you must wear the feradge over it in the carriage."

"Fine, fine, whatever you say." Sarah stood gingerly and waited for the world to tilt, but it remained upright.

So far, so good.

By the time she was bathed and dressed, her head felt as if it was as thin and delicate as an eggshell, but she made her way through the door, determined to walk through the halls unaided. Memtaz followed at a discreet distance, but they both stopped short when they saw a palanquin with a striped awning standing in the corridor, flanked by four eunuchs.

"What is this?" Sarah asked.

"My master instructed us that you should ride in this conveyance to the Bird House gate," one of the eunuchs replied.

Sarah did not protest, since she already felt fatigued from her preparation for the outing. She waved to Memtaz as she was carried away in the litter, lulled by the swaying motion into a sort of peaceful lassitude. She had always resisted being transported in this way, for it seemed the ultimate in Eastern excess, but today she was grateful for the ride.

Kalid's elaborate carriage was waiting on the

cobbled walk outside the gate. He was wearing a loose jersey sweater in an ivory waffle weave, with tight-fitting brown trousers; he looked like an Oxford rugby player. He dismissed the eunuchs, then came around to the side of the palanquin and pulled its tasseled curtain back all the way, sticking his head inside.

"Now you look like the ikbal," he said teasingly. Before she could protest, he reached down and lifted her, slipping an arm beneath her knees and swinging her into the air. It seemed the most natural thing in the world for Sarah to put her arms around his neck and let her head fall to his shoulder.

He carried her to the coach and set her inside it gently, pulling a rug over her knees and closing the door on her side. Then he vaulted into the driver's seat and called down to her, "Relax and enjoy the ride. It isn't far."

Sarah sat back and did as she was told, glancing out the window every so often at the passing scenery but mostly resting with her head back against the padded satin seat cushion. She was almost asleep when the carriage jolted to a halt and she looked out the window at the most beautiful expanse of beach she had ever seen.

They were on a rise above an estuary of the Bosporus, the green field below sheltered by palms and walnut trees and leafy sycamores. A fountain splashed near the shore and a lacy white gazebo planted all around with flowering bushes stood on the grassy verge where the white sand began to reflect the sunlight. Sarah was dazzled; she held her hand up to shield her eyes as Kalid opened the door of the carriage to get her.

"How do you like it?" he asked, throwing a blanket over his shoulder.

"It's gorgeous," Sarah replied.

"The Sultan had the gazebo built and the fountain installed for Roxalena's mother, Nakshedil."

He lifted her out of the carriage.

"I can walk, Kalid," she said.

"You can walk tomorrow," he said. "For today, you ride."

"You sound like me, after you were shot," Sarah said. "When you think of it, we've spent quite a lot of time taking care of each other," she added, after a long moment.

He looked down at her as he carried her over the worn path to the beach. "When we weren't arguing," he said ruefully.

Sarah nuzzled into the solid warmth of his body. Why couldn't he always be like this? When he wasn't trying to dominate or control her, he could be so . . . nice.

He reached a level spot on the sand and flung the blanket out, then set her down on it. "I'll be right back," he said.

He climbed up the hill and returned with a reed basket. He dumped it on the blanket and then sprawled full-length next to her, sighing luxuriously. Sarah studied his long lean legs encased in the tight trousers and then looked away.

"What's in there?" Sarah asked, pointing to the basket.

"Food."

"Oh, a picnic! I missed my last one."

"When was that?"

"On the outing to the bazaar. We were supposed to have a picnic on the way back."

"But you, of course, had more important things to do," he said dryly.

"Do we have to talk about that now? It could lead to another disagreement."

"I'm not going to disagree with you any more," he said, in a tone of resignation Sarah had never heard him use. She looked at him sharply, wondering what he meant.

"Are you hungry?" he asked, changing the subject. "I checked this menu with Doctor Shakoz. It's all approved invalid food."

"What's that insignia on the clasp of the basket? I've never seen it before," Sarah said.

"Oh, the animal depicted there is a leopard in the black phase. A panther, you would say in English. It's the old Greek word for the Shah family, *leontopardus*."

"Who called you that?"

"The Greeks who were always trying to conquer us."

"I'll bet they never did."

He grinned. "You're right."

"Panther. Its suits you. Dark and lithe and dangerous," Sarah said softly.

He reached for the basket and winced.

"Is your shoulder still bothering you?" Sarah asked.

"Not often, only now and again. My permanent gift from the bedouins."

"Why did they shoot you? I never asked."

"Oh, they're always shooting somebody," he said wearily. "They identify me with the government, so I'm a target."

"They don't like the government?"

"They don't like anyone trying to collect taxes from them. They're nomads, gypsies. They roam from district to district and answer to no one. The Sultan is always trying to pin them down and assign tithes, and in this area I'm the Sultan's man." He handed her an envelope of pita bread filled with vegetables. "They make good bread, though," he said, and grinned.

Sarah accepted the sandwich and took a bite, waching him uncork a bottle of boza and pour the liquid into two tumblers. "Are the bedouins Turks?" Sarah asked.

He shook his head. "Arabs. That's the problem. They don't consider themselves subjects of the Empire, a situation the Sultan would like to change."

"Where do they get pistols?"

"They steal them, barter for them, raid caravans for them. They do whatever is necessary to get arms. That's why they're so dangerous to the Sultan."

"What do you think of him?" Sarah asked.

"The Sultan?"

"Yes."

"Oh, he's a scoundrel."

Sarah giggled.

"What's funny?"

"You have the same opinion of him that I do. Doesn't it bother you that he's your . . ." she stopped.

"Boss?" Kalid suggested, and they both laughed.

"Well, yes," Sarah said.

Kalid shrugged. "He doesn't bother me much in Bursa. I make my required state visits and pay enough duties to keep him off my back, so he lets me run my district my way."

"It was on a state visit that I first saw you," Sarah said.

"And I saw you," he replied simply. "Which brings me to the subject of this little trip." He took a long swallow of his drink and then said, "I have decided to let you go."

Chapter Ten

Sarah couldn't have been more stunned if he had slapped her.

"Let me go?" she said stupidly.

"Yes. I'm giving you what you want, what you've wanted since you came here. I did a lot of thinking while you were ill and came to a hard conclusion. As soon as Doctor Shakoz says that you are fully recovered and well enough to travel, I will bring you to the American embassy myself."

Sarah stared at him. "You once said that you would never give me up."

"I once said too damn many things," he replied darkly.

"Why did you change your mind?"

241

"For two reasons. The first is that what I wanted has not happened."

"What did you want?"

"I wanted you to fall in love with me."

Sarah looked back at him, too shocked to say another word.

"I thought if I kept you here long enough and spent time with you . . . well, you know what I thought," he went on evenly. "But I either overestimated my charm or underestimated your determination. You have demonstrated more than once that I cannot force my will upon you. So. It is *kismet,* and I accept."

"What's the second reason?" Sarah asked quietly, hardly able to believe her ears.

"You almost lost your life here, because of me. This is not a safe place for you. Your poisoning opened my eyes to my own stupidity. I would rather have you alive and well and teaching in Boston than dead in my harem. You should go home."

"It was Fatma who poisoned me, not you, Kalid. And she's gone now."

"For a woman in your position, there will always be another Fatma," he said.

"My position?"

"The beloved of the pasha," he replied.

Sarah looked away from him, too moved to speak. Why was he saying these things now? Because he had already decided that it was too late?

"An Eastern woman would be able to survive the intrigues of the harem," he went on. "After your first encounter with Fatma, you vowed that you would fight her on her own terms, but instead you almost died. You are too . . . straightforward, Sarah. You can't resort to deceit and trickery, not even to save yourself. The Ottoman Empire is not for you. And neither, apparently, am I."

"How long have you known this?"

"I suppose I've known it all along, but I resisted accepting the situation. I thought if I had time, I could . . ."

"What?" she prompted.

"Win you over?" he said, with a smile that indicated how foolish that idea had been. "But it was not to be. So now you will be a virgin bride for your American husband."

"Don't be ridiculous. I don't have an American husband."

"You will," he said shortly, not looking at her.

"Why did you bring me here to tell me this?" Sarah asked, undone by his resigned attitude. He was like a different person, not the man she had known.

"I wanted to spend a last afternoon with you. It will give me something to remember."

"How long will I remain in the harem?"

"Until Doctor Shakoz releases you from his care. A few days, I should think."

There didn't seem to be anything left to say. Neither one of them was very hungry.

"Are you ready to go back?" Kalid asked.

Sarah nodded.

He tossed everything back into the hamper and took her up to the carriage.

Sarah couldn't understand why she felt like crying all the way back to the palace.

"Leaving!" Memtaz said, amazed. "No one leaves the harem unless they are sold. Or die."

"Well, I've been given my walking papers," Sarah said.

"What means this? What papers?"

"It means that the pasha is bringing me to the American embassy as soon as I'm well enough to go."

Memtaz looked very sad, her small face crumpling. "I will miss you terribly, mistress. But I am happy that you are getting what you want. You must be joyful to know that you will soon be returning to your country."

Sarah said nothing. She didn't feel very joyful.

"I thought you would be growing old with us," Memtaz said, stacking pieces of jewelry in a box and setting it on the ikbal's vanity table.

Soon it would belong to someone else.

Sarah didn't want to think of Kalid with another favorite, even if it wasn't Fatma.

"It will be difficult to have a new mistress," Memtaz said, tears welling. "I will always think of you that way."

Sarah patted the maid's shoulder, unable to think of a single comforting thing to say. What could she tell Memtaz—that she would write?

Even if such a thing were possible, the little servant could not read.

The khislar appeared in the doorway of Sarah's antechamber, his face solemn.

"My master requests the presence of the ikbal," he said.

Sarah looked at Memtaz. What fresh torture was this?

"When?" Sarah said.

"Now."

Sarah followed the khislar through the halls of the palace to the mabeyn and into Kalid's suite. The eunuchs assigned to her waited outside the pasha's door.

Kalid turned from his window as she entered. He was wearing a loose dark-blue cotton shirt and gray trousers that complemented his dusky coloring, the open collar of the shirt revealing the long, slender lines of his muscular throat.

He had never looked more attractive to Sarah. Was this because she knew she was leaving?

"You're very prompt," he said quietly.

"I saw no reason to delay."

"I have something for you."

"You've given me quite enough already."

"This is special. I think you'll like it much better than harem jewelry."

Sarah watched as he withdrew a package wrapped in paper from a drawer. He handed it to her silently.

"Open it," he said, when she stood with it in

her hands, unmoving, looking at him.

Sarah obeyed, smiling when she saw that it was a copy of Twain's *Life on the Mississippi.*

"I told you I would get it for you," Kalid said. "Look inside the cover."

Sarah lifted it and saw that the flyleaf was inscribed, "Samuel Langhorne Clemens."

"It's a signed first edition," Sarah said, amazed.

"Signed with his real name," Kalid added.

"How did you find this?"

He smiled.

"Oh, yes. I forgot. You can get anything you want for the right price."

"Except you," he said, holding her gaze.

Sarah didn't know what to say.

"I don't know if I should accept this," she finally managed.

"Why not?"

"It just doesn't seem right."

"Because you're leaving?"

"Among other reasons."

"I want you to have something to remember me by," he said quietly.

"I won't need this to remember you," she said.

"You'd rather forget me."

"I didn't say that."

"You will forget me if you go back to the United States," he persisted, watching her closely. "You will go back to your former life, and after a while your time here will seem like a dream,

246

a troubled dream from which you were glad to awaken."

"I won't go back to my former life," Sarah said softly, shaking her head. "I can't."

"Why not?"

"Because I have changed."

"Did I change you?"

"My feelings for you changed me."

They were standing facing one another, like debaters in a secondary school classroom.

"How?" he said huskily.

"You were my introduction to . . ." she stopped.

"Passion?" he suggested.

"If you want to put it that way."

"Is there another way to put it, kourista?" he asked with a wry smile.

"I suppose not."

"Do you think you will ever regret that we didn't make love?" he asked.

"We did make love," she said flushing.

"You know what I mean."

"I already regret it."

He crossed the distance between them and took her chin in his hand, turning her face up to his.

"What are you saying?" he demanded.

"Just that when I finally do . . . sleep . . . with a man, I won't feel the same way about him as I feel about you."

"You expect that your husband will be boring?"

"I expect that he won't be you," she said quietly.

He put his arm around her and drew her into the curve of his shoulder, nuzzling her hair. "You are undoubtedly the most impossible woman I have ever met. How do you expect me to keep my hands off you when you say something like that?"

Sarah wrapped her arms around his waist and closed her eyes, not thinking, not caring about anything but this man and this moment. When he bent his head to kiss her, she looked up and met his mouth with hers.

Sarah gripped his hard shoulders, fitting her body to his, tilting her head back as his mouth traveled from her lips to the shell of her ear, the base of her throat. He ran his hands up her bare arms and across her back, crushing her breasts to his chest. She tugged his shirt loose from the waistband of his pants, seeking the satiny texture of his warm skin with her hands.

Kalid found her mouth again with his, aware that he was kissing her too hungrily, but unable to restrain himself. He tugged at the slender belt of her gown and the silken material parted; his hands sought her flesh, caressing, his fingers hot, moving everywhere as Sarah swayed in his embrace, her eyes half closed. When he released her, she would have fallen but for the arm he slipped under her knees as he carried her to his couch.

He set her on it and then ripped off his shirt; buttons flew everywhere as Sarah held out her arms, eager for the renewed sensation of his skin against hers. When he joined her, she clung to him, running her lips over the smooth line of his shoulder. He groaned and pulled her into his lap as she sank her hands into his lush hair, sighing luxuriously. Her touch drove all reason from his mind as she strained against him. Sarah felt the tension in his powerful body as the panther he was named for readied itself to spring. She shifted her weight, making a small sound of satisfaction as she felt him full and ready against her.

"I can't wait any longer," he gasped, lifting her into position, his hands on either side of her slender waist. "I will try to be gentle, kourista."

"Gentle?" she said, opening her eyes.

"When I take you," he muttered, pushing her down on the couch, reaching for the top button of his trousers.

Suddenly she was looking up at him with a clarity that belied her previous ardor. "I know what you're doing," she said.

"What?" he panted, bewildered.

"You want to get into me just once before you pack me off to Boston. Then you can still feel that you've won."

He let her go and stood abruptly, walking to the other side of the room to put some distance between them. When he could talk again, he said tightly, "*I* pack you off to Boston? *Me?*

You are deranged, do you know that? That's your problem—not virginal reticence, not some drivel about being a captive or coming to Bursa against your will. I don't know why I didn't see it before. I must have been blinded by desire. The real difficulty here is that you are completely and totally insane." As always when he was angry or excited, his British accent intensified, making the last word sound like "insign."

"And you, I suppose, are the picture of stability, paying a king's ransom for a woman you'd seen once and then resorting to the basest tactics to have your way with her," Sarah retorted.

"What base tactics? What? Were you tricked or misled in any way tonight? If you were, I must have missed it."

"Getting that book for me . . ." she said, sitting up and pulling her gown around her, tightening the sash.

"That's a base tactic?" he demanded, staring at her. "Thoughtfulness is now a crime?"

"It wasn't thoughtfulness," Sarah said, standing.

"Then what the hell was it?" he inquired furiously.

"Duping me. You know just what to do in order to soften me up, make me susceptible to your charms. You're a past master at it with all women, and you're particularly effective with me. I have no idea why, but it's true. I've read that there is one man in the world that each individual woman will be helpless before, and for me that man is you."

"You are not helpless, Sarah, never less so than at this moment," he replied darkly.

"I'd like to leave," Sarah said primly.

"You may go. You have my promise that I won't try again. There will be no more interviews, presents, or tormented embraces. Your business with me is concluded. You won't see me until you are ready to be taken to the American embassy."

Sarah strode out of the pasha's suite and walked back to the harem, her eunuch escort nipping at her heels.

Kalid downed another slug of raki and stared down at his hands, the hands that had so recently caressed Sarah until she was at the point of submission.

But she had not submitted, and he was now getting drunk to forget that.

Nothing was going as he had planned.

He had thought that telling Sarah she was free to leave him would make her realize that she did not want to go. He had thought that expressing concern about her after Fatma's attempt on her life would make her realize that she meant more to him than just another woman to take to bed. He had thought that she felt more for him than just the passion two beautiful people would naturally stir in each other.

He had thought that freeing the caged bird

would make it fly happily back to its perch.

He had thought wrong.

She was actually going to leave, and he had no one but himself to blame for it.

Why did he always misjudge the situation when she was concerned? Was she really so different from the other women he had known? She always reacted in an unanticipated way, leaving him baffled and frustrated.

And alone.

He finished the liquor in his glass and filled it again from the jug.

She would go back to America—marry some clerk or salesman or teacher, a faceless nobody who wouldn't know the first thing about making her moan with pleasure, who would never see the slow flush creep up her neck as she gave herself over to passion.

The very thought of it made him want to reduce every stick of furniture in the palace to splinters.

Instead, he threw his glass against the wall, where the liquid splashed and the glass shattered into a crystalline profusion of tiny pieces.

"Thank you for agreeing to accompany me on this little farewell trip," Kosem said to Sarah. "My grandson told me how much you enjoyed the Sweet Waters, and I thought you might like to see it again before you left us."

Sarah pulled her feradge back from her face and studied the old woman sitting next to her.

They were traveling in Kosem's luxurious carriage, the cushions so soft that sitting on them was like sinking into a cloud. Two halberdiers rode on either side of them, and the khislar trotted on his palomino behind the coach.

"Why do you look at me so?" Kosem asked.

"When you are about to spring a trap, you resemble Kalid very much," Sarah replied.

"He resembles me, no? I came first."

"So you don't deny that this little excursion has an ulterior motive?" Kosem's invitations always did.

"What is an interior motive?" Kosem asked.

"Ulterior. It means a secret motive, other than the one expressed."

"You think I'm tricky?"

"It runs in the family."

"Since you have made an observation, may I make one?" Kosem said, enjoying the parrying.

"Certainly."

"For a woman who is about to achieve her heart's desire, you don't seem very happy."

Sarah turned away from her and looked out the window of the coach.

"Sarah, if you leave us and go back to the United States, you will never see my grandson again as long as you live. Is that what you really want?"

"I have to go."

"Why?"

"Kalid doesn't love me." If she weren't certain

of that, she could never leave.

"You stupid girl, of course he loves you. Love sometimes finds expression in self-sacrifice," Kosem said urgently. "He loves you enough to let you go, and that's more love than I have ever seen him show for anybody."

"He has never told me so," Sarah said.

"Deeds mean more than words, or isn't that true in the U.S. of America?"

"That's true anywhere."

"So? Has he behaved as if he loves you?"

"He has behaved as if he *wants* me, which is an entirely different matter."

The coach hit a rut, and both women jounced on the seat. Kosem leaned forward and pounded on the roof of the carriage with her jeweled walking stick.

"This driver is an idiot," she grumbled. "He finds every hole in the road as if he is searching for them." She looked at Sarah. "You can't tell the difference between affection and desire?"

"Kalid can't. Any time I think he feels something real for me, it turns out that he just wants to get me into bed."

"Is there something wrong with that? Did you think that his interest in you was . . ." She searched for a word.

"Platonic?" Sarah supplied.

"What is that?"

"Just friendly."

"Yes," Kosem nodded vigorously.

"You don't understand. Of course I know that

254

he has always desired me." She hesitated. "I feel the same."

"So exactly where is the problem?"

"He has desired Fatma and I don't know how many others. It has to be more than that for me."

"You want to be special."

"Yes. And I'm afraid his only interest in me is the challenge I represent."

"You think you will be discarded once he has achieved his goal?" Kosem said.

"Kalid is accustomed to getting what he wants," Sarah said. "Since I resisted him, chasing me was a novel experience. What will happen when he no longer has to chase me? If there is no real love between us, I'll be cast aside like a toy which no longer interests him because it has become too familiar."

"And if there is love?"

"If there is love, I've seen no evidence of it."

"How can you say that? He drove Dr. Shakoz day and night when you were ill. He tore apart the palace to find those responsible for your poisoning."

"To keep me alive so I could warm his bed in the future," Sarah said flatly.

Kosem examined her soberly as the coach slowed to a stop. "You cast a very cold eye on my grandson's behavior."

"He bought me, valide pashana, and then kept me here, locked me up like a convicted criminal. As much as I react to his physical presence, I've never been able to forget the cynical, calculated way in which he selected me as if I were a piece of fruit that looked particularly appetizing, paying the price to obtain me like a customer in a bazaar."

"It is the way things are done here in the Empire," Kosem said simply.

"Kalid knows better. He has spent time in the West."

"Never believe that. In his soul, he is Turkish to the core. It is why he wants to possess you. For him, there is no other way."

The driver opened the door of the coach and let down the steps. Kosem alighted and turned to wait as Sarah followed her.

"It's a lovely day," she observed, as they started down the path to the beach. "Will you miss our balmy weather?"

"I'm sure I will. It can get very cold in the winter in Boston. Though I confess there have been days when the heat here has been too much for me."

The khislar and the two halberdiers took up their positions on the road as Kosem led the way to the gazebo built for the Sultan's kadin, Nakshedil.

"Did you know her?" Sarah asked, sitting on one of the stone benches inside and looking out to sea.

"Who?" Kosem replied, sitting across from her.

"Roxalena's mother."

"Yes, she was a very powerful woman. Willful, beautiful. She exerted a great influence on the Sultan."

"Roxalena sounds a lot like her."

"The Princess Roxalena is a spoiled child. She refused to marry my grandson."

"I don't think either one of them was really interested," Sarah said, smiling.

"*I* was interested," Kosem said, and Sarah laughed.

"I'm going to miss you," Sarah said.

"And Kalid? Will you miss him?"

Sarah looked down at her hands. "Yes," she said.

"You will never meet another like him."

"I know that," Sarah said quietly.

"Nor anyone who stirs your blood in the same way."

Sarah was silent.

"Are you prepared to make this sacrifice?"

"I must."

Kosem shook her head. "I don't understand you."

"Yes, I know."

"You could live out your life here in comfort, even if Kalid did give you up in later years."

"I could never stand that."

"To be discarded?"

"To be unloved."

"I think you are too proud, Miss Sarah of Boston."

"Maybe."

"It is why you anger Kalid."

"I'm too much like him?"

Kosem smiled. "He would never say so."

"He'll have another favorite before my ship docks in Boston," Sarah said tersely.

"The thought of it bothers you?"

"Of course."

"American women are a mystery," Kosem said, sighing.

"I'm sure Kalid agrees with you. He'll find it restful to deal with women who aren't such a puzzle."

"He might be bored," Kosem said, smiling devilishly.

"Not for long. Variety is the spice of life."

"I don't imagine you will be replaced so easily."

"It would be nice to think so."

Kosem placed her hand over Sarah's. "I had hoped you would be the mother of the next pasha."

"It is written on my forehead that I will leave this place," Sarah replied.

"Ah, now you sound like an Ottoman woman." Kosem rose and tucked Sarah's hand through her arm. "Come, let us walk along the beach. I find it very peaceful."

The two women, one at the beginning of her life, the other at the end of it, walked for some time along the strand, their guards following at a discreet distance. When it was time to return to the coach, they walked up the hill slowly, both seeking to prolong what would probably be their last visit.

Suddenly, just when they reached the road, the sound of pounding hooves overtook them. The khislar ran toward them, drawing his sword, and the two guards raised their halberds, looking around for the source of the noise.

Three horsemen were bearing down on them, swathed in dark robes, their faces covered with hoods that revealed only their eyes. Sarah watched in horror as the first horseman ran the khislar down, striking him with a truncheon and knocking him to the ground. She grabbed Kosem's hand and tried to run, but the old lady stumbled and they both fell to their knees.

Sarah looked up to see one long arm swoop down and grab her. She struggled as she was hauled bodily onto the racing horse. Kosem stared after her, screaming. The halberdiers tried to give chase, but the riders were already vanishing into the distance, the horses' hooves sending up a cloud of dust.

It was all over in seconds. Kosem sat on the ground, weeping, crawling toward the bloodied and unconscious Achmed. The halberdiers ran back to assist her, helping her to stand.

"Who was that?" she gasped.

"Bedouins," the first halberdier said, as his partner knelt next to the khislar. His expression was bleak as he looked at Kosem; he knew how the pasha would react to this news.

"What?" Kosem said.

"The ikbal has been kidnapped by the bedou-ins."

Chapter Eleven

Kalid looked up from a schematic for a dam he was building and saw Turhan Aga standing at the door. Two of his halberdiers were right behind him, and they all looked frightened.

Kalid stood abruptly. "What is it?" he demanded, his heart beating faster.

"Master, there has been an . . . incident," Turhan Aga began.

"Sarah?"

The captain looked ill.

"My grandmother?"

"Both," Turhan said.

Kalid stared at him, trying to absorb the enormity of such a disaster. Then, "Tell me," he said tersely.

Turhan Aga nodded at his lieutenant, who

said, "The valide pashana and the ikbal were just about to leave the Sweet Waters when we were set upon by bedouins. The khislar was badly injured defending the women. My partner and I tried to stop them, but the pashana fell to the ground and they kidnapped the ikbal."

Kalid was already running toward the door. "How long ago?" he called.

"About an hour."

"My grandmother?" he said to the halberdier.

"A few scrapes. I think she is sound physically, but of course very upset."

"And Achmed?"

"Doctor Shakoz is with him." The men were dashing after Kalid as he burst into the anteroom of his suite, shedding his ceremonial clothes.

"Tell the groom to saddle my horse immediately and bring him to the Carriage House gate," he called to a eunuch outside the door, who broke into a run.

"Did you see anything about the men who took her?" Kalid asked the halberdier, who looked pained.

"There were three of them, but they were all swathed in dark, heavy robes. Only their eyes were visible."

"What kind of horses?" Kalid said, tearing off his caftan and strapping on his sword.

"The leader was riding a sorrel. The others had gray mares," the halberdier replied.

"The leader took the ikbal?" Kalid pulled out

a drawer and removed his pistol, cocking it and loading it, draping a strap with extra bullets in it around his neck.

"Yes, master."

"Then he is my man," Kalid said under his breath. He pointed to a servant who was dusting his bookshelves, pretending not to notice the commotion, and said, "You. Go to the kitchen and tell them to prepare me food and water for three days. Bring it to the Carriage House gate as soon as it's ready."

The servant bowed and vanished as Turhan Aga said, "Master, you don't mean to go after her alone."

"I mean to bring her back. This is my task, and I won't endanger anyone else in pursuing it."

"Let me come with you," Turhan Aga said.

"I need you here," Kalid replied shortly.

"Then at least take some of my men with you—"

"No. This is my woman and my fight."

"The bedouins are very dangerous, master. Perhaps your feelings for this woman—"

Kalid whirled on him, and he stopped.

"Hold your tongue! They took her because of me!" he said to Turhan heatedly. "They knew she was my favorite, don't you understand?"

"Perhaps not, master. Maybe they just saw the yellow hair and thought she would bring a high price at the slave auctions."

Kalid shook his head, now strapping a short

knife to his thigh. "They were following her. This was planned. They waited for the right moment, when she was lightly guarded, and then struck. They tried to kill me, and that attempt failed. This is just another tactic to bring me to heel."

"Do you think they will demand a ransom?"

"I'm not waiting to find out. I know those hills almost as well as they do, and they can't have gotten far. On Khan I might be able to catch them."

He grabbed a cloth from his dresser and tied it around his neck. He turned to the halberdier captain and said, "Guard my grandmother with your life. Tell Dr. Shakoz that I hold him responsible for the khislar's health. He is not to leave Achmed's side."

Turhan nodded.

"And I charge all of you," he said, raising his voice and looking at each man individually, "to keep the faith with me while I am gone and protect the house of Shah."

He dashed from the room, and Turhan Aga looked around at his abashed halberdiers, then gestured abruptly for them to follow the pasha.

Sarah could not tell if it was day or night, but she thought that it was night. Everything was quiet, and the air was cool. She was blindfolded and gagged, and her hands were tied to some sort of pole, but she could tell that she was alone.

Whoever had kidnapped her must be some-where else, plotting her sorry fate.

She didn't even have the strength left to cry. Exhausted from an endless ride over rough country and a futile struggle with her captor, who finally struck her smartly several times in order to end her resistance, Sarah's head was ringing from the blows. She was viciously thirsty and her shins were scraped raw from being dragged across the ground; her wrists were chafed from the rope that bound them.

In addition, she was miserably sure that Kalid would not come after her.

Why should he? As far as he was concerned, she was a nuisance and he was well rid of her. Whether he was planning to dump her off at the embassy or let these hooligans have her, he had clearly cut his losses.

And there was nothing she wanted to hear more at this moment than the sound of his voice.

Sarah tried to change her position and couldn't; she'd been forced into a kneeling position, and her legs were cramping. She moved her left foot a couple of inches and groaned. She listened, waiting for the babble of voices to resume at the sound she had made, but nothing happened.

No one must be near.

She was dreadfully afraid that the language they had been speaking was Arabic and that her kidnappers were bedouins.

She whimpered and then bit her lip to keep from crying out loud. What was going to happen to her? She remembered the stories she had heard of rape and torture and murder and closed her eyes behind the cloth that bound them.

Why had she ever thought that Kalid was mistreating her? No matter how much she had teased and taunted and tormented him, he had never raised a hand to her, had endured her endless rejection in the face of his ardent pursuit with nothing more harmful than a few harsh words, and in the end had planned to give her the freedom that she wanted.

She was sure that she could expect much different treatment from her current captors.

Sarah tried to find some ray of hope, some positive prospect to cling to, and came up empty.

She had a good idea what would happen to her when her kidnappers returned.

Her future looked bleak indeed.

Kosem gestured for the eunuchs to part ranks and admit James Woolcott to her presence. She was receiving him in her grandson's audience room, with Turhan Aga at her side.

James looked at the wizened old lady, dwarfed by the pasha's ornate throne, then glanced around in bewilderment.

"I wanted to see Kalid Shah," he finally said, in carefully grammatical Turkish.

"You may speak English," she replied in that language. "Kalid Shah is not here. I am the valide pashana, his grandmother. I understand that you have been trying to bribe your way into the palace for the last several days. The captain of the halberdiers has been bringing me reports. I finally decided to see you myself, since it became apparent that you were not going away."

"I tried the usual diplomatic channels, pashana. I went to see the Sultan, even sent a leter to the Pasha asking for an audience about my cousin. Nothing worked, so here I am."

"Who is your cousin?" Kosem asked smoothly, as if she did not know.

"Sarah Woolcott. She was a tutor in the Sultan's harem, and he sold her to the . . . to your grandson." James waited for the pashana to launch into the same stonewalling routine he had heard from the Sultan, but she surprised him. She turned her head for a long moment, and when she looked back at him, he was stunned to see that her eyes were filled with tears.

"Sarah is gone," she said softly.

"Gone?" James echoed.

"She went on a beach excursion with me, and while there she was captured by the bedouins."

James was speechless for several moments, then covered his face with his hands. "The bedouins?" he murmured despairingly. This just got worse and worse; Sarah's life was in ruins, and it was all his fault.

"Yes. I am very sorry to tell you this, but I felt it was something you should know. I think it may have been my grandson's intention to conceal her presence at the Orchid Palace from you, but he is very much in love with her and this is affecting his judgment."

"In love with her?" James said, staring.

"Yes. He has gone after her, alone, to reclaim her from the gypsies who took her."

"I take it you don't feel that he has much of a chance," James said dully.

"My grandson is very resourceful. If anyone can do such a thing, he can."

"He has a whole palace full of men here—why didn't he take anybody with him?"

Kosem sighed. "You would not understand. It is *inshallah*, a matter of honor. When your woman is taken, you go alone to do battle with the one who took her."

"The bedouins travel in packs! Are they going to respect your grandson's tradition?" James asked incredulously.

Kosem said nothing.

James sighed, near tears himself. "I don't know what to do," he said aloud, voicing his thoughts.

"Nor do I," Kosem said quietly.

"Should I go after them?"

"You would not last a day in those hills," Kosem replied.

"But the pasha will?"

"He knows them very well, since he was a boy."

"So I just have to wait and see if he comes back with her?" James said resignedly.

"As we all have to wait," Kosem agreed.

"Will you contact me if you hear anything?" James said, wondering why he trusted her. But she obviously cared about Sarah, and that had to be enough for him.

"You have my word," Kosem said solemnly. "Leave your address with my captain of halberdiers. I will send a messenger as soon as there is news."

James nodded. *"Tessekur ederim,"* he said.

"You are welcome."

Kalid crouched behind an outcropping of rock and looked down on the bedouin camp. The tents were close together, with an extinguished cooking fire in the middle, the horses tied in a string at the edge of the clearing.

Sarah had to be in one of those tents. But which one?

Kalid had tracked the tribe for a full day, racing Khan to catch up with them and then following at a safe distance, waiting until they had bedded down for the night before approaching close enough to see details. He knew that they rose and retired early, sometimes even traveling by dark and sleeping during daylight to avoid the worst of the heat. But that was in high summer; now they were on their autumn schedule, which meant going to bed soon after sundown and awakening at sunrise.

He had about two hours before the women would be up to start cooking.

He tied Khan to a tree, carefully marking the spot, then moved slowly down the slope, traveling by inches, careful not to make any noise. He knew there would be guards posted, but he had no idea where they might be, so he cleared the space in front of him a foot at a time, his knife at the ready. Almost an hour passed before he reached the level of the camp, and then he was even more cautious, moving from tent to tent like a shadow, inspecting each one for a sign that Sarah might be inside it.

If he chose the wrong one, the alarm would be sounded and all would be lost.

He was circling the largest tent, one embroidered with burgundy and navy Tikal designs, when he stopped short.

Tied up next to it, apart from the other horses, was a splendidly groomed sorrel, his mane braided and gleaming in the moonlight.

This, then, was the leader's tent.

Kalid felt for his pistol in his belt. If he were lucky, he would not need it.

A knife was swift and silent, and he was an expert with one.

He knelt and began to cut through the back of the tent; the flap was at the front, where he might be spotted more easily. It was tedious and painstaking work. By the time he had cut a hole big enough to admit his body, his wrists ached and he was bathed in sweat. He fell full-length to the ground and snaked into the tent, remaining frozen in a prone position until his eyes adjusted to the total darkness.

A man and a woman were sleeping on cushions to his left, still wrapped in their robes, ready to move at a moment's notice, like all nomads. The leader and his first wife, most likely. Kalid looked to his right and saw Sarah, tied to the central tent pole, blindfolded and gagged, slumped like a bag of wet laundry.

It took every ounce of will power he possessed not to kill her bedouin captor immediately. But he had to be careful; he was outnumbered and he would be risking Sarah's life as well as his own if he followed an emotional impulse. He had to take this one step at a time or it might cost him dearly.

Kalid crawled to Sarah's side and put his hand over her mouth. She started and began to struggle. He cut away her blindfold and let her see who he was.

Kalid would never forget the look in her eyes when she recognized him. He removed her gag swiftly and then held his finger firmly to her lips.

She nodded, her eyes flooding with tears.

He cut the rope binding her hands and then rubbed her wrists briskly to restore circulation. He helped her to stand and she stumbled; they

271

both looked toward the sleeping pair, who didn't move.

Kalid led her by the hand to the hole he had made in the tent and pointed. She crouched and crawled through it, and he followed. He was almost out when the man sleeping behind him sat up and said something in an alarmed tone in Arabic.

Kalid whirled and threw his knife with deadly accuracy. It landed in the bedouin's throat, and blood began to jet rhythmically from the wound, bathing the nomad in a scarlet flood. The Arab gurgled and grabbed his neck, coughing wetly. The woman at his side rolled over and gazed at him sleepily, then jumped up, gasping. A second later, she looked around at Kalid and screamed.

Kalid dove through the tent after Sarah and grabbed her hand, running with her toward the leader's horse. He cut its tether and jumped up on it, then hauled Sarah up behind him.

"Hang on!" he yelled. As he kicked its flanks, the camp erupted around them, the women wailing, the men bursting from the tents, pistols at the ready.

"Get your head down!" Kalid called, as the horse pounded through the camp and gunshots burst around them. Kalid pulled out his pistol and returned the fire as Sarah ducked and clung to him, feeling the trained response of his body as he twisted and turned, aiming at the bedouins closest to him. The last two dashed out of his way as he drove the horse past them, out of the camp into the open countryside and then farther up into the hills.

They rode at full gallop for some time, the wind whistling past their ears, Kalid turning frequently to look for pursuers until he was certain they were not being followed. Then he slowed the horse to a walk and led it to a grove of trees by a stream, where he moved to dismount.

Sarah clung to him, preventing him from stepping down to the ground.

"It's all right now," he said gently, prying her arms loose from his waist. "Let me get down, Sarah. You're safe."

Sarah relaxed her grip and he slid to the ground, then reached up for her. She allowed him to set her on the grass and then she flung her arms around his neck again.

He held her for several minutes and then said quietly, "Let me go, Sarah. I have to tether the horse."

She sat on the ground and watched as he tied up the bedouin sorrel and then rubbed it down with his shirt, finally giving it a drink in his cupped hands. Then he stretched out with his bare back against a tree and extended his arm.

"Come here," he said, and she snuggled in next to him, her head on his shoulder, her eyes closed.

"Did they touch you?" he asked quietly, his breath stirring her hair.

She knew immediately what he meant. "No."

"They were probably still deciding what to do with you."

"What were the choices?" she asked, shuddering.

"Sell you, hold you for ransom, use you themselves. The leader would have been first until he tired of you, then the others would have followed in turn."

Sarah moaned faintly.

"Don't think about it," he said soothingly.

"Why did you come after me?" she whispered.

He held her off to look down at her in amazement. "You didn't think I would?"

"You were so angry with me," she murmured, looking away from his penetrating gaze, his eyes luminous in the moonlight.

"So I would abandon you to the horrible fate of a bedouin whore? You have a very low opinion of me, kourista."

"I know I've been a great deal of trouble."

"Yes, a great deal. Maybe I should take you back."

"That isn't funny," she said, nuzzling into his shoulder again. The scent of his exertions was on his skin, and under other circumstances this would have stimulated her to further action, but she was simply too exhausted to respond.

"Are you sure they aren't following us?" she said drowsily.

"They would have been here by now if they were."

"What about Kosem and Achmed? Are they all right?"

"Kosem was more frightened than hurt. Dr. Shakoz is with Achmed. He has a head wound."

"Is it serious?"

"I didn't stay to find out. We'll learn more when we return."

"Did you kill him, Kalid? The one who kidnapped me?"

"Unless he's immortal," Kalid replied dryly. "An ordinary human could not survive that wound."

"I was hoping we could just slip away," Sarah whispered, almost asleep.

"It just saved me the trouble of going back and killing him another time," Kalid said grimly.

Sarah didn't answer, and he thought she was asleep. Then she said in a small voice, "Thank you."

He kissed the top of her head, and in seconds he was breathing deeply also.

When Kalid awoke, it was mid-morning and Sarah was gone. He sat up quickly, looking around, and then relaxed when he saw her splashing in the stream where he had watered the horse.

His relaxation changed to intense interest when he saw that she was naked. He got up and walked a little closer, leaning against a tree, ignoring the protests of his body, which had slept on the ground after engaging in mortal combat the previous night.

The scene before him was enough to drive all other thoughts from his mind. Sarah had discarded her clothes, the ones she'd been wearing on the outing with Kosem when she was kidnapped, and they fluttered on the riverbank like a pastel snowfall. A few feet away, standing in water up to her knees, she raised her arms and rivulets of water ran down them. The droplets sparkled in the sun as her breasts rose, taut and firm, the nipples stiffening in reaction to the cool water. Kalid was riveted, his mouth going dry as he watched.

Sarah bent over to rinse her back, and his eyes traveled along her spine, admiring the arc from slim shoulders to narrow waist, the dimpling of flesh at the swell of her buttocks. She turned, and he saw the tangle of sandy curls at the apex of her thighs, darkened now with water, and he sagged against the tree, his stomach knotting with desire. He stared helplessly, spellbound, as she lifted her dripping hair from her neck and her rosy skin tightened with the movement, exposing the outline of her ribs. He found himself walking toward her almost involuntarily, and when he said her name his voice was hoarse.

She looked over her shoulder as he stepped into the water and slid his hands under her arms, enclosing her breasts from behind. She went limp as he pressed his lips to the nape of her neck, sighing as he stroked her nipples, then moaning as he put his hands on her hips and forced her back against him so that she could feel his excitement.

He grasped her waist and spun her around to face him, kissing her wildly, his skin now wet from contact with hers. Sarah's mouth opened under his, and she responded in kind, running her hands urgently over the hard surface of his back. He picked her up and carried her to the riverbank, bending to lift her feradge from the pile of her clothes. He flung it wide on the soft patch of grass under the tree where they had slept and set Sarah down upon it. When he lay next to her, she wrapped her arms around his neck and fitted herself against him, rubbing her face against his bare shoulder.

"You know what I want, Sarah," he said softly, stroking her damp hair.

She nodded. He felt the motion rather than saw it.

"Will you give me what I want?" he asked.

"Yes," she whispered. It was like a sigh.

"Not because I rescued you last night," he said into her hair. "You don't owe me anything."

She nodded again.

"Only because you want it too," he said.

"I do," she whispered. "I always did."

"Oh, Sarah, you have nearly driven me mad," he said hoarsely, pushing her gently into a prone position and nuzzling her neck, then moving lower to take her nipple in his mouth. Sarah arched her back, sinking her fingers into his hair and holding him as he sucked gently, increasing the pressure until she was tossing her head from side to side. When he raised his head, she clutched at him, trying to stop him, then sighed as he laid his flushed cheek against the smooth surface of her belly.

"Do it again," she whispered.

"What?" he said, tonguing her navel. But he knew.

"What you did to me last time," she said, her eyes closing as she felt his warm breath on her sensitive skin.

"Did you like that?" he said softly, slipping his hand between her legs. She made a small sound and pressed against his caressing fingers, yearning toward him.

"Did you?" he said again, and she seized him, pulling his head down as her legs fell apart. When his mouth finally touched her, she whimpered with gratification, writhing as his cheeks, roughened with stubble, abraded the skin of her inner thighs and then succumbing to ecstasy as his lips caressed her. His arms and shoulders knotted with the strain of controlling himself in order to pleasure her. She lay supine, awash in sensation, until the need to join with him was so overwhelming that she dug her fingers into his shoulders fiercely, trying to raise him.

"What?" he said, looking up at her, his eyes slitted, his amber skin flushed deep crimson, his mouth wet.

"Come inside me," she gasped.

"Are you sure?" he said huskily. If she stopped him this time, he would not be responsible for what he might do. But he could see that she was too far gone to resist him; she was dewed with perspiration, her eyes almost closed, her nipples pebble-hard and darkened to a rosy hue with excitement.

"Please," she moaned, reaching for him. He bit his lip as she cupped him, her inexpert caress more erotic than the skilled enticements of the most experienced courtesan. He closed his eyes as she felt him through the cloth of his trousers, stimulating him until he rolled away from her, unable to take it a moment longer.

"Kalid?" Sarah said questioningly.

"Wait," he said, his breath coming harshly as he stripped off his pants and threw them aside. Then he lay next to her again, stroking her flank, marveling once more at the intensity of her response. She reached up and hooked her arms around his neck. His skin was slick with sweat and he felt hot to the touch, the cords in his throat full and taut, his muscles fairly vibrating with tension.

"Sarah," he said, his voice almost unrecognizable.

"Yes," she said. "Now."

He rolled her under him, positioning her, and he knew he would retain the memory of the way she clung to him trustingly, giving herself up to him completely, forever.

He meant to be careful, to take her slowly and gently, but he had waited so long and he wanted her so much. He plunged into her too quickly, too deeply, and she froze, gasping. He stopped, his arms rigid and trembling as he held himself poised above her.

"I'm sorry," he gasped. "Are you all right?"

"Yes," she said in a small voice, but she felt stiff and unyielding in his arms. He withdrew and cradled her against him.

"It often hurts the first time. I should have told you," he said soothingly, kissing her reassuringly, cursing himself. It was many years since he had taken a virgin, and he had never in his life been so emotionally involved with the object of his desire. It made more of a difference than he could have anticipated.

Despite what seemed an eternity of thinking about it, he really wasn't prepared for this.

"I knew that," she said, not wanting him to feel responsible for her pain.

"Should I stop?" he asked, as his body urged him onward, impelling him to do just the opposite. She had fitted him so well, the sensation of entering her had been so fulfilling, that his offer to end the pursuit when the quarry was so near was costing him every shred of restraint he had left.

"No, no," she replied, wrapping her arms around his torso, feeling the wide shoulders tapering to the slim waist, the silken mat of black hair on his chest pressing her breasts.

"I want you so much, and I want it to be you."

"It?" he said, lifting her against him.

"My first lover," she said shyly.

"Only," he replied fiercely. "Your only lover." He began to stroke her thighs, slowly, luxuriously, until she was weak with need, opening her legs invitingly for his more intimate caress. It was some seconds before she said, in a slurred tone, "Again."

He poised above her. "Sure?" he said.

She reached for him, encircling him with her fingers, and he groaned helplessly.

"Please," she said.

This time when he entered her, his throaty sound of satisfaction was echoed by hers.

"Yes?" he said, beginning to move slowly within her, barely able to speak.

"Oh, yes," she sighed, wrapping her legs around his hips and digging her heels into the backs of his thighs.

He dropped his head to her shoulder and closed his eyes, taking her along with him on the ancient journey of discovery.

"Let's never leave this place," Sarah said dreamily. "Couldn't we stay here forever?"

Kalid didn't respond. She lifted her head from his shoulder and gazed into his face.

"Are you asleep?" she demanded.

His eyes opened. "Not any longer."

"It's the middle of the afternoon!"

"I'm tired."

She smiled. "Are you saying that I've worn you out?"

He sighed and adjusted his position more comfortably. "Draw your own conclusions."

"Well, you've disappointed me. All you did was rescue a fair maiden from a band of evil gypsies and then deflower a virgin. That should be an easy day's work for the Pasha of Bursa."

"That's all very well for *you* to say," he intoned in his best British accent, and she giggled, then stretched like a satisfied cat. "I think I'll start a new career."

Kalid grinned. "As what?"

"Your lover." She turned her head and kissed his shoulder.

He lifted her hair off her neck and wound it around his hand. "I always knew it would be like this," he said quietly.

"How could you tell?"

"From the way you looked at me."

"How did I look at you?"

"With a very hot eye," he said, smiling.

"I thought you were the most beautiful man I had ever seen."

He snorted. "Men aren't beautiful."

"You are."

"What about all those investment bankers back in the United States?" he asked.

"What makes you think I would want one of them?"

He took her hand and held it to his lips. "Some people would say a man like that is more appropriate for you."

"I know what I like," she said, tracing the full lines of his mouth with a fingertip.

"It took you some time to admit it."

"I'm stubborn. You've said so yourself. In fact, you isolated me so that I could think about it."

"I'm sorry I locked you up in the harem," he said softly. "I was afraid that you would get away before . . ."

"Before this happened," she finished for him.

"Yes."

"It's all right. It was almost like being in a convent. Or a girls' school. Safe and boring."

"No one bothered you there?"

She knew he was referring to the sexual play she had seen with Roxalena in the Sultan's harem.

"No, that was the one advantage to being the hated foreign ikbal. Everyone left me alone."

"Everyone left you alone because I made it known through the khislar that anyone who even approached you would be answerable to me."

Sarah stared at him. "I see."

"I wanted to keep you for myself," he said.

"You did." She ran her hand along the hard line of his thigh, roughened with dark hair. "I guess we have to forgive each other for quite a few things."

"I forgive you for driving me to the brink of madness," he said piously.

"And I forgive you for Fatma," she said promptly.

"Fatma?"

"I think you remember her," Sarah said.

"There's nothing to forgive."

"Kalid, please. You were sleeping with her while I was under house arrest in the harem."

"I was not."

Sarah sat up and glared at him. "Are you going to lie about it now? Memtaz told me you were sending for her. I saw her vest in your room!"

"I recall the circumstances vividly," he said dryly.

"Well?"

"I saw her, yes, and she brought that thing she was embroidering with her and left it behind. But it wasn't sexual. I was consulting her on another matter."

"What?"

"I wanted her to mix a love charm for me."

"A love charm?" Sarah was dumfounded.

"Yes, she was skilled in such things. All the people in her area of the Caucasus study the effects of potions and philtres."

"And poisons. But you don't believe in love charms, do you?"

"I was willing to try anything," he said shortly.

"To win me over?" Sarah asked softly.

"Yes."

"You wanted me that badly?"

"You like to hear me say it, don't you?"

"I do."

"Then yes, I wanted you that badly."

"But Kalid, don't you see how cruel it was to bring Fatma into it? She was in love with you herself, and you were asking her to dream up an elixir to help you win me!"

"I was desperate," he said.

"But that's why she treated me so badly, can't you see that? That's why she eventually poisoned me. You must have driven her wild with jealousy."

"I know I handled it badly. I wasn't thinking clearly. I don't know what else to say."

"Why didn't you tell me what was going on when I saw that piece of her underwear in your room?"

"I was angry, frustrated, and disappointed—not to mention in physical pain. I saw no reason why you shouldn't suffer a little too, kourista."

"I suffered a lot, imagining you entwined with Fatma while I was playing Mah-Jongg with Memtaz in the harem."

"I never touched Fatma, or anyone else, after I met you. You have my word on that."

"Fatma worked very hard to make me believe otherwise. I was completely miserable thinking that you had resumed your affair with her."

"And all I wanted from her was a little piece of magic," he said in reply.

Doreen Owens Malek

Sarah leaned against him and kissed his cheek. "Actually, I think it's very sweet. Consulting her for a love charm, I mean. It's very . . . Turkish."

He closed his eyes. "Yes, my stupidity is *so* charming, so amusing, isn't it?"

"Why, Kalid? Why was it so important to win me? Why did you want me so much?"

He looked down at her, his dark eyes full of feeling. "I don't know. I have learned not to question such things. We here in the East believe in fate."

"Yes, I know. *Kismet.*"

"Why do you say it so scornfully, kourista? Isn't it possible that we were destined for one another? Why did you come so far from your home to wind up in the Sultan's harem? Why were you there at the precise moment I came for my state visit? Don't you ever think about it?"

"I think about it," Sarah admitted.

He kissed her. "Kismet, Sarah. Surrender to it or it will destroy you."

"I surrender," she whispered.

He guided her hand to him and closed his eyes as her fingers encircled him.

"Are you all right?" he said thickly, as she caressed him. "Are you still bleeding?"

"I'm just fine," Sarah said. "Do you want to make love to me again?"

"What do you think?" he said quietly.

She moved across his body to straddle him

286

and said softly, "Show me how to do it this way."

He lifted her hips and eased her onto him. She made an animal sound and fell forward, tucking her head into the curve of his shoulder as he set his cheek against her hair.

"You learn quickly," he said hoarsely, as she moved sinuously in his arms.

"I want you to teach me everything," she replied, running her tongue along his collarbone.

"Everything," he said, and began another lesson.

When Sarah awoke this time, it was evening and the sun was setting. She and Kalid were curled up like puppies under the tree, the darkening sky above them streaked with purple and crimson and gold. She felt sticky and sweaty and in need of another dip in the river.

As she sat up, Kalid's long fingers encircled her wrist.

"Where are you going?" he said.

"Just to rinse off in the river."

He got up and ran his hands through his hair, looking very tall and very male and very nude. Sarah suddenly felt embarrassed, standing there with both of them stark naked, as they had been all day. She ran the few steps to the river and plunged in, gasping as she hit the chilly water. When she raised her head, Kalid was next to her, and he took her in his arms.

"Don't pull back from me," he said softly. "Sex is natural. You can't think back on what we've done and feel skittish about it. There should be no shame."

Sarah clung to him, wondering how he could read her thoughts so accurately. When he took her by the hand and led her back to the riverbank, she followed obediently, looking up at him in the fading light as he handed her items of her clothing.

"Much as I hate to see you get dressed," he said, "it is turning colder and we have to think about getting back."

"Now? It will be dark in an hour."

"Aren't you at all hungry?" he asked, thumbing his hair back from his face. It sprang into ringlets when wet, later drying into thick waves.

"Starving."

"Well, Khan is tied up about two miles from here, and my pack with all the food I brought with me is on his back. If you want anything to eat tonight, we have to find him. We'll go the rest of the way in the morning."

"Can we ride double on the bedouin horse?"

"That's the plan." He handed her the wide-sleeved blouse she'd been wearing when she was kidnapped and then grasped her arm, holding it aloft.

"Your skin looks translucent in this light," he said softly. "Like mother of pearl."

"My real name means 'a pearl'," Sarah replied, buttoning the blouse.

"Your real name?"

"My given name is Margaret Sarah, but from childhood everyone called me Sarah, to distinguish me from my mother. She was Margaret too."

"And so what does 'Sarah' mean?" he inquired, fastening his trousers.

"Gift of God."

"A God-given pearl. I like that." He draped his shirt over his shoulder and put his arm around her, kissing her forehead. "Come along, pearl, it's time to eat."

She walked at his side back to the horse.

Chapter Twelve

"Captured by the bedouins," Roxalena moaned. "Oh, no. What will become of my American friend?"

"Kalid has gone after her," Osman said.

"Are you sure?" Roxalena asked sharply.

"Yes. Turhan Aga was present at the audience Kosem granted to her cousin James, and she told James that her grandson had set off alone to rescue his ikbal. Turhan repeated this to me himself when I met him at the bazaar in Bursa."

"Then Sarah has a chance," Roxalena said with relief. "If anyone can bring her back, Kalid can."

"I thought you didn't like him," Osman said, feeling a twinge of jealousy at her confidence in the other man.

"I didn't want to marry him any more than he wanted to marry me, but I have the utmost respect for his abilities. He's very determined when he wants something." She paused. "And apparently he wants Sarah very much," she added thoughtfully.

"Your friend must be tougher than she looks. She has already survived a poisoning by the Pasha's former favorite."

Roxalena sighed. "Sarah wanted to learn about harem life. I think she knows about it now."

"Turhan said the rumor at Orchid Palace is that Kalid Shah was planning to execute the poisoner and her accomplice in the old-fashioned way, but the valide pashana persuaded him to merely banish them."

"Why would he listen to Kosem?"

Osman shrugged. "Supposedly Kosem told the pasha that Sarah would not like it if he killed them out of hand."

Roxalena nodded. "Sarah would not like it. In America, they have trials about such things, and no one is ever executed on the word of one man."

"What is a trial?"

Roxalena shrugged. "A group of Americans sit in a box and listen while the authorities discuss the case and examine witnesses. Then they decide if the prisoner should be punished or go free."

Osman made a disbelieving face.

"It's true. Sarah told me all about it. She thinks it's a system far superior to ours, and I have to admit, I'd rather trust the judgment of several average Turkish citizens than the whim of a man like my father."

They both drew back as a guard on patrol passed within a few feet of them, his rifle on his shoulder. They held their breath until they heard his footsteps fade into the distance.

"You'd better go," Osman whispered. "I'll see you tomorrow night in the boathouse."

Roxalena stood on tiptoe to kiss his cheek, then drew her feradge over her face. She stepped out of the shadows and slipped onto the path that led through the Garden of the Kadins, heading back to the harem.

"I think you should go to see Secretary Danforth again," Beatrice Woolcott said firmly.

James took another sip of his Boodles gin before replying irritably, "I've told you before, Bea, that man is not going to help me. He is only concerned with not making waves and keeping his job. The last thing he's going to do is buck the local authorities over an insignificant tourist like my cousin Sarah."

"Then what are you going to do?"

"Wait for some news from the valide pashana."

"Do you really think that old woman is going to tell you what's happening? If the pasha wants to keep Sarah, as it appears he does, you won't hear another word even if he does bring her back from the bedouins."

"If you have any other suggestions, Bea, I would certainly like to hear them," James said wearily, draining his drink. "I've already spent three days just getting inside the Orchid Palace, and the only information I was able to obtain is what I've just told you."

Beatrice fell silent, glancing around their parlor as if she might find an idea hidden in one of its corners.

"I'll wait a week and try again," James said, relenting.

Beatrice nodded.

The stillness in the room was overpowering.

"Welcome home," Kosem said, embracing Sarah warmly. "You look very well for someone who has survived such an ordeal. We were so worried about you."

"I'm feeling very well, thank you," Sarah replied, stealing a glance at Kalid, who smiled at her. Sarah colored faintly.

Kosem did not miss the interchange.

"Would you like to have a bath and a rest in the harem?" Kosem asked. "Memtaz is waiting for you."

Sarah nodded.

"I will see you in my quarters after the evening meal," Kalid said to Sarah, who looked at him, and then away, almost shyly.

"Take the ikbal back to the harem," Kalid said to the waiting eunuchs.

He watched Sarah depart the audience room with her escort and then threw himself onto his throne, one leg over the arm of the chair, grinning at Kosem.

"I gather it went well," Kosem said dryly.

"She gave herself to me," he said.

Kosem nodded sagely. "Yes, I can tell. She follows you everywhere with her eyes, touches you as often as she possibly can, and behaves in every way like an initiate wildly in love with her instructor."

He closed his eyes. "I can think of nothing but her."

Kosem withdrew a slip of paper from her capacious sleeve and held it out for him to see.

"What is that?" Kalid asked.

"The Constantinople address of her cousin. He was here while you were gone, and I gave him an audience. I promised to contact him if I had any news of Sarah."

"Give me that," Kalid said sharply. Kosem handed him the scrap of paper. He glanced at it and then tore it up, flinging the bits on the carpet.

"Why did you admit that man to the palace?" Kalid demanded furiously of his grandmother. "He has already sent me a letter through the American embassy, and I replied that I wouldn't be able to see him for some time."

"I was distraught, Kalid! I didn't know if I would ever see either one of you again, and I could understand very well how Sarah's cousin feels. How can you let that poor man go on wondering if she is all right?"

"You've just seen her! Does she look ill or unhappy? Just when I have finally won her, you expect me to bring in this relative who will try to persuade her to leave with him?"

"If she loves you, she will stay."

"Don't be ridiculous. The pull of her old life is very strong. I need time, time to bind her to me, time to make her see that she will have no future without me."

"So you will not tell her about her cousin's visit."

"No. And I forbid you to say anything about it to her."

Kosem opened her mouth.

"I forbid it, do you understand?" Kalid said, rising and shoving his forefinger under her nose.

"I advise against this," Kosem said quietly.

"When I want your advice, I will ask for it," Kalid said tersely. "Now go."

Kosem stood before him regally, staring him down, her raisin eyes boring into his.

"Go and leave me to think," he said, and she obeyed reluctantly, looking back over her shoulder at him.

Kalid saw a fragment of paper on the rug and kicked it away viciously.

Nothing would stand in the way of his life with Sarah.

Nothing.

"Ah, you are so beautiful, mistress. My master will be very pleased."

Sarah was wearing a smock of fine white silk tissue, with wide sleeves and mother-of-pearl buttons down the front, the sleeves and hem edged with gold, her body visible through the gauzy material. Over it, she wore a rose-brocade caftan with a satin girdle of deep rose pink, fastened with an amethyst clasp. A cap of wine velvet embroidered with pearls perched on her hair, which flowed down her back in a silken profusion. Pearl earrings falling from amethyst studs and white kid boots completed the ensemble.

"Such lovely clothes," Memtaz said. "Though I think you will not be wearing them for very long." She giggled.

Sarah smiled and shook her head. Nothing was secret from Memtaz.

"You look so happy, mistress. Why did you resist the Pasha for so long?"

"It's . . . complicated, Memtaz."

"What means complicated?"

"It means that there were many issues involved and I . . . oh, forget it. Just call the eunuchs to take me to the mabeyn."

Kalid was waiting for her in his austere ante-room. When he saw Sarah come through the door, he opened his arms and she flew into them.

"Go, you're dismissed," he said over her shoulder to the servants, who fled, exchanging knowing glances.

"I missed you," Sarah sighed.

Kalid was already unfastening the girdle at her waist. "Why so many clothes?" he asked.

"Memtaz insisted that I be properly dressed," Sarah replied, laughing.

Kalid tossed the girdle and the caftan to the floor, removed her shoes, and began to unbutton the silk shift. As soon as one creamy breast was revealed, he had the nipple in his mouth. He wrestled with the smock for several seconds, shoving it down to her waist to allow him access. Then Sarah gasped as he grabbed the shift by its open neck and ripped it from her body impatiently, flinging the rent garment aside.

He lifted her quickly into his arms and carried her into his bedchamber. He set her on his sleeping couch and tore off his shirt, but before he could undress any further Sarah stood up and put her arms around him.

"Let me love you," she whispered, kissing his chest, then the line of dark hair that bisected his torso, disappearing under the waistband of his trousers. He leaned back against the wall next to the bed as she worked her way down his body, finally kneeling before him and undoing his trousers. His head fell back, his eyes closed, his fists clenched on his thighs, as she took him in her mouth, acting on instinct rather than knowledge. She caressed him until he was groaning, his breath coming in short bursts, his body so tense she could feel an immediate reaction to her slightest movement. Finally, he sank his fingers into her hair and pulled her head back, his chest heaving.

"I want to be inside you. Now," he gasped, lifting her bodily and putting her on the bed. He stepped out of his pants and joined her, turning her face-down and embracing her from the rear.

"Kalid?" she said questioningly, and he said, "Follow me," as he pushed her knees up gently and then slipped his hands under her, lifting her to him. In the next second he entered her, and Sarah closed her eyes, transfixed with pleasure. He was so deep inside her that she seemed to feel him at the mouth of her womb.

"All right?" he gasped, moving, taking her with him.

Sarah moaned helplessly in response.

"Do you want me to stop?"

Sarah whimpered in wordless protest. Then, "Don't stop," she managed to say.

He didn't, and by the time they were finished, they were both covered with a light film of sweat, exhausted like long-distance swimmers at the goal line. They lay supine for several minutes as their breathing slowed and heartbeats returned to normal. Then Kalid rose and pulled on his pants, pushing open the doors to the terrace. Sarah listened for several seconds but heard nothing further. She got up and slipped into Kalid's discarded shirt, since her silk shift was in tatters on the floor. She followed him outside and found him leaning over the stone balustrade, looking down at the tiled courtyard below him.

"Kalid?" she said, and he turned to look at her, holding out one arm to embrace her. She came to him and he enfolded her, standing with his arms crossed over her breasts and her head tucked under his chin, her back against his chest.

"What are you doing out here?" she asked. "It's so chilly after sundown."

"Desert climate," he responded. "Hot all day, cold at night. Do you think you can get used to it?"

"I'm already used to it. Boston isn't exactly paradise, you know. It's humid in the summer, freezing in the winter."

"Do you miss it?"

"Not anymore."

Kalid closed his eyes in relief at her response. He rubbed his hands up and down her arms, saying, "What is this thing you are wearing?"

"Your shirt. You didn't leave me much else."

"You're trembling, kourista. Should we go in now? Are you chilled?"

"No. It's just . . . I don't think I have recovered yet. My legs are still weak."

"I like to make you weak, kourista," he said, his lips moving in her hair.

She was silent for so long that he finally asked, "What's wrong, Sarah?"

She shrugged, but when he said quietly, "Tell me," she responded by turning around and looking up at him.

"You've made many women feel the way I did tonight. I can't help thinking about all of your past lovers, wondering how I fit in with them."

"None of them were like you."

"But surely they were . . . better at it?" she asked.

"Better at what?" he said teasingly, but when she didn't smile, he said, "No, they weren't."

"But they were trained, skilled in the art of love . . ."

"And that's exactly why it's so different with you. Can you imagine what it does to me to know that I'm the first man who has touched you this way? That I'm the first man to receive your intimate caresses?"

"But that's exactly what I mean, Kalid. I don't know what I'm doing."

"Yes, you do. Desire guides you, and desire is the best teacher of all."

"You're the best teacher of all," Sarah said, and stood on tiptoe to kiss him lightly on the mouth.

"That's because I've never wanted anyone the way I want you," he said simply, pressing her to him fiercely.

She relaxed into his arms, and it was several seconds before he realized that she was laughing.

"What's so funny?" he said, holding her off to look at her. The oil lanterns at the corners of the terrace cast flickering shadows on her face.

"I was thinking about the first night I was here, after you took me from the Sultan's harem. I was so afraid of you when I was brought to see you." She lifted a lock of lustrous black hair from his brow and stroked it into place.

"You didn't seem afraid. As I recall, you slapped me."

"It was an act."

"You were very convincing. I thought you hated me."

"I never hated you, Kalid. I wanted to, which is a very different thing."

"And why did you want to hate me, Miss Margaret Sarah Woolcott of Boston?" he asked.

"Because of the way you got me here. Because of the way you made me feel."

"I made you feel the strong urge to kill me," he said smilingly, swinging her in his arms.

"Sometimes. But more often you made me feel that I would melt if you touched me."

"And that scared you?"

"Of course."

"Why 'of course'? Some women would be thrilled to have such a reaction to a man."

"A man who had drugged and kidnapped them?"

"I didn't kidnap you. I purchased you, according to the practice of my country."

"Well, it's not the practice of *my* country. Can't you understand that I was horrified to feel myself so drawn to a man who had behaved in such a primitive way?"

"And now you no longer think me primitive?" he asked, looking down at her.

"Now I think of you as my lover," Sarah said and rubbed her face on his bare shoulder, luxuriating in the scent and texture of his warm, satiny skin. She ran her tongue along the line of his collarbone, then kissed the hollow of his throat.

"Keep doing that and there will be no more conversation," he said tightly.

"I think we've talked enough, don't you?" she replied, running her hand under the waistband of his pants.

He sucked in his breath. "I agree," he said, and taking her by the hand, he led her back inside.

"So you will be staying with us, Sarah?" Kosem said, puffing on her pipe.

"I can't imagine leaving Kalid now," Sarah replied. They were sitting in Kosem's suite as the older woman went through one of her many jewelry boxes, deciding which of the sparkling items no longer interested her. They could then be passed on to the other women of the harem.

"Because he rescued you from the gypsies?"

"Because I want to be with him all the time."

"But what about your family?" Kosem asked carefully, not looking at Sarah.

"My cousin James obviously doesn't care about me," Sarah replied sadly, thinking about the note from Roxalena brought to her by the bundle woman. "I have been gone for some time, and there's been no word from him. I guess I should forget about my past and make a new life here."

Kosem said nothing, raising her eyes.

"Why are you looking at me that way?" Sarah said. "You've been trying to persuade me to stay from the moment I arrived."

"It's true that I want you to remain with Kalid and produce an heir," Kosem said.

"So?"

Kosem didn't answer, merely held up a diamond clip for Sarah's inspection.

Sarah shook her head.

Kosem tossed the clip onto the discard pile. "If you knew you were missed at home, would it make a difference?" Kosem said casually.

Sarah eyed her narrowly. "What are you getting at?" she asked suspiciously.

"Getting at?"

"What do you want to know?" Sarah translated.

Kosem shrugged. "What about your job?"

"When I didn't show up for the start of the new school year, I think the school board figured out that they had to hire somebody else," Sarah said dryly.

"What is the school board?"

"Never mind about that. Why are you asking me all these questions?"

Kosem stood abruptly, setting the jewel box aside. "Isn't it time for you to dress for your riding lesson? My grandson will be waiting for you."

Sarah rose also, more slowly. "I suppose so," she said, still wondering what the wily old lady had on her mind.

"Go, then," Kosem said, making a shooing motion.

Sarah left, and as soon as she was gone the valide pashana summoned one of the eunuchs from the hall.

"Send Turhan Aga to me in the pasha's audience room," she said to him.

When the captain of the halberdiers arrived, Kosem said to him briskly, "Turhan, I want you to take this letter to the address I have written on the front. It's in Constantinople." She withdrew an envelope from her hanging sleeve.

"Constantinople, mistress?" Turhan said. It was some distance away.

"Yes, and I want you to take it yourself. Don't send one of your men, and don't tell anyone else where you are going."

"Including the pasha?"

"Especially the pasha."

Turhan looked worried. "Mistress, I cannot take such a big responsibility. . . ."

"I will take the responsibility."

"How shall I explain my absence?"

"I will explain it, I will handle everything. I would trust this mission to no one but you, Turhan. Now go. I want you to leave immediately."

Turhan accepted the envelope and bowed his way out of the room.

Kosem watched his exit with a concerned expression, lacing her fingers tightly.

She didn't know if she had made the right decision. Kalid planned to conceal the truth from Sarah; he didn't want her to know that her cousin had been trying to see her. But Kosem's respect and affection for Sarah had grown over the time they had known each other; as much as she wanted Sarah to stay, she found that she could not be a party to this deception. Sarah should be able to make her decision based on all the facts. If the knowledge that her family was pursuing her persuaded her to go back to Boston because she still had a life there, then it was in the stars that she should leave. Kalid was a man desperately in love, willing to do anything to keep his woman with him, but Kosem saw the situation clearly. Sarah deserved to be treated like an adult making a decision based on all the facts, not like a child whose life had to be organized for her.

Kosem stood and folded her arms into her sleeves. Her hands were trembling. If Kalid found out what she had done, and Sarah left as a result of it, his wrath would be terrible. Even his long-standing affection for his grandmother would not bar him from punishing her, and his word was the final one in Bursa.

But Kosem still felt a curious satisfaction in taking action. From birth, all decisions had been made for her by men, and Sarah had shown her that there was a different way to live. As much as she shook her head and chided the younger woman for her independence, Kosem had come to admire it.

With this action, she had adopted some of it for herself.

Kalid watched as Sarah approached the jump, then called out, "Show some confidence, kourista. The horse can tell if you're afraid to run with him."

Ousta ran at the obstacle and then pulled up short, dodging to the side and running around it. The horse slowed to a walk and then trotted to a stop next to Kalid.

"I'll never be able to do it," Sarah said, sighing as Kalid lifted her down to the ground and handed the reins to a groom.

"Yes, you will. You've only been riding a short while and already you want to take the highest jump in the paddock. You must be patient, Sarah. It takes time to learn any skill." He put his arm around her shoulder and hugged her to him.

"I didn't think I would like it this much," she admitted.

"Riding?" he said, arching one black brow.

She dropped her head to his shoulder. "Speaking of new skills," she murmured.

"Yes?"

"I think I'd like to practice."

"Practice what?" he said, grinning.

"Don't be obtuse, Kalid," she said, dragging him by the hand toward the barn.

"Obtuse? Is that an American word?"

Sarah pulled him through the double wooden doors and said to the guards in Turkish, "Don't let anyone come in here unless it's an extreme emergency."

The guards looked at Kalid, who nodded.

"You're getting very good at giving orders," he said to her, laughing as the horses stamped in their stalls and a startled groom's boy looked up from polishing a saddle as they entered.

"Go outside. Ousta needs to be rubbed down and watered," Kalid said to the boy, who bowed and fled.

Sarah helped Kalid bar the door from the inside. Then she flung herself on him and tore at the buttons of his shirt.

"Where is shy Sarah?" he said teasingly, as she pulled the shirttails loose from his pants. "Where is that oh-so-proper New England miss?" He held her loosely as she undressed him, enjoying her eagerness.

"She's dead," Sarah replied, shoving aside the material of his shirt and kissing his chest, tonguing the flat nipples surrounded by dense, dark hair. "We buried her in the bedouin hills."

Kalid stood still as she pulled the sleeves off his arms and tossed the shirt aside.

He could only hope that was the truth.

She reached for the buttons of his fly, and he stayed her hand. "Let me," he said. "You always fumble with it."

"My hands shake," she said.

"And why do your hands shake?" he asked rhetorically, taking one of them and placing it inside the opening he had created. She touched him and he closed his eyes.

"Where?" he said thickly.

Sarah looked around and saw an empty stall. "There," she said, nodding toward it.

He grabbed a horse blanket and spread it on the straw, then tumbled her onto the makeshift bed. In seconds he had disposed of her riding blouse and split skirt, flinging them aside and pulling her to him.

"I can never seem to get enough of you," he said, yanking her chemise down to her waist and pressing his face to her breasts, his mouth busy. His free hand crept up her hip and over her thigh, finding the secret place between her legs that drove her mad with pleasure. She yearned toward him, gasping as he caressed her.

"Don't make me wait," she whispered, pulling him on top of her, reaching for him greedily, feeling him pulse in her hand.

"Tell me what you want," he said, moaning as she guided him into her. She wrapped her legs around his hips, but he held back.

"Tell me," he said. "I need to hear you say it."

She whispered in his ear, and he entered her forcefully at the same time.

"Yes," he said hoarsely. "Yes, I will."

After that they forgot everything but each other.

"What's that sound?" Sarah said drowsily, rubbing her cheek on Kalid's chest.

"Mmmnh," Kalid said. He was almost asleep.

"Can't you hear that? It sounds like water dripping."

Kalid listened obediently. "It's the horse trough," he said. "It's just under that window behind us."

Sarah raised her head. "I don't know how I'm going to walk past all those people outside, Kalid. They must know what we've been doing in here."

Kalid chuckled. "You weren't worried about that earlier, as I recall."

She punched his shoulder. "Don't make fun of me."

"I'm not making fun of you. They're servants. They're trained to keep their mouths shut."

"But what will they think?"

"Who cares what they think?" Accustomed to the presence of servants, he had long ago ceased to see them except when he wanted something.

"Send them all away."

He stared at her. "What?"

309

"You heard me, Kalid. Send them someplace before I have to go out there."

Muttering to himself, he got up and pulled on his clothes, then unbarred the door. She saw him go out and heard his voice issuing commands in rapid succession. Seconds later, he returned, shaking his head.

"You are ridiculous, kourista."

"Yes, I know. Just chalk it up to false modesty."

"Everyone at the palace knows you are the ikbal. They have already figured out what we do together."

"Not five feet away in a horse barn."

"It was you who wanted to come in here!" he said, exasperated, his hands on his hips.

"Stop being so logical," Sarah said, irritated. She was throwing on her clothes, pulling pieces of hay out of her hair and turning up her nose at the horsey smell she had recently acquired.

"Just when I think you have gotten over all that Victorian nonsense, you have an episode like this," he said, watching as she stepped into her skirt.

"Blame it on my Puritan ancestors," she said.

"Who?"

"The Puritans came from England and settled in Massachusetts about two hundred years ago. They were very strict about . . ." She stopped.

"Sex?" he suggested.

"Among other things," she said, buttoning her blouse.

"And I suppose you have inherited those tendencies?" he said, amused.

"Not inherited. It's in the atmosphere, in the way you are raised. Like you growing up knowing that you would be the pasha one day and everyone in Bursa would have to obey you."

"I fail to see what that has to do with your attack of shyness before a bunch of servants."

"Well, there's a connection, believe me," Sarah said, shaking out her hair.

"You must learn to do whatever you want, whenever and wherever you want to do it."

"That sounds like the philosophy of a spoiled child," Sarah retorted.

"Or a pashana," he said.

She looked at him. "What?"

"Never mind. Come to me this evening, and I will tell you all about it." He lifted her hand to his lips and kissed it lingeringly. "My finance minister will be waiting for me by now, so I must go. I will see you tonight."

He left, and the eunuchs escorted Sarah back to the harem, where Memtaz was in a lather. She was going through Sarah's garments, pulling open drawers and trunks.

"Memtaz, what is going on?" Sarah said from the doorway of her suite.

Memtaz whirled to face her and bowed. Sarah waited for her to straighten up, resigned to the fact that she would never break the Circassian woman of the habit.

"I must make you ready for a special evening,

mistress," she said breathlessly. "I was looking for the blue-and-silver caftan that looks so well on you."

"What special evening?"

"I received a message that you are to present yourself in the mabeyn, dressed for a state occasion."

"A state occasion?" Sarah said. What was this? Why hadn't Kalid said anything about it?

"Yes, mistress."

"Memtaz, I'll wear the caftan but just with a shift. No earrings, no girdle, no cap. I'm tired of wearing twenty pounds of clothes every time I get dressed."

Memtaz looked distressed.

"All right, we'll compromise," Sarah said, relenting. The little maid felt she was not doing her job if Sarah didn't leave the harem beribboned like a birthday present. "You dress me, and then I'll take five items off," Sarah added.

"Five?" Memtaz said.

"Yes."

Memtaz nodded happily.

By the time Sarah had her evening meal and had bathed and dressed, it was time for her to visit Kalid. As per agreement, she had disposed of the jewelry and the ornate girdle Memtaz had selected, but she was still gaudy enough to satisfy the maid that she was satisfactorily attired. She left the harem wondering what Kalid had planned for the night, but he gave no sign as he admitted her to his suite and dismissed the servants.

Sarah watched him turn down the oil lamps and then face her. He was wearing Western clothes, as he almost always did now when he was with her, resulting in a curious case of turnabout—she was dressed like an Eastern concubine and he like a London playboy in tweed trousers and an ivory lisle shirt. He gestured for her to sit down and then presented her with a scrolled box sealed at the clasp with yellow wax.

"What is this?" she asked.

He sat at her feet and reclined on one elbow. "Open it," he said.

Sarah obeyed, thinking that he was always giving her presents. It was difficult not to get used to it.

The box contained a pair of ornate velvet slippers, trimmed with gold thread and studded with precious gems. She picked up one shoe and studied it, the crystals sparkling in the lamplight.

"They're very beautiful. Are they for me?"

"Of course. I had them made. They were measured from your kid boots."

"Thank you."

"Do you understand the significance of this gift?"

"Uh, no."

"That's what I thought. I'm asking you to marry me."

Sarah stared at him, speechless. "By giving me a pair of shoes?" she finally said stupidly.

He smiled. "It is the custom."

"Why?"

"It signifies that I will be supplying all of your necessaries for the rest of your life. The custom demands slippers for all the members of your household. I had a pair made for Memtaz too."

Sarah sat holding the shoes, looking down at him.

"What is your answer?" he said.

Sarah was silent.

"You are still free to go back to America, if that is your choice," he said quietly. "I am asking you to stay here in Bursa with me and be my wife."

Sarah bent to touch his face, and he pulled her down into his arms.

"Can you leave me?" he asked, cradling her tenderly against his shoulder. "Can you, kourista?"

"No."

"Then why do you hesitate?"

"It's just such a complete commitment, abandoning a former life for a completely different new one. I will never see my home again, will I?"

"Perhaps you will. We can travel."

"That's not all, Kalid."

"What else?"

"I don't want to be the pashana."

"I'm afraid there's no choice about that."

"But all these people bowing and scraping to me, it makes me nervous. It was bad enough as the ikbal, but as your wife . . ."

"I could tell them all to spit on you if it makes you feel any better," he said dryly.

"I don't think that's very funny."

"Sorry."

"Can't we just go on as we were?" Sarah asked. "I've been so happy, haven't you?"

"Do you really want to spend your time here as a concubine?" he demanded.

"No, I suppose not."

"Do you want to see me take another wife? I will have to eventually, for the safety of the title."

"I could never stand to see you marry anyone else," she said quietly.

"Then you have no choice. I want you to be my wife and have my children. I want you to be the mother of the heir," he said.

The thought of having Kalid's children gave her butterflies in her stomach. What would they look like? Would they have his slender body, dark eyes, and lustrous black hair? Would they be as beautiful as their father?

"What are you thinking?" he said.

"About the future."

"I want you to share it with me," he said.

"I never thought, when I met you, that we would be having this conversation," she said.

"I did."

"You knew you wanted to marry me the moment you saw me?" she asked.

"I knew you would be important in my life. More than that it was impossible to say."

"I guess I felt the same, but I didn't want to admit it," she said softly.

"Then your answer is yes?" he asked, taking her hand and holding it to his cheek.

"Yes, Kalid. I'll marry you."

He kissed her forehead lightly. "I'll make the arrangements right away," he said.

"What arrangements?"

He smiled. "I am still the pasha of this district, and I must have a formal wedding so that my heir will be recognized."

"What does a formal wedding involve?"

"Well, let me think. You will arrive at the Orchid Palace heavily veiled and dressed in a red silk wedding gown. Then you will come through a silk tunnel stretching from your carriage to the door. Kosem will lead you to the bridal throne set up on a dais. Once I lift the veil and see you, I will throw coins at the spectators to signify my acceptance of you as my bride."

"Why do you have to accept me?"

"In marriages among commoners, the husband often does not see the wife until the wedding day."

"Oh, no, that's awful. You mean he can reject her if he doesn't like the way she looks?"

"Yes."

"But the wife has no such option."

"No."

"Lovely custom. What else?"

"Then there is a feast, and after it you are delivered to my room by your male relatives. Since you have none here, your escort will be a selection of my halberdiers."

"And then?"

"Then you enter my bed from the foot to signify that I am your master," he said, grinning.

"We'll skip that part. Anything else?"

"In the morning, we display the bloody sheets from my balcony," he said casually.

Sarah stared at him. "We might have a little trouble with that one," she finally said.

He laughed. "You *were* a virgin bride, kourista. We just didn't wait for the formal ceremony, and that, to me, is a matter of no consequence."

"Your subjects might not see it that way."

"They won't know. No man touched you before me, and that is what counts."

"So what do we do about the sheets?"

"We'll kill a rooster and then smear the animal's blood on the bed linen."

Sarah was speechless, appalled. "I hope that's a joke," she eventually managed to whisper.

"No. It's often done. Virgins are not as plentiful as they once were."

Sarah closed her eyes. "Kalid, are you making all of this up?" she asked, almost hopefully.

"I am not. In the rural areas, if the bloody

sheet is not displayed, the husband can repudiate the wife."

"What? Again?"

"Yes."

"It's so . . ."

"Barbaric?" he said, watching her face.

"I know you don't like that word."

"But that's part of my attraction for you, isn't it?"

Sarah glanced at him but didn't reply.

"I'm not exactly what you might encounter back home at a tea dance given by the Daughters of the American Renovation."

"Revolution," she corrected him.

"Whatever. You know what I mean."

Sarah looked away from him. She did. "How do you know about tea dances?" she said.

"I attended a few of them at Oxford," he replied, sighing exaggeratedly.

"I gather you found them boring."

"I found them very . . . Western. Lots of chit-chat and not much action."

"You must have caused quite a sensation among the finger sandwiches and canapes."

"I was a curiosity. I think some of the young ladies expected me to arrive with a knife clasped in my teeth."

"Or they were hoping," Sarah said under her breath.

"What?"

"It doesn't matter. When will the ceremony take place?"

"In three days."

"Three days! That doesn't give me much time."

"To do what?"

"Well, I have to get ready."

"And what exactly would that involve, kourista?" he asked, amused.

Sarah considered it. There wasn't a single person for her to invite, she had no personal effects other than those at the palace, and everything she needed was here.

"Thinking about it?" she offered lamely.

"I understand. Brides-to-be always have their dreams. What are yours?"

"To be with you forever," she said promptly.

"That I can guarantee."

"To have children as handsome and brave and smart as their father," she added.

He didn't say anything, merely took her chin in his hand and ran his thumb lightly over her lips, his dark eyes lambent in the softly lit room.

"And to be your best friend," she added.

"You *are* my best friend," he said, his voice catching on the second word. He eased her down onto the carpet and began to undo the outfit Memtaz had so carefully assembled.

"Do you think you will ever tire of me, want to send me back to Boston?" she asked, running her fingers through his hair.

"You'll be too old to travel by then," he replied, bending his head to kiss her.

*   *   *

"Oh, mistress, there never was such a lovely bride," Memtaz said, clasping her hands together and staring at Sarah's reflection in the pier glass.

Sarah looked too, unable to believe that the woman in the mirror was herself. She was dressed in a long-sleeved, high-necked silk gown with frog closures of golden thread, embroidered all over with golden flowers and cinched with a gold mesh belt. A diamond tiara held a short veil of silk gauze trimmed with gold. Fastened to it was the *abayah*, or long veil, and her earbobs were golden circlets with huge, dangling pearls. Over it all she would wear a red velvet feradge when she traveled by coach to enter the palace by the Carriage House gate. It lay on her sleeping couch, a reminder that in an hour she would be the new pashana of Bursa.

"I'm so glad you'll be able to attend the ceremony," Sarah said to Memtaz.

The servant nodded happily. "The pasha said all may come. And Dr. Shakoz said the khislar is well enough to be up for a few hours as well."

"Good." It wouldn't seem like an Orchid Palace event without Achmed.

"Is there anything else you needed?" Memtaz asked.

"No. Please tell Kosem that I'm ready."

Memtaz went to get the valide pashana, who would accompany Sarah to the coach, and thence to the throne room, where Kalid was already waiting.

The pasha paced back and forth in front of his throne, oblivious to the crowd of his subjects who waited for the ceremony to begin, to the halberdiers and janissaries who stood in attendance, to the khislar who occupied a chair by the door, permitted to sit in the presence of the pasha because of his injury. Kalid looked repeatedly at only one spot—the door through which Sarah would enter the throne room to become his wife.

It seemed an eternity before she finally appeared, standing tall and regal behind Kosem, who was also outfitted in her finest, looking like a tiny doll. He watched as the women walked toward him and Sarah took her place at his side. He smiled tenderly and lifted the abayah, looking down into her face.

At the same moment, Turhan Aga stepped out of the crowd and banged his halberd on the floor.

Kalid whirled on him furiously, growling something in guttural Turkish.

Turhan said something in ancient, ceremonial language that Sarah couldn't understand, but there was a murmur in the crowd, and Kalid left Sarah's side abruptly, moving rapidly through the assembled people to the door.

"What is it?" Sarah said to Kosem, whose expression was wooden. "What's wrong?"

321

Doreen Owens Malek

"Someone objects to the marriage," Kosem said evenly. "It is our custom that the ceremony should not take place until the grievance is aired, even if the groom is our pasha."

Kosem did not seem surprised by the turn of events, and Sarah said to her, "Do you know something about this?"

Kosem made no reply, and then Sarah was stunned to see her cousin James appear at the entrance to the throne room. As she watched, aghast, Kalid made a gesture and two halberdiers seized her cousin and held him fast.

"Don't worry, Sarah," James yelled over the excited babble of the wedding guests. "You don't have to marry this man!"

"Take him to the dungeon!" Kalid called, and the halberdiers began to drag James away.

"You can't stop me!" James shouted. "The American embassy knows I'm here! I have come to take Sarah home."

Chapter Thirteen

Sarah ran up to Kalid and seized his arm. "If you have him arrested, I'll never speak to you again," she said tightly. "I want to hear what he has to say."

Kalid jerked his arm away from her, but gestured for the guards to release James. They did so, and James shook himself, then straightened his coat and tie, his eyes on his Sarah.

"Clear the room of the guests," Kalid said harshly to the janissaries. "There will be no wedding today."

They all stood awkwardly as the people filed out, and then Sarah said, in as normal a tone as she could manage, "Just what exactly is going on here?"

"I've been trying to get in to see you since you disappeared from the Sultan's harem, Sarah," James said in a rush. "I finally sent a letter to the pasha here, and he replied that he would be busy for a month and unable to grant me an audience."

Sarah looked at Kalid in astonishment, but he avoided her gaze, his expression grim.

"Then I tried to bribe my way inside the palace, and when the valide pashana heard about it, she sent for me."

Kalid turned to glare at his grandmother, who met his gaze defiantly.

"She told me that you had been kidnapped by the bedouins, and that the pasha had gone after you. She promised that if you came back here, she would get word to me."

A vein in Kalid's temple was throbbing as he looked at the old lady. Sarah moved to Kosem's side and took her hand, staring malevolently at Kalid.

He looked away.

"A few days ago, I got a note from the valide pashana saying that you were in Bursa, and well, and planning to marry the pasha today," James went on. "I left Constantinople and got here as soon as I could. This morning I sent a message to the pasha saying that I wanted to see him immediately. He refused an audience and barred me from the palace."

Sarah's eyes filled with tears of rage. She couldn't even look at Kalid.

"How did you get in?" she whispered to James.

"The captain of the halberdiers was honor-bound to obey the custom of admitting anyone who objects to a wedding to the ceremony. That's why I'm here."

Sarah looked at Turhan Aga, who was staring morosely at the floor. Not even for the pasha would he shirk his duty. He truly was an honest man.

"James, I will be with you in a few minutes," Sarah said calmly. "Kosem, would you see that my cousin is made comfortable while he waits for me? I would like to speak to Kalid alone."

Kosem looked at Kalid, who said flatly to the khislar, "Achmed, make sure that the ikbal's wishes are fulfilled. Kosem will entertain our guest. The rest of you may go."

When they were alone, Sarah said to Kalid, "How could you do such a thing? How could you?"

He looked back at her stonily, saying nothing.

"You allowed me to think that my family didn't care about me! You allowed me to think that I had been abandoned to whatever fate befell me here. You lied to me!"

"I didn't lie. I merely didn't tell you about your cousin's inquiries," he finally said.

"It's the same thing!" She felt the fullness of more tears in her throat and fought them back. "When you told me I didn't have to sleep with you in payment for my rescue from the bedouins, I thought you had changed. When you said I was still free to go home to Boston when we got back here, that it was my choice to stay with you, again I thought you had changed. That's why I decided to marry you. I assumed you had learned to respect the feelings, and the free will, of someone other than yourself. Now I find out that all along you knew James was trying to contact me, and you never even told me. You haven't changed, Kalid, you were merely saying what you knew I wanted to hear in order to pacify me."

He looked away from her.

"Can you give me one reason why you didn't tell me?" she persisted.

"I thought if you assumed no one outside the palace was looking for you, then you would be more likely to stay with me," he said tonelessly.

"In other words, you tried to remove the element of choice," she said.

He did not deny it.

"Kalid, maybe it's too much to expect from someone who was raised to believe that he is superior to everyone else, but I should have a choice. What you want is not the only thing that matters. I matter too. Didn't you ever consider the implications of your silence on me? I knew James had received a message that I was here, and I thought he didn't care enough about me to pursue it!"

"I care about you," he said shortly. "That should be sufficient. And who sent your cousin James a message that you were here? Was it Kosem?"

"Leave Kosem out of this. It's between you and me. It's about respecting me as a mature human being and not thinking of me as property to be managed or a child to be controlled. How can I marry someone who views me as a chattel?"

For the first time, he looked alarmed. "What are you saying?" he demanded, his eyes wary.

"I'm saying that I can't marry you," Sarah replied, crying openly now, removing the tiara from her head and setting it on a table. "I'm leaving with my cousin James."

"What are you talking about?" Kalid said, seizing her arm in a viselike grip. "You love me, I know you do. You never would have slept with me if you didn't. How can you even think of leaving?"

"I didn't say I didn't love you, I said I'm not going to marry you. Now will you please let me go?"

His hold on her arm tightened.

"What are you going to do, Kalid?" Sarah asked wearily. "Throw me in the dungeon, threaten to whip me—or Memtaz—again? Tell me that you'll line up a row of draftees and shoot them in the head if I don't do as you say? No matter what you do, or claim you will do, you can't force me into the mold of the compliant little sex toy you so obviously want."

"That's not what I want," he said bitterly, his fingers biting into her flesh.

"Oh, no?"

"No, Sarah. No man in his right mind would get involved with you just for sex; you are far too much trouble. I have a whole harem full of women willing and eager to warm my bed, but it is my sorry fate that I am besotted with you."

"Then that's our shared misfortune." She tugged, and he finally released her so suddenly that she stumbled. She took off the rest of the gold rings and bangles she was wearing and set them next to the tiara.

"You are really going?" He seemed to be having some trouble absorbing it; after all of his time with Sarah, for it to come to this just when they were about to be married was an incomprehensible blow.

"Yes. I'll go back to the harem to change. And I hope you're honorable enough not to punish Kosem or interfere with my cousin's business in this country after I'm gone. They did what they thought was right, and I hope that when you calm down you will understand that."

He said nothing.

"I'll leave anything else I have in the ikbal's suite," Sarah said, depositing her earrings in the pile of jewelry. "I want to go just as I came, with nothing."

"Except memories," he said.

She started to walk away from him, barely able to see for the tears in her eyes.

"I'll haunt you," he said, his voice breaking.

Sarah turned to face him one last time, dressed in his wedding day finery, looking as handsome as he had on the first day she saw him.

"No, you won't. You'll miss me."

She ran out of the room and he stared after her, shaken to the roots of his soul.

"So he wasn't forcing you to marry him?" James asked incredulously.

"No. I know this is difficult for you to understand, James, but I love him. I just can't be the kind of wife he really wants. He doesn't see that now, but maybe he will, in time."

James looked at this woman he had known all his life and felt as if he were staring at a stranger. They were waiting in the Carriage House for the escort to take them off the Orchid Palace grounds. Sarah had said painful good-byes to Memtaz and Kosem and was now dressed in her split skirt and riding blouse, the only things she was taking with her. Her tear-stained face was sad, but resolute.

She had not seen Kalid again since she left him in the throne room.

"But he kidnapped you, Sarah. He paid the Sultan for you and drugged you and spirited you away in the dark of night!"

"That's the way it began, yes. And I was as outraged as you are about it, at first. But after I got to know him . . . well, he can be quite

329

different from what you saw today."

"He's very handsome," James said. "In the Western way, I mean. I was surprised when I saw him. I suppose that contributed to your feelings for him."

Sarah sighed. "The situation is . . . complex, James. I just know that preventing me from hearing that you were trying to find me was unforgivable."

"He did it because he wanted to keep you with him."

"His reasons don't excuse his behavior. And it wasn't just this incident, there's a whole pattern that I thought he had abandoned where I was concerned, but I was wrong. He once threatened to whip a friend of mine, the servant assigned to me at the Palace, when I wouldn't do something he wanted."

"He threatened to whip a servant to get *you* to do what he wanted?"

"Yes."

"He understood you very well."

Sarah nodded resignedly.

"I just don't see how you can go back to Boston and resume your old life after this experience," James said.

"I probably can't. I've changed too much."

"I don't know if you'll still have your job."

Sarah looked at him in surprise. She hadn't even thought about that.

"I wrote the school board after you disappeared and said that you had been . . . unavoidably detained," James said.

"That's one way of putting it."

"They wrote back and said that if you returned by the spring semester, they might still have a place for you."

Sarah put her hand on his shoulder. "James, thank you for everything that you have done for me."

He reached up and patted her hand. "Bea will be so glad to see you. She's been very worried."

"James, maybe we'd better not tell her about the wedding or my relationship with Kalid. I don't think she'll understand, and I don't want to upset her."

James nodded.

Turhan Aga appeared in the doorway. "The coach is waiting to take you to the train station, Miss Sarah. The next train for Constantinople is in two hours."

"Thank you, Turhan." She and James both rose.

"Say good-bye to the khislar for me," she said to Turhan.

"I will." He took her hand and held it to his lips. "We will all miss you," he added. "Many women come and go from the harem, but none as memorable as you."

Sarah smiled at him. "What a lovely thing to say."

He withdrew an object from his tunic pocket and handed it to her. "From Memtaz."

It was an icon of one of the Russian saints,

intricately carved, the border inlaid with bits of colored glass. "For good luck, she said," Turhan added.

Sarah closed her fingers around it. "I will need it."

Turhan nodded and opened the door to the coach lane. Sarah looked around the room briefly, trying to memorize it. She would never forget this place, or the people she had met here.

"James, I'm ready to go," she said finally, and he walked at her side through the door.

"Would you like a cup of tea, dear?" Beatrice said. "I'll bring it over to you."

"I'm not an invalid, Bea. I can get it for myself." Sarah rose, pouring from the pot on the trolley in the Woolcott sitting room, and then took the china cup back to her seat. It felt strange to be wearing her own clothes once more. She had never realized before how confining they were; the stays of her corset pinched and the high stiff collar of her dress almost immobilized her neck.

Harem clothes were much looser, more sensual, and she found that she missed them.

"What are you thinking, Sarah?" Beatrice said.

Sarah shrugged.

"Don't dwell on that experience. Try to put it out of your mind," Bea added.

"I am trying."

Bea stirred sugar into her tea and said quietly, "If there's something you want to talk about, I'm here to listen."

"Thank you."

"Would you like to speak to our minister? There's a Christian church here, founded for the European colonials, and I'm sure Dr. Hastings would be happy to give you some time."

"I'll think about it."

There was a long pause before Bea said, "You seem so sad, dear. I wish I could help you."

"You are helping, just by being here and giving me a place to stay until I can book passage back home."

"Was it awful?" Bea finally said, looking at her directly for the first time that day.

"No, it wasn't."

"But weren't you . . . violated?"

"I wasn't raped, if that's what you mean."

"But you were in the harem, weren't you?"

"Yes."

"But isn't that the purpose of the harem, to provide bedmates for the Pasha?"

"Yes, but he didn't force me."

"You mean he didn't choose you?"

"He chose me, but I was willing." There, it was out.

Bea colored slightly. "Oh. I see."

"James hasn't told you very much about what happened to me there."

"No."

"I asked him not to, but it seems you want to

333

know about it. I was about to marry the Pasha of Bursa when James finally was able to see me."

"Marry him!" Beatrice was stunned.

"Yes."

"What, in some barbaric rite?"

"In a wedding ceremony, the Ottoman version of one. But when I found out that my intended husband had let me think that James wasn't interested in finding me, I realized that there was no real future for us."

Beatrice was silent, unable to think of a reply.

"I know you're shocked, Beatrice. I wasn't going to tell you any of this, as I said, but it's obvious that you are curious and I would rather you know exactly what happened than imagine things far worse than the reality."

"Do you want to go back to him?" Bea finally said.

"Every minute," Sarah replied grimly.

"Then why don't you?" Bea asked, surprising Sarah.

"Because nothing has changed. I thought it had, I thought I had helped him to see things differently, but I was wrong. I can't spend my life with a man who views me as property, property to be hoarded, to be coveted and hidden lest someone take it away."

"That's the way they all are here," Bea said wearily. "Haven't you learned that?"

"Yes, I suppose you're right. His upbringing

was just too difficult to overcome."

"But you love him."

"Yes," Sarah admitted. "I know you must find that shocking, but it's the truth."

"I'm not in the judgment business," Bea said briskly, rising. "It's true that I've found the adjustment to living in the East difficult, but I don't expect everyone to feel the same way. Now let me see how Listak is doing with dinner."

Beatrice had barely left the room to confer with the servant before James entered it, sweeping off his tie and heading for the sherry on the sideboard.

"I'm afraid I have bad news," he said, pouring some of the amber liquid into a glass.

"What's that?"

"I can't book you on the Orient Express to Paris for another month," he said.

"Why?"

"There's some kind of convocation in Paris on the twenty-ninth. All the seats on the train are reserved until then. You'll just have to wait."

Sarah was silent.

"I'm sorry, Sarah," James said in a defeated tone. "I know that sitting around here with nothing to do but think about the Orchid Palace and listen to Bea complain won't be much fun for you."

"It's all right. I'm sure that Boston will still be there when I get back."

"And we're heading into the bad weather, too,

I'm afraid," James added. "It rains all the time in the late fall. You won't be able to take many walks or get out much."

"I'll catch up on my reading," Sarah said lightly.

James sat heavily in one of Bea's overstuffed chairs. "I guess that your vacation in the Orient didn't turn out exactly as you'd planned."

"No."

"If I haven't said so already, let me say it now. I'm so sorry, Sarah. It was my bright idea to get you into the harem in the first place. I feel responsible for everything that happened to you afterward."

"I'm a grown woman, James. I made my own decisions and must face the consequences."

"Do you have regrets now?"

"No. I don't think you should ever regret loving somebody. It didn't work out because we were just too different, but I'll probably love Kalid until I die."

"He meant that much to you?"

"Yes."

"Then how could you leave him?"

"I don't know. The strength came from somewhere. He's very intelligent, and he had me fooled. He had me believing what he wanted me to believe, but when you arrived, I suddenly saw what a sham it had all been. He can't change, and I can't stay with someone who thinks of me as an accessory."

"Were you afraid he would discard you?

They often do. That's why the harem exists, for variety."

"I wasn't afraid of that, not really. In his own way, he was very . . . devoted."

"Then what? Was the cultural gap too wide? I know Bea has never been able to bridge it."

"I guess that was part of it. After all, his culture made him what he is."

Beatrice appeared in the doorway and said, "Oh, hello, James. I didn't realize you were home. Listak will be serving dinner in ten minutes."

Sarah and James rose to follow her into the dining room.

"Get out of my sight, old woman, before I have you drawn and quartered and served up to the janissaries in their soup," Kalid said darkly, not looking at Kosem.

"I have to talk to you," his grandmother replied stoically, disregarding the halberdiers who stood ready to throw her out of the Pasha's suite if Kalid inclined his head.

"I think you've already said enough."

Kosem sat next to him and patted his hand. "All is not lost," she said.

Kalid muttered something under his breath and snatched his hand away.

Kosem surveyed him, shaking her head. He had three days' growth of beard, his shirt was open to the waist, revealing that two buttons were missing, and his eyes were bloodshot from lack of sleep. He looked dissolute, disagreeable, and dangerous.

"Leave us alone," Kalid barked to the guards.

They disappeared.

"I know where she is," Kosem said.

"I know where she is too. She's at her cousin's house in Constantinople. I have four of Turhan's men watching the place at all times. That doesn't mean she is coming back to me."

"I can help."

"Oh, really? The way you 'helped' Sarah to go away with her cousin? I don't understand you, donme pashana. You must be losing your mind. Before Sarah came here you could talk of nothing—*nothing*—but my getting married and presenting you with an heir. Then the perfect opportunity to achieve both those goals presents itself and what do you do? You tell James Woolcott where Sarah is so he can come and take her away. I don't know why you're still alive. Why haven't I executed you?"

"Perhaps because you've been too preoccupied with getting Sarah back to do anything else," Kosem said primly. "The chief of your mint has been waiting two days to see you."

"If you even attempt to lecture me now, I'll have you thrown into the dungeon," he snapped.

Kosem said nothing.

He turned to look at her fully for the first time. She saw that his expression was more bleak than even she had imagined.

He was taking Sarah's departure very hard.

"Why did you tell her cousin that she was back here?" he asked softly, his gaze narrow and hard.

"She deserved to know that her family was looking for her. Did you really want her to stay with you because she thought she had no alternative?"

"I just wanted her to stay!" he exploded. "You knew she would be angry when she discovered my deception—what did you think would happen then?"

"I didn't think she would leave you," Kosem said quietly. "Honestly, Kalid, I didn't. I knew it was possible, but I really thought she would just be reunited with her cousin and relieved that he knew she was all right. I thought that her strong feelings for you would keep her here."

"I guess we both underestimated her, didn't we?" he said bitterly, saluting his grandmother with two fingers held together and a sarcastic nod.

"So are you just going to sit here? Aren't you going to do anything about it?"

"I am formulating a plan."

"And what is that?"

"I haven't finalized it yet."

"Kalid, this inactivity is not like you at all.

When Sarah was taken by the bedouins, you were on your horse in ten minutes to go after her."

"When she was taken by the bedouins, I was worried for her safety and certain she would be glad to see me. This situation is very different."

"You are in power here. You are the pasha. You can do anything you want!"

"And where have all my high-handed tactics gotten me so far? Sitting here in deep despair, having this miserable conversation with you!"

Kosem was silent a moment, and then said, "When is Sarah leaving Turkey?"

"Not for several weeks. I had Turhan bribe the stationmaster so that when the cousin inquired, he was told that all the seats on the Orient Express were booked for a month."

"High-handed tactics?" Kosem said, raising her brows.

"Sarah won't find out about that one. But she'll know if I have her arrested or impound her passport and so bar her from leaving the country."

"I take it these are possibilities you have considered?" Kosem inquired.

"Yes, but they won't work. She must make the decision herself. She wants me to behave like a civilized Western gentleman, not an Ottoman tyrant."

"The problem with that is you *are* an Ottoman

tyrant. And Sarah would be bored to distraction by a civilized Western gentleman. She only thinks that's what she wants."

"It's what she thinks that I'm battling, not what she feels. If her heart ruled her head, she would still be with me."

"How are you going to keep her here?"

"Merely keeping her in this country won't make her come back to me," Kalid said musingly, shaking his head. "I think she used her cousin's sudden appearance as an excuse, though she doesn't recognize it herself. What she's really afraid of is committing herself to a way of life that's so foreign to her. She loves me, and as long as she is with me she's sure, but I can't be with her every minute of every day. I have a whole district to run."

"Not that you have been running it lately," Kosem replied pointedly.

"I'll get back to it once this crisis is past," he said.

"So you think you will get her back?"

"I must."

"Then compromise. Tell her you will take her back to her family once a year, at that winter holiday she loves so much."

"Christmas?"

"Yes, yes. You can spare the time once a year. There's nothing happening here during that period anyway, except a monsoon. Let her see that you don't expect her to give up everything in order to be with you, that she doesn't have to abandon her whole past life to become the pashana."

He stared at nothing, pondering her words.

"You have always been arrogant, son of my son. You assume that for any woman, having you is enough. If Sarah marries you and stays here in Bursa, she gives up everything and you give up nothing. She has no trace of her former life, and you go on exactly as before, isn't that right?"

He looked at her. He was listening intently.

"She's not a trinket that you can acquire and put on a shelf and then take down every so often when you remember it is there and feel like playing with it."

"You sound just like her."

"Well, I have learned something too. Sarah needs a purpose in life beyond being your companion. The idea that she will spend all of her time here as the harem women do terrifies her."

"I have thought of asking her to take over the palace school," Kalid said.

"Wonderful!" Kosem said, beaming. "Why didn't you do that before she left?"

"I suppose I was being greedy and wanted her all to myself," he admitted.

"But you just said you can't be with her every minute! You know already that she is not the sort of woman to bathe in the hamman and plait her hair until you decide you want to see her. Let her get involved with domestic matters. Let her help you. I have always thought you were intelligent, Kalid, but I shouldn't have to tell you these things, you should have realized all this for yourself."

"I was concentrating only on what I wanted, all right? No other woman had to be persuaded that being with me was the right thing for her."

"And none of them held your interest for longer than thirty seconds."

He smiled slightly and looked away.

"What is it?" Kosem asked.

"My mother was a challenge for my father, and it seems that history is repeating itself."

"You are like him in many respects. He never desired anything to be too easy, either."

Kalid leaned forward and kissed her cheek. Kosem looked at him, surprised. He was usually not so demonstrative.

"Go now, and let me think," he said.

She rose.

"And grandmother? Thank you," he added.

She smiled to herself and left.

Sarah realized that she was pregnant about three weeks after she left the Orchid Palace. She had missed her period, which at the time she ascribed to stress, but now there was a strange tenderness in her breasts, and with each passing day the prospect of breakfast looked less appealing. She could no longer avoid the conclusion when she tried to button her skirt over her shirtwaist and the button flew across the room.

She sat down heavily on the edge of the bed in James's guestroom and analyzed her feelings. Even though she knew that this baby was going to be a problem for her single and unmarried future, she was elated.

Kalid's baby. She was carrying his baby, and it must have happened the first time he had made love to her completely, after he rescued her from the bedouins. Now she was returning to Victorian Boston with an illegitimate child in her womb, the child of an exotic foreign ruler, the great love of her life, whom she would never see again.

But she was happy, very happy. Even though she had no job and would probably wind up living in her father's old house alone with her child, she had never felt more hopeful in her life.

She decided to tell James and Beatrice about her news right away. She would be in Boston before she began to show, but they would hear about her condition from the letters of relatives, and if they ever came home to stay, as Bea wanted, they would have to deal with the ramifications of her situation.

New England in the latter half of the nineteenth century was not known for its tolerance of unwed mothers.

At dinner the next night, she waited until dessert was served and then said, "I have something to tell the two of you."

James and Beatrice looked at her expectantly.

"I'm pregnant."

James closed his eyes, and Bea paused with a forkful of lemon cake halfway to her mouth. Under other circumstances, their expressions would have been comical.

"I was afraid of this," James said.

When Bea had recovered enough to speak, she whispered, "What on earth are you going to do?"

"I'm going to have it."

"In Boston?" Bea said. The second word came out as a mouselike squeak.

"It looks like that's where I'll be."

"Sarah, that will be social suicide," Sarah said. "And you'll never get another teaching job. Your morals will come into question, and the school board won't sanction it."

"Then I'll do something else."

"Like what?" James said.

"I don't know—take in washing, take in boarders. Father's house is mine and it has several extra bedrooms. And he left me some money. I won't be impoverished."

"But what about the child?" Bea asked.

"What about him?"

"My dear, he won't fit in, he'll be an outcast."

"Why? Because he'll be illegitimate?"

"Not only that. Won't he be . . . dark?"

"Bea!" James said warningly.

"That's all right, James, let her say it. I'm sure it won't be the first time I'll hear it. Yes, Bea, he may be dark, as you put it, or he may look just like me. Of course it's impossible to say about that now. For my part, I hope he looks just like Kalid, who is the most beautiful man I ever met."

Bea looked down at her plate, silenced.

James rose and came to her chair, bending to kiss her hair. "You have a great deal of courage, Sarah. I have always admired it, but never more than at this moment. You'll let me know whatever I can do to help you, won't you?"

Sarah nodded, biting her lip, feeling a little misty at his supportive words.

James left the dining room and Bea said, "Sarah, I didn't mean . . ." she stopped.

"I know what you meant, Bea, and I understand. Don't worry about it."

Bea shoved her chair back from the table and ran out after her husband.

Sarah stared down at her empty dessert plate and then took another sip of coffee.

She knew that Bea's reaction would be the typical one back home; Sarah would certainly have her work cut out for her. But curiously enough, she was not afraid.

It was worth enduring anything to have Kalid's child.

Chapter Fourteen

"There's someone to see you, Sarah," James said.

Sarah looked up from her book, her eyes darting to the doorway of the sitting room, which was empty.

"No," James said quietly. "It's not him."

He stepped aside and Roxalena came up behind James, breaking into a huge grin when she saw Sarah.

"My American friend," she said dramatically and threw open her arms.

Sarah rose to embrace her, surprised to find that tears were filling her eyes. She found that she was very weepy lately; maybe it was her condition.

James bowed slightly and said, "Stay as long as you like, your highness. Ladies, I'll leave you alone." He went out, closing the door behind him.

"He thinks I am a highness, too," Roxalena said, laughing and removing the face piece of her veil as James left. She was wearing a sky-blue silk shalwar with a sapphire-blue blouse and a girdle embroidered with pearls and gold thread. A blue velvet cap stitched with pearls perched on her head.

Sarah laughed too. "It's so wonderful to see you. How did you get away from Topkapi?"

"I told my father I was going to the bazaar at Saint Sophia," Roxalena replied, folding her gold-fringed feradge and dropping it on a chair.

"And?"

"And he sent Osman as my escort," Roxalena added, winking broadly.

Sarah smiled. "And where is Osman?"

"Down in the street, with my coach."

Sarah took Roxalena's hands and led her to the loveseat by the window. "How did you find out I was here?"

"Turhan Aga told Osman what happened at your wedding," Roxalena said. "I didn't understand it at all, Sarah. At first you were so desperate to get away from Kalid Shah, and then you were going to marry him?"

"Yes, well, it's a long story."

"Did you get the note I sent with the bundle woman?"

"Yes, I did, and you can't guess how much it meant to me to know that you were out there, trying to get word to my cousin. It gave me hope."

"So how did you agree to marry Kalid? Or didn't you agree? Was he forcing you?"

"He wasn't forcing me. I love him, Roxalena."

A slow smile spread over Roxalena's face. "I knew it. I told Osman that you had fallen in love with the pasha. I knew it when I heard he was going after you to rescue you from the bedouins. I guessed it would happen when I saw him react to his first sight of you. Few women can resist his charm when he wants something. Or someone."

"Well, I'm resisting it now. That's why I'm here."

"What happened?"

Sarah briefly recounted her history since Roxalena had last seen her. Roxalena listened raptly, interrupting occasionally with a pertinent question.

"And you have not heard from him since you left?" Roxalena finally asked.

Sarah shook her head.

"Were you hoping that you would?"

"I don't know."

"If it helps you to know it, he has a continuous guard posted on this house."

Sarah stared at her. "What?"

Roxalena nodded. "Turhan Aga told Osman."

"You mean he is having me watched?"

"Yes."

"What does he think I am going to do?"

"Leave early, before he is ready to stop you?" Roxalena suggested. "I know something else. Kalid told Turhan to bribe the stationmaster when your cousin James came to buy your ticket."

"What do you mean?"

"The stationmaster said that the seats on the Orient Express were booked for a month. That is not true. Kalid was trying to keep you here."

"And he succeeded," Sarah said softly, thinking about James's reaction to the news.

"Do you really think you can just go back to the U.S. of America and forget Kalid?" Roxalena asked.

"I never thought I could forget him."

"But you do plan to go home? Why not stay here in Turkey with your cousin?"

"I can't stay here, Roxalena. I'm pregnant."

Roxalena's eyes widened.

"And Kalid does not know?" she whispered.

"No. I didn't know myself until recently."

"He would never let you go if he knew you were carrying his child," Roxalena said quietly.

"That's why he must not know. If he comes after me, I want it to be for me, not for the Shah heir."

"Then you are hoping he'll come after you?" Roxalena said, leaning forward eagerly.

Sarah bit her lip. "I never thought I would miss the man so much, Roxalena. I reacted hastily when I found out about my cousin's attempts to contact me, but the prospect of the rest of my life without Kalid now seems very bleak."

"Then why not go back to him yourself?"

Sarah's mouth hardened. "No. He has to want me enough to think about what happened and choose to work it out with me. I can't go back to him and spend the rest of our lives together with him behaving as he has in the past. If I have to make a future alone, at least I will have his child."

"You're very brave," Roxalena said.

"I don't feel very brave."

"And very stubborn."

Sarah smiled. "You sound like Kalid."

"That's why I knew you would be a match for him," Roxalena said, laughing.

There was a knock at the sitting room door, and Listak came in, bowing deeply.

"My master would like to know if you ladies desire refreshments," she said, sneaking glances at the dazzling princess on the sofa. "Perhaps some tea?"

"Tea would be lovely," Sarah replied.

Listak bowed her way out again, and Sarah said teasingly, "She's very impressed with you."

Roxalena sniffed. "People are very impressed with my father also, and he is a cheat and a liar."

"He never admitted he sold me to Kalid?" Sarah said, marveling at the Sultan's gall.

"He acted as if it had all happened beyond his knowledge, as if the khislar had acted without his sanction. Oh, I hate him."

Sarah covered Roxalena's hand with her own. "I will miss you when I go back to Boston."

"Perhaps I will come and see you one day," Roxalena said mysteriously.

"What does that mean?"

"Osman and I are making plans," Roxalena replied, smiling radiantly.

"To get away from Topkapi?"

"To get out of the Empire altogether."

"How?"

"Osman is making arrangements to go to Cyprus and get a job there. If he can work it out, I will go with him."

"Roxalena, will you be able to give all of this up?" Sarah said, lifting the princess's silken sleeve with a forefinger. As much as she loved her friend, Sarah suspected that Roxalena was fond of the trappings of Ottoman royalty.

"In a second," Roxalena said firmly. "I am a prisoner at Topkapi, just like the men in my father's dungeons. The only difference is that I am better dressed."

Sarah laughed. "Then good luck with your plans."

Listak came in with the tea tray, and both women fell silent, waiting to continue their conversation until the servant had left the room.

"So when is the train leaving?" Kalid asked Turhan Aga.

"At two in the afternoon."

"So it should be going through the Greek mountains a day and a half later," Kalid said musingly. "And then reach Paris on the tenth. Where does it stop?"

"Gare St. Lazare. And she has a reservation at the Hotel Delacroix for that night."

Kalid nodded.

"Master, I counsel against this plan," Achmed said.

Kalid looked at his khislar, who had recovered from his encounter with the bedouins, except for a two-inch bandage on his head to cover his healing wound.

"I am not interested in your opinion," Kalid replied.

"You have no jurisdiction in France!" Achmed said anyway. "If the ikbal resists you, you can be prosecuted by the French government on any number of charges."

"The French are not going to prosecute me. They owe the Sultan four million francs in loans," Kalid said darkly.

"You could create an international incident," Turhan said warningly.

"Be quiet," Kalid replied testily. "I remember your role in breaking up my wedding."

"I did my job, master," Turhan said quietly.

"Yes, well, you can go. You can both go."

When they had left, he paced back and forth, his expression absorbed.

He would take an earlier train and be in Paris on the tenth, when Sarah arrived.

"Why can't you stop in England and see Aunt Emily on your way home?" James asked, watching as Sarah folded a scarf and placed it in a suitcase.

"My plans are already made, James."

"But she says here," James went on, waving a letter, "that you can get a boat from Calais to Dover and be across the Channel in a day. You haven't seen Mother's sister since you were ten. Don't you think it's worth going out of your way a little bit on your return trip to renew the family tie?"

"James, I know what you're doing. I thank you for the effort, but it's really not necessary."

"What are you talking about?"

"I'm sure you wrote to Emily and asked her if I could visit. You're trying to provide me with a distraction and I appreciate it, but I can hardly descend on a relative who hasn't

354

seen me since I was a child and unpack my bags."

"Why not? For a few days? Don't you think you could use a rest in the English countryside?"

"I've had a rest here."

"Then for your mother's sake? Emily was her favorite sister, you must remember that."

"Why is it so important to you that I go?" Sarah asked, lowering the lid of the suitcase.

James sighed. "You need to be among allies, Sarah. Bea and I could only do so much, and watching you sitting here day after day, waiting for that—scalawag—to show up here, growing paler and thinner by the minute—"

"I expect the 'thinner' part will change quite soon," Sarah said dryly.

"Forget him," James said sharply.

"Easier said than done."

"Then go back to him. Existing in this half world is sapping your health, and that isn't good for the baby."

"You know why I can't go back to him, James. We've discussed it endlessly. And sitting in an autumn English garden with Mum's middle-aged sister isn't going to change anything."

"How do you know that? Maybe you will feel better. And don't forget, this may be your only opportunity to see Aunt Emily. She isn't getting any younger, and she rarely leaves England since her husband died."

Sarah stared at him, exasperated, then burst out laughing, shaking her head helplessly.

"What?" James said, shrugging.

"You are relentless, do you know that? All right, I'll go to Dover and see Emily."

James grinned.

"You didn't tell her anything of my situation in your letter?" Sarah asked.

"No, of course not. I just said that you enjoyed an extended visit here and were now returning to Boston."

Sarah nodded. "I'll have to change my itinerary. Instead of staying in Paris and going on from there, I'll need transportation from Paris to Calais."

"I'll arrange it," James said briskly, and left the room, whistling merrily.

Sarah walked over to the window and looked down at the bustling street, wondering again why she hadn't heard from Kalid. Why was he bothering to have the house watched, why had he delayed her departure, if he didn't plan to contact her? Had Roxalena's information been wrong?

She would never know. She was leaving Turkey in the morning and she would not see him again.

"You will write to us often?" Bea said, dabbing at her eyes with a handkerchief. In the background, boarding passengers said good-bye to their companions at the station

356

while the locomotive steamed restlessly, ready to depart.

"Yes, I will," Sarah replied.

"We'll be so concerned about the . . . you know."

"Baby, Beatrice. You can say the word." Sarah leaned forward to kiss her cheek.

"And give our best to Aunt Emily," James added.

"I will."

"You look very pretty," he added lamely, glancing at the porter who was walking away with Sarah's bags.

"Thank you." In a vain attempt to lift her spirits, Sarah had splurged on a traveling outfit in one of the Constantinople shops that catered to Western visitors. It was a street dress of gray and black striped bengaline with a modified bustle and an apron skirt. A fitted black jersey jacket buttoned over it, and a matching gray hat trimmed with raven's feathers and edged with black grosgrain ribbon sat on her upswept hair.

In two months' time, the only item still fitting her would be the hat.

"All aboard!" sounded in their ears. The command was repeated in French, then Turkish, as the last straggling passengers climbed aboard the train. The whistle hooted shrilly, and the engine belched a cloud of acrid smoke.

"I must go," Sarah said, extracting her fingers with difficulty from James's grip.

He embraced her again, tears standing in his eyes.

"If you need anything . . ." he said for the hundredth time, searching her face.

"I will write, I promise," Sarah said.

Bea hugged Sarah in her turn, and then husband and wife stood back and watched as Sarah ascended the mobile steps to the passenger car and turned in the doorway to wave again. Then she vanished inside as the porter whisked the steps away.

"I feel as if I am sending her off to certain disaster," James said huskily.

Bea said nothing, her expression mournful. In her own repressed and childless way, she was very fond of Sarah.

They stood there until the train had departed and disappeared around a bend in the tracks.

Kalid looked around the sumptuous presidential suite at the Hotel Delacroix with satisfaction. The three rooms were banked with flowers, a bottle of the finest champagne stood in a silver ice bucket in the reception area, and two elaborate fruit baskets sat on a side table. He glanced in the gilt-edged mirror on the silk-covered wall and adjusted the vest of his Saville Row suit. He was in his Oxford mode, dressed by the best British tailors and speaking the King's English.

If this didn't work, he was out of ideas.

He looked at the clock on the mantel and frowned. Sarah's train should have been in an hour ago, and the hotel was near the station. He had asked the desk to notify him when she arrived, but so far he had heard nothing.

Kalid left the suite and walked along the lavish figured carpet to the newly installed Otis elevator, a slow contraption powered by steam which closed with an iron grille across the door. The immense Baccarat chandelier hanging from the enameled plaster ceiling vanished as the elevator descended to the lobby level.

Kalid walked to the registration desk and looked around him as he waited for the desk clerk to appear. A black walnut main staircase at the rear of the lobby swept down from a central platform which led to the second level of the hotel. The stairs were fitted with a red plush carpet and all the gas jets had shades designed by Louis Comfort Tiffany. The reception desk where Kalid waited was of the same black walnut as the staircase.

He hit the bell with the flat of his hand.

The clerk appeared from a side door immediately.

"May I help you, Mr. Shah?" he said in French with the intonations of Marseilles.

"Yes. I am waiting for the arrival of a Miss Woolcott, and she should have been here by now. Can you check for me?" Kalid replied in his British-accented French.

"*Mais oui,*" the clerk said, and flipped open the ledger, then turned to a pile of telegrams stuck on a spike to his left. He riffled through them and then said, "*Voilà!*"

"What is it?"

"Miss Woolcott canceled her reservation. She will not be arrving today."

"What do you mean? I checked when I got here yesterday morning, and the clerk on duty then said that she was due to check in this afternoon!"

"I'm sure that was true at the time, *monsieur*. We only received the telegram this morning."

"And you don't know anything else?"

"I'm afraid not."

Kalid whirled from the desk and sprinted across the lobby.

"Is there anything else I can do for you?" the clerk called after him.

Kalid ignored him as he ran out the door.

The clerk sniffed and closed his ledger.

Foreigners.

What could one expect?

Chapter Fifteen

Kalid rushed up to an iron-grilled ticket window at Gare St. Lazare and said rapidly in his university French, "I need to track a passenger who arrived here two hours ago on the Orient Express from Constantinople."

"I'm sorry, *monsieur*, that information is confidential. We do not share the passenger manifest with the public."

Kalid whipped a two-hundred-franc note from his vest pocket and shoved it under the man's nose.

The ticket seller snatched it and said, "You would have to see the stationmaster. His office is just beyond that arch."

Kalid ran in the indicated direction, passing through crowds of men and women dressed in the latest European fashions, past newsboys in corduroy jackets and felt caps hawking their wares, past peanut and ice-cream vendors and the uniformed porters who seemed to be everywhere. He heard the distant rumble and hiss of an arriving train as he knocked on the frosted glass door marked *Maitre d' gare* and then yanked it open abruptly.

The stationmaster looked up from his lunch of *rondelet* bread with sardines and *brie* and stared at Kalid in shock.

"I need information about a passenger who arrived on the Orient Express today," Kalid announced. "The ticketseller said you would be able to help me."

The stationmaster put down his glass of burgundy and opened his mouth to speak. At the same time Kalid produced a five-hundred-franc note and held it aloft.

The stationmaster's expression changed. "What do you want to know?" he asked, rebuttoning the tunic of his uniform.

Kalid explained his mission, and the stationmaster rose to retrieve the passenger manifest from a drawer. He ran his finger down a column and then nodded.

"Yes, *monsieur*. She arrived here several hours ago, as you say. At least she had a seat in her name, and someone used it."

"But she never came to her hotel."

The stationmaster gave a particularly Gallic shrug.

"Can you tell from that list what car she was in, who might have been the porters?"

"*Mais oui.* Henri Duclos and Pierre Montand."

"Then summon them here. If she hired a coach or went to another hotel, she would probably have asked one of them to help her."

The stationmaster sighed.

Kalid produced another five hunded francs.

"Duclos is on another run. You will have to wait until he returns to the station to see him."

Kalid nodded.

"But I will call Montand now. Wait here."

Kalid nodded again.

The stationmaster went out, and Kalid began to pace the small room, oblivious to the train schedules and posters and notes tacked to the peeling plaster walls, to the overpowering smell of garlic and sardines from the stationmaster's lunch.

He had to find Sarah.

By the time Sarah reached Dover, it was late evening and she decided to spend the night at a local inn called the Leaping Stag. James's letter was not likely to reach Aunt Emily before she herself did, and although Sarah had sent a wire, she knew that Emily's house was in a small village which did not have a telegraph office, so service was always delayed. She thought it impolite to barge in late at night unannounced, so she planned to hire a carriage in the morning and arrive at a reasonable hour.

Her room was cozy with a cheerful fire, and although she had missed dinner, the innkeeper said he would send up an order of "starry gazy pie," a local delicacy on the order of shepherd's pie. Sarah found that she was very hungry, which followed the pattern of her days now. She couldn't think about food in the morning but by evening was ravenous, but because of the traveling and pregnancy-induced seasickness, she had skipped lunch on the boat. She was warming her feet before the fire when there was a tap at her door and the barmaid entered with a tray, the plate on it covered with a checkered napkin.

"All cozy now?" she said, when she saw Sarah with her feet up on the embroidered footstool.

Sarah nodded. It was wonderful to hear voices speaking her native language, even if it was with a thick Kentish accent sometimes difficult to decipher.

"I saw you when you arrived tonight, and you looked all done in, if you don't mind my saying so," the barmaid added, bending to place the tray on a table by the fire. "Cut up quite nasty outside, hasn't it? Rain, rain, rain, this autumn, nothing but storms and showers, and now it's gotten cold too. Did you have a long trip?"

"Yes, from Turkey on the Orient Express, and then to Calais to take the packet to Dover."

The barmaid clucked her tongue sympathetically as she whipped off the napkin and poured a tankard of ale into a glass mug. "You have had a long trek, pet, small wonder you looked all at sixes and sevens. Better now, though, eh?"

"Yes, I think so. That food smells good."

"Oh, indeed, Albie serves up the best tucker in the district and no mistake. You'll enjoy that, and it'll put some color back in your cheeks. Go ahead, don't let me stop you."

Sarah took a bite of a biscuit and a sip of ale as the barmaid looked on approvingly, her reddened hands folded over her apron and her kindly face wreathed in smiles.

"You're not British, are you?" she said, as Sarah chewed enthusiastically.

"No, American."

"Have you been away from home long?"

"Several months. It seems long."

"You must be missing the States, I expect."

"I didn't realize how much until I got off the boat in Dover and saw all the signs printed in English. It was like a . . . welcoming sign, somehow."

"Oh, it would be. I've never traveled abroad myself. If you're happy where you are, I think you should stay there."

Sarah put down the biscuit and looked out the streaming window at the dark. "There are times I wish I'd stayed at home," she said softly, and to her horror, she started to cry.

The barmaid sat on the edge of the featherbed and patted her hand.

"There, there, miss. Have you got troubles?"

Sarah nodded, wetly.

"Something to do with your trip?"

"Yes."

"Did you meet a man?"

"How did you know it was a man?" Sarah inquired, her eyes streaming.

"With pretty young ladies, it usually is. Have you left him, then, is that the problem?"

"I've left him, and what's more, I'm pregnant," Sarah replied, sobbing louder.

The barmaid sighed. "You are in a pickle, aren't you?" she said quietly.

Sarah wiped her eyes with her fingers, and the barmaid handed her the checkered napkin. Sarah blew her nose, wondering how much lower she could sink.

She was now having weeping fits in front of strangers.

The barmaid handed her the mug of ale and Sarah drank deeply, closing her eyes.

"My name is Ethel," the barmaid said, "and in this job I've heard everything, so you can tell me all about it."

Between bites of her dinner, Sarah did.

"So you thought he would come after you," Ethel said twenty minutes later, as Sarah pushed aside her empty plate and picked up an apple.

"In the beginning, I was too angry to think

about anything. I just wanted to get away from him. But then I began to miss him terribly, and when I heard from Roxalena that he was watching James's house, I thought . . ."

"Roxalena is the princess?" Ethel said.

"Yes. She said that he arranged it so I couldn't get a train ticket, and I thought that meant he was delaying my departure so he could intercept me. . . ."

"But he didn't."

"No, he didn't. And now here I am, and I'll never see him again and I'm going to have his baby and I'm just . . ."

"Miserable?" Ethel suggested.

"Pretty much. I mean, I'm happy about the baby, but the thought that I have to live the rest of my life without him is overwhelming. Do you understand?"

Ethel nodded. "But why did you come to England? Aren't you going home?"

"I'm visiting my aunt. She lives in Gilly-on-Strait. How far is it to the village?"

"About two miles straightaway down the post road. What's her name?"

"Emily Hepton. She's a widow now. She was married to Giles Hepton, the cabinetmaker? He had a store in Dover."

"I knew him well. He used to stop off here for a pint on his way back from the market. Never met the wife, though."

"She kept the house and stayed on alone. We all thought she'd come back to Boston, but she prefers to remain where she lived with her husband."

"People get set in their ways, love."

"But she must get so lonely," Sarah said, threatening to lapse into tears again.

"Then she'll be very glad to see you," Ethel said, standing. "I've got to go down and do the washing up for the night or Albie will be getting after me. You're our only guest tonight, but we get the old duffers in the bar until all hours, and the glasses will be standing there waiting for the cloth."

"Yes, yes, go ahead, I understand. I've kept you too long already. Please forgive me."

Ethel gathered up the tray and bent to put another log on the fire. "Got to keep you and the little one warm," she said.

"It was so hot in Turkey, I can't get used to the change of weather here," Sarah said.

"You're a long way from Turkey now."

Sarah sighed in agreement. "Do you know where I can hire a coach in the morning?" she asked.

"There's a livery stable just down the road. My boy Henry works there—you can ask for him and tell him I sent you. He'll take care of you right enough."

Sarah looked up at her and smiled. "Thank you for your kindness, and I'm sorry about—you know, the little scene I made."

"Stuff and nonsense," Ethel said. "Don't give it a thought. You're just going through a bad patch, and we all hit them. I'll set you up with a hearty English breakfast in the morning, and you'll feel much better when you see your auntie."

Sarah nodded, trying not to think about breakfast, especially a hearty one, since she knew she would be in no mood for it when the sun rose.

When the door closed behind Ethel, the room seemed suddenly very empty.

Sarah let her head fall against the plush back of the overstuffed chair and stared morosely into the fire.

"Calais?" Kalid said, staring at the porter. "What do you mean, she went to Calais?"

Henri Duclos spread his hands. "Just what I said, *monsieur*. The American woman you described asked me to arrange transportation for her to Calais."

Kalid was stymied. Why would Sarah be going there, when she could sail for New York or Boston without traveling a mile out of her way?

"Did she say anything else?" Kalid asked.

"She inquired about the sailing times for the packet from Calais to Dover."

"Well, why didn't you say that in the first place? She must have been going to Dover!"

Duclos shrugged. "It's possible."

Kalid stared the man down, exasperated. The next one of these Frenchmen who shrugged at him was going to get punched.

"Did she say anything about why she was going there?" Kalid demanded.

"She said nothing about Dover. You did."

Kalid looked over at the stationmaster, who was watching the byplay with a detached expression.

He had already been paid.

Kalid handed Duclos a two-hundred-franc note and said, "*merci*." Then he stalked out of the stationmaster's office and hailed a hansom cab at the curb outside the station.

"Take me to the docks," he said.

It took him a couple of hours and a good deal more *baksheesh* to determine that Sarah had indeed sailed for Calais and to get a ticket for himself. He was leaning over the railing, studying the churning waves from the deck of the last boat of the day before he stopped to examine what he was doing.

He had now pursued Sarah through several countries, gone without sleep for two nights, and spent an untold amount of money. He wasn't even sure Sarah would listen to him if he found her, and in the meanwhile his own country was rudderless as he ran around the globe anonymously trying to track her down. He had come by himself, against the wishes of his grandmother and his closest advisors, because he thought this personal mission should be his alone. But he was now bone-tired, exasperated with Sarah for unwittingly leading him on this merry chase, and, if the truth be told, weary of being treated like an ordinary citizen when he was used to special handling. His passport carried only his name and a sepia-toned daguerreotype, and without his robes and his entourage, foreign travel was a different event altogether from what he had previously experienced. Only his fierce desire to see Sarah again kept him from turning around and going straight home.

He looked into the distance in the fading light, idly watching the gray clouds merge with the gray sea.

Across the water was England, which he knew well from his time at Oxford.

He hoped Sarah was there.

"My dear, this is such a surprise!" Emily Hepton said, kissing Sarah on both cheeks. "When I didn't hear anything further from James, I assumed you weren't coming to see me."

"I got here before his letter did," Sarah said, removing her hat as Emily gestured for her umbrella.

"How did you get here?"

"I hired a coach at the livery in Dover. The driver dropped me off at the end of the lane."

"Then you must be wet quite through. Let's get those things off you." Emily hung Sarah's jacket and other effects on a clothes tree next to the door and then led the way inside the house into a cozy sitting room. It was still raining, and the wind blew through the eaves of the cottage as they sat before the fire and Emily put aside her knitting. A striped tabby rubbed up against Emily's legs luxuriously and then bolted down the hall.

"Samantha is a little shy with strangers," Emily said, smiling fondly. "She'll come sneaking back in here shortly to take another peek at you."

Sarah laughed.

"Now let *me* look at you. I haven't seen you for—how long is it?" Emily asked.

"Ten years."

"Yes, and you've become a lovely young woman."

"And you haven't changed at all."

"Telling fibs is a sin, child."

"I'm not telling fibs. You look exactly the same as I remember you, right down to the cameo brooch."

Emily fingered the pin fastened to the bunch of lace at her throat. "Yes, Grandmother Gibson's brooch. I always wear it."

Emily was soberly dressed in a navy fitted dress with a sweeping apron front and the full bustle of some seasons past. Her graying reddish hair was swept up on top of her head in a loose knot and held in place with two ebony hairpins like skewers that Sarah remembered from her childhood.

"Now, what would you say to some tea?"

Emily asked. "I've already fired up the stove for lunch, so I'll just go and put the kettle on now. Then we can settle down and have a nice, long chat."

"Tea sounds wonderful," Sarah said.

Emily disappeared through an archway, and Sarah looked around at the main room of the cottage. The fireplace dominated the space, with an oak mantel laden with family collectibles, knick-knacks, and stiffly posed photographs. The furniture was old and comfortable, with hand-tatted doilies on the back of each chair and knotted fringe along the skirt of the sofa. The wallpaper was typically Victorian, pink-and-white stripes embellished with cabbage roses, and the organdy curtains draped across the front window were tied back with gold tassels. It was a room like Emily—prim, fussy, but essentially serene.

Emily came back and said, "The tea is steeping. It should be ready in a few minutes. I'm afraid I've become like the English about tea, spending too much money on special blends from Ceylon and China and squabbling with clerks about the size and color of the leaves."

"It's the national pastime here, isn't it?" Sarah said, and Emily laughed.

"I suppose it is. I got the taste from my husband."

Emily sat across from Sarah and picked up her knitting again. "Now you must tell me

373

what's been happening at home."

Sarah filled her in on the Woolcott family's recent history, skillfully editing those items she knew Emily would find shocking. She did not discuss her time with Kalid, leading Emily to believe that her visit to Turkey had consisted only of sightseeing and visiting with James and Beatrice. Her aunt interrupted with questions and got up several times to fetch and renew the tea. By the time the pot was empty, Emily said, "I'm hungry, aren't you? It's past time for lunch. Why don't you join me in the kitchen and we'll see what we can rustle up for us?"

Sarah rose, and as she passed the older woman, her aunt hugged her suddenly.

"Isn't this nice? I've missed seeing family, and I'm so glad you decided to stop here for a visit. How long can you stay?"

"Only for tonight. I have to be on the *Atlantic Star* sailing for Boston tomorrow. After that, all the sailings are for New York and nothing's going direct to Boston for a month."

"Oh, I was hoping you could stay a few days at least. I'm alone here since Giles died, and I'm so grateful for the company."

"We'll have tonight," Sarah said kindly and followed Emily into the kitchen.

Kalid looked around at the paneled walls of the third inn he had visited and sighed. There had to be ten of these places in the Dover area, and he had no idea which one Sarah had patronized, or if she had set out for some other destination immediately upon her arrival in England. He thought that unlikely, since she would have disembarked in late evening, but Sarah had always been one to surprise him. He looked around at the clutch of early drinkers, who were eyeing him suspiciously, and then approached the innkeeper, who was wiping down the bar.

"Are you the landlord?" Kalid asked him.

The man nodded curtly.

"I'm looking for an American woman who might have passed through here," Kalid said. "Tall, with blond hair, fair skin, and blue eyes. Have you seen anyone like that?"

The barman stared back at him, still wiping.

Kalid sighed, took out his wallet and held up a note with Queen Victoria's picture on it.

The barman turned to look at a woman who was passing behind Kalid carrying two mugs of ale. She stopped and said, "What?"

"This gentleman wants to talk to you," the barman said and disappeared through a swinging door behind the bar.

Ethel put down the mugs and wiped her damp hands on her apron. She surveyed the stranger—a tall, slim man with dusky skin, luxuriant black hair, and riveting dark brown eyes. She took a step forward, then stopped.

"Help you, love?" she said cautiously.

"I'm looking for an American woman who may have stayed here," Kalid said. He was taking another bill out of his wallet when Ethel said, "Put your money away."

Kalid looked up alertly.

"Why do you want to see her?" Ethel asked.

"She's my fiancée. Or, she was."

"Then why isn't she with you?"

"It's a long story."

"It must be."

"We had a fight and she left me. I've come after her."

Ethel looked back at him stonily.

Kalid ran his hand through his hair. "See here, madam, I've come a long way, and I'm very tired. It's extremely important that I find this young lady, but if you aren't going to help me, I wish you would just say so. I haven't time to waste."

"Keep your shirt on, sonny, I'm going to help you. I just want to make sure that you're not planning to cause more trouble for Sarah."

Kalid lunged forward and seized her arm in a viselike grip. "You know Sarah?"

"She was here."

"Where is she now?" he demanded, looking around wildly.

"She's not hiding in the pantry, laddie, I can assure you," Ethel said dryly.

"Tell me!"

"Tone your voice down, or Albie will be out here in a second to give you what for," Ethel said crisply.

Kalid released her.

"That's better," Ethel said, rubbing her arm.

She studied Kalid with a detached air. "Are you really a king or something in your own country?"

"Or something."

"Well, that don't cut much mustard around here."

"I understand that."

"If you want information from me, you'll have to talk to me real respectful," Ethel said, folding her arms, relishing her moment of power.

Kalid startled her, and the rest of the patrons of the Leaping Stag, by going down on one knee and bowing his head.

"Please tell me where Sarah is," he said quietly.

"Here, what's going on, Ethel?" Albie said, appearing from the back room and staring at Kalid as if the younger man were having a frothing fit.

"Get up, sonny, get up," Ethel said nervously, looking around her in distress. She had not anticipated this.

Kalid rose, never taking his eyes from Ethel's. She sighed and relented.

"She's visiting her auntie in Gilly-on-Strait," Ethel said.

"Where is that?" Kalid called over his shoulder, already heading for the door.

"Down the road a mile or two. Just ask anyone."

"Where can I hire a horse?"

"There's a livery stable three doors away. My

boy Henry works there, and he probably took your lady out to Mrs. Hepton's. Ask for him. He'll know the way."

Kalid turned on his heel and ran back to Ethel, taking her in his arms and planting a kiss firmly on her lips. When he released her, she staggered back, amazed.

"Thank you, thank you, I'll never forget you. What was the name, Hepton?"

"That's right."

Kalid dashed out the door without another word, leaving everyone in the room staring after him.

"Who the hell was that?" Albie said to Ethel.

"A man in love," Ethel replied, and touched her fingers lightly to her lips.

Emily was heating water to do the breakfast dishes when her cat streaked out of the kitchen and shot into the front room. Emily wiped her eyes with the corner of her sleeve and went to see who was coming down the lane. She was feeling a little teary since Sarah's departure and was not really up to having visitors.

When she opened the door, a most exotic-looking young man was standing on her brick paving stones.

"May I help you?" she said, wondering if some new neighbors from India or the East had moved into the area.

"I'm looking for Sarah Woolcott," he said bluntly.

"I—I'm her aunt," Emily replied, staring.

"May I speak with her?"

"She isn't here. She left about an hour ago to return to America," Emily said.

Kalid crashed his fist through her front door.

Emily shrieked and tried to run back into her house, but Kalid caught her and spun her around to face him.

"Which dock is she leaving from? What's the name of the ship?" he demanded, holding her fast.

Emily's eyelids fluttered and she sagged into his arms. Her skin was very pale.

Kalid swept her up and carried her inside, cursing the impatience which had caused him to manhandle her. Now she might pass out before he could get the information he needed.

He set Emily on the sofa and chafed her wrists briskly, waiting until some color came back into her face before saying, "I'm not going to do your niece any harm, Mrs. Hepton. I have been looking for her for a long while, and I was just frustrated that I had missed her again, that's all."

"What do you want with her?"

"I want to marry her."

Emily's eyes widened. "Marry?"

"Yes. We were about to get married when we had a disagreement and she left me."

"Where?"

"In Turkey."

"She said nothing of this to me."

"Well, I can understand why she wouldn't, but it is the truth. I don't have a lot of time to convince you, Mrs. Hepton. I assume that her boat will be sailing very soon?"

Emily looked back at him silently.

"At least give me the chance to talk to her."

"You're not British?" Emily said suddenly.

"No."

"But you have a British accent."

"I went to school here. Please, Mrs. Hepton."

"How did Emily meet you?"

"I'm the Pasha of Bursa, a district in Turkey. She was visiting there," he replied, imagining Sarah's reaction if she heard that description of their meeting.

"And she had agreed to marry you?"

"Yes, yes, you can check all of this with her cousin James if you like, but right now I have no time to go into a long explanation about it."

Emily said nothing.

"Mrs. Hepton, I'm alone, I'm unarmed, and the only thing I have right now is a rented horse tied up outside this house. All I'm asking for is the opportunity to talk to Sarah for a few minutes. Will you please tell me where she's going?"

The intensity of his plea convinced her. "Dock four, off Wellington Street," Emily said. "The ship is the *Atlantic Star*. She took my neighbor's coach because she didn't want me to see her off. You might be able to outdistance her on a fast horse. She left at nine o'clock, and the sailing is at eleven."

Kalid seized her hand and kissed it. "I'm out of money, but I'll send you a wire to pay for the door," he said, springing up and dashing outside.

Emily followed more slowly, watching him mount the horse at a dead run and take off at a pelting pace down the lane, kicking the animal's flanks.

Emily sagged against her splintered door, wondering if she had done the right thing.

Sarah stood at the railing of the ocean liner and looked down at the bustle below her. Late passengers were still arriving, climbing up the wooden walkway with their luggage, and the pier was clogged with their friends and relatives, crowding the departure platform and staring upward at the ship looming above them. The horn behind the twin smokestacks sounded once and she jumped, then was about to turn away when she caught sight of a moving figure cutting through the throng.

She looked more closely. It was a man on a horse, galloping across the pier, and people were diving out of the way as he plowed through the crowd like a shark's fin slicing through water. As he got closer, she could hear the astonished cries of those he passed and then watched in amazement as the horse jumped the ropes sealing off the embarkation area and step-danced up the planking.

People on the boat were running to the railings to see the cause of the commotion, and several sailors started for the lower deck. On the bridge, the captain gestured for one of his officers to go down and see what was happening.

A security man who reached for the horse's bridle missed and fell into the water, and shrill police whistles sounded as bobbies converged on the scene, making their way toward the ship.

Sarah's eyes widened, and her hand went to her mouth as she recognized the rider.

It was Kalid.

Chapter Sixteen

Sarah began to push her way down to the gangway area, her heart pounding, a thousand thoughts rushing through her head. By the time she reached the ship's entrance, Kalid was being restrained by two bobbies and a third was holding the reins of his horse.

"Sarah!" he yelled when he saw her, struggling with the policemen. "Sarah, you have to listen to me. I love you, and I'll do anything you want to make you stay with me!"

"Do you know this man, miss?" a ship's officer said, gazing down at her, as everyone else stared at the spectacle, intrigued.

"Yes," Sarah said.

"Sarah, I'm being arrested. Please come down to the police station," Kalid called.

"May I speak with him?" Sarah asked.

The purser looked at the two bobbies dragging Kalid away. They were now being assisted by a British sailor, as Kalid kicked and twisted, trying to break their hold.

"Hold on a minute," the purser said, and the policemen stopped. The purser led Sarah to Kalid, signaling with his eyes for the bobbies to continue holding their prisoner.

"Kalid, what on earth are you doing here?" Sarah asked, taking in his disheveled appearance and heavy beard.

"I followed you from Paris. I had a hotel suite for us there, but when you didn't show up, I found out that you were going to Calais and then to Dover. I spoke with your aunt."

"Is she all right?" Sarah asked, imagining Emily's reaction to Kalid's appearance. Sarah knew what he was like when he wanted something.

"I think I startled her," Kalid said.

"She probably had apoplexy."

"Look here, can we do this down at the station?" one of the bobbies said in a Cockney accent.

The purser looked at Sarah, who nodded.

"I don't suppose you'll be traveling with us, then?" he asked, smiling.

"Not today. Will you be so kind as to remove my luggage from cabin 12B?"

"Yes, madam. It will be held for you at the Greenhouse Station, and you can redeem your ticket at the bursar's office."

"Will you be accompanying the prisoner to the lockup?" the second bobby said.

"I suppose so," Sarah said resignedly.

The little procession—Kalid, Sarah, and several policemen—wended its way across the dock as the crowd cleared a path for them, applauding wildly. Sarah could feel her face flaming as Kalid was handed into a black mariah and she followed with another bobby in a paddy wagon. The clopping of the horses' hooves punctuated her musings as they traveled the several cobbled city blocks to the police station.

Once there, Kalid was kept away from her and she waited for several hours as a series of telegrams established Kalid's identity. A few minutes later, Scotland Yard warned the local constabulary that it would have an international incident on its hands if it proceeded against him. Kalid was released in short order, and Sarah rose slowly as he came into the waiting room, his eyes fixed on hers.

"Will you stay with me?" he said to her, as if the arrest had never taken place.

"Kalid, we can't talk about this here."

"Why the hell not? I've just traveled the globe to track you down, and I want an answer."

"Don't order me about, Kalid, or you'll find that your trip was wasted."

"All right, all right, I'm sorry. I'm trying to change, but it takes time. You don't really want to go back to America and never see me again, do you?"

Sarah said nothing.

"Do you?"

"No."

"I love you, Sarah. I'll do anything, be anything you want. Just don't leave me."

He touched her face and she put her hand over his, her eyes filling with tears.

"No more making decisions for me, treating me like a child?" she said.

"No more."

"And if I disagree with you, I can say so and you won't have a conniption?"

"No conniptions," he said solemnly.

"And I won't have to lead an idle life in the harem?" she said, searching his face.

"No. You can run the palace school. I was going to talk to you about it anyway, but I never had the chance."

"And my relatives can see me any time they want? James can come and visit?"

"Any time. Anything else?"

"I want you to free Memtaz."

"Done."

"She'll probably want to continue at the palace, as she doesn't know anything else, but you have to pay her a salary."

"Fine."

They were beginning to attract attention, standing in the middle of the tiled entry area of the police station, negotiating like two barristers.

"Let's go to a hotel," Kalid said, putting his arm around Sarah's shoulders. "I haven't any money at present, but Achmed can wire me some by the time I have to pay the bill."

They went outside and Kalid hailed a cab. Sarah sat with her head on his shoulder during the ride, and Kalid booked them a room at the best hostelry in Kent, the Southington Arms. His piratical appearance attracted some glances, but his upper crust accent convinced the clerk that he was an acceptable guest, especially when he sent a telegram to Turkey and received a prompt, and fulsome, reply.

The second they entered the room, he turned to her and took her in his arms.

"I missed you so much," he said, kissing her, his beard scraping her cheek. "The thought that I might not be able to stop you was driving me wild."

"I wanted you to stop me," Sarah replied. "I was devastated when I calmed down and realized that you weren't coming after me."

"But I was! I did! I was just one half-step too late all along the way."

"It doesn't matter now. We're together, and I'll never leave you again."

Kalid began taking off her clothes, tossing them on the floor, and when he got down to her whalebone corset he stared at it in pure amazement.

"How can you Western women wear these

things?" he asked. "It looks like an instrument of torture."

"It is."

"Then why bother?" he asked, unlacing her.

"To have a tiny waist."

"You have a tiny waist without it," he said, spanning hers with his hands. He bent to take a nipple in his mouth.

"You don't understand women," she sighed, sinking her fingers into his hair.

"That's certainly true," he replied, raising his head and scooping her up in his arms. He deposited her on the bed and flung himself down next to her, embracing her immediately.

"I ached for you," Sarah whispered, clutching him to her and closing her eyes.

"Never again," he replied, and made exquisite love to her to prove it.

"Why do they call this Yorkshire pudding?" Sarah said to Kalid, around a mouthful of it. "It isn't pudding, it's a kind of roll."

"Why do the British do anything?" Kalid countered, topping off her glass of wine from the carafe they had ordered brought to their room with dinner. "Why is Magdalen College called 'Mawdlin' and Caius College 'Keez'? They ruin their own language."

"You must have had quite a time with English when you first came here."

He shrugged and bit into a carrot. "I knew some English from my mother. It was the local expressions that defeated me. I sounded very much the foreigner until I got acclimated."

"But you did pick up your useful Oxford accent. I've noticed that the natives find it very impressive."

"It's a class distinction the British revere. Here, your station in life is determined by the way you speak. In my country, we are more open about it."

"Yes, slavery is pretty hard to mistake," Sarah said dryly.

"Are we going to have that discussion again?"

"Would you really have whipped Memtaz when I wouldn't obey you that time you wanted to go riding?" Sarah countered.

He grinned. "You'll never know."

"I don't think you would have. You were just manipulating me, weren't you?"

He went on smiling mysteriously.

She threw her napkin at him, and he laughed.

"I have something to tell you," she said.

"You want me to convert Bursa to a democracy and turn the Orchid Palace into a hospital for the indigent."

"That would be nice, but that's not it."

"Well?"

"You remember that discussion we were having about the size of my waist?"

"Mmh?" He was buttering a slice of bread.

"It's going to be expanding."

"What is?"

"My waist."

He dropped the knife and looked up at her.

"Sarah," he said soberly.

"Yes?"

"You're—?"

"Pregnant. Yes, I am."

He shoved his tray aside and came to kneel at her feet. He put his head in her lap, and she stroked his hair.

"I didn't think I could be any happier, but now I am," he said, his voice muted by the folds of the hotel's dressing gown. "How long have you known?"

"Since before I left Turkey."

"And you were just going to go home to Boston and say nothing about it to me?"

"I thought you didn't want me."

"My son would have grown up in America," he said.

"Or daughter."

"It will be a boy."

"How do you know?"

"Kosem's fortune teller said that my firstborn would be a male," Kalid replied seriously.

"Kosem's fortune teller? Well, with that reliable source on our side, we should start picking out boy's names right now."

"Whatever we call him, he will be the next Pasha of Bursa," Kalid said.

"He will be yours and mine, and that's more important."

"I love you, Sarah," Kalid said.

"I waited a long time to hear that."

"I will say it every day from now on, for the rest of our lives," he replied.

"For the rest of our lives," Sarah repeated contentedly, and smiled.

DISCOVER A NEW WORLD OF HISTORICAL ROMANCE!

By Love Betrayed by Sandra DuBay. Rebecca Carlyle agrees to become a spy for the British to avenge her husband's death. But she never expects to find passion in the strong arms of American Beau McAllister. How can she remain true to her cause when all she wants to do is surrender to the ecstasy she has found in the tender caresses of the enemy?

_3282-1 $4.99 US/$5.99 CAN

Mistress of the Muse by Suzanne Hoos. When young Ashley Canell returns to the Muse, her family home, she is faced with dark secrets—secrets that somehow involve her handsome stepcousin, Evan Prescott. And even as she finds herself falling in love with Evan, Ashley fears he might be the one who is willing to do anything to stop her from unraveling the shocking mysteries of the Muse.

_3417-4 $4.50 US/$5.50 CAN

Island Flame by Karen Robards. Young and beautiful, Lady Catherine Aldley was raised by England's most proper governesses, but Jonathan Hale makes her feel like a common doxy. When the lustful pirate attacks Catherine's ship, he spares her life but takes her innocence in a night of savage longing.

_3414-X $4.99 US/$5.99 CAN

LEISURE BOOKS
ATTN: Order Department
276 5th Avenue, New York, NY 10001

Please add $1.50 for shipping and handling for the first book and $.35 for each book thereafter. PA., N.Y.S. and N.Y.C. residents, please add appropriate sales tax. No cash, stamps, or C.O.D.s. All orders shipped within 6 weeks via postal service book rate. Canadian orders require $2.00 extra postage and must be paid in U.S. dollars through a U.S. banking facility.

Name _____

Address _____

City _____ State _____ Zip _____

I have enclosed $_____ in payment for the checked book(s).

Payment <u>must</u> accompany all orders.☐ Please send a free catalog.

FABULOUS HISTORICAL ROMANCE BY LEISURE'S LEADING LADIES OF LOVE!

Where The Heart Is by Robin Lee Hatcher. Fleeing a loveless marriage, Addie Sherwood becomes the first schoolteacher in Homestead, Idaho. But within days of her arrival in the frontier town, she receives another proposal, this time from handsome rancher Will Rider. Although Will is everything Addie has always wanted in a man, she will not accept his offer unless he believes, as she does, that home is where the heart is.

_3527-8 $4.99 US/$5.99 CAN

A Wilderness Christmas by Madeline Baker, Elizabeth Chadwick, Norah Hess and Connie Mason. Discover the old-fashioned joys of a frontier Christmas with this collection of holiday short stories by Leisure's leading ladies of love at their heartwarming best!

_3528-6 $4.99 US/$5.99 CAN

The Tiger Sleeps by Fela Dawson Scott. It was a tawny minx not a proper English lady who once aroused Dylan Christianson's burning desire. Years later, as the only man who can save Ariel from a loveless marriage to a ruthless predator, Dylan will forfeit all he possesses to awaken her sleeping passion and savor the sweet fury of her love.

_3529-4 $4.50 US/$5.50 CAN

LEISURE BOOKS
ATTN: Order Department
276 5th Avenue, New York, NY 10001

Please add $1.50 for shipping and handling for the first book and $.35 for each book thereafter. PA., N.Y.S. and N.Y.C. residents, please add appropriate sales tax. No cash, stamps, or C.O.D.s. All orders shipped within 6 weeks via postal service book rate. Canadian orders require $2.00 extra postage and must be paid in U.S. dollars through a U.S. banking facility.

Name _____

Address _____

City _____ State _____ Zip _____

I have enclosed $_____in payment for the checked book(s).

Payment **must** accompany all orders.☐ Please send a free catalog.

Top-selling Historical Romance
By Leisure's Leading Ladies of Love!

Savage Embers by Cassie Edwards. Before him in the silvery moonlight, she appears as if in a vision. And from that moment, a love like wildfire rushes through the warrior's blood. Not one to be denied, the mighty Arapaho chieftain will claim the woman. Yet even as Falcon Hawk shelters Maggie in his heated embrace, an enemy waits to smother their searing ecstasy, to leave them nothing but the embers of the love that might have been.

__3568-5 $4.99 US/$5.99 CAN

Winds Across Texas by Susan Tanner. Once the captive of a great warrior, Katherine Bellamy finds herself shunned by decent society, yet unable to return to the Indians who have accepted her as their own. Bitter over the murder of his wife and son, Slade will use anyone to get revenge. Both Katherine and Slade see in the other a means to escape misery—and nothing more. But as the sultry desert breezes caress their yearning bodies, neither can deny the sweet, soaring ecstasy of unexpected love.

__3582-0 $4.99 US/$5.99 CAN

LEISURE BOOKS
ATTN: Order Department
276 5th Avenue, New York, NY 10001

Please add $1.50 for shipping and handling for the first book and $.35 for each book thereafter. PA., N.Y.S. and N.Y.C. residents, please add appropriate sales tax. No cash, stamps, or C.O.D.s. All orders shipped within 6 weeks via postal service book rate. Canadian orders require $2.00 extra postage and must be paid in U.S. dollars through a U.S. banking facility.

Name _____

Address _____

City _____ State _____ Zip _____

I have enclosed $_____ in payment for the checked book(s).
Payment **must** accompany all orders.☐ Please send a free catalog.